He wanted her.

He wanted her more than he'd wanted anything in a long time. The knowledge slammed into Neil like a bullet, and he clenched his teeth and called on all his self-control to banish the dangerous desire.

Laura was off-limits. But he couldn't get her out of his mind. Something in her called out to him, and something in him responded.

His body ached with need. His soul ached with loneliness. His heart ached with guilt.

The truth reverberated through him, stark and undeniable.

He wanted Laura Sebastian—the woman his brother loved.

Dear Reader,

Welcome to Silhouette **Special Edition** . . . welcome to romance. Each month, Silhouette **Special Edition** publishes six novels with you in mind—stories of love and life, tales that you can identify with—romance with that little "something special" added in.

June has some wonderful stories in bloom for you. Don't miss *Silent Sam's Salvation*—the continuation of Myrna Temte's exciting *Cowboy Country* series. Sam Dawson might not possess the gift of gab, but Dani Smith quickly discovers that still waters run deep—and that she wants to dive right in! Don't miss this tender tale.

Rounding out this month are more stories by some of your favorite authors: Tracy Sinclair, Christine Flynn, Trisha Alexander (with her second book for Silhouette **Special Edition**—remember *Cinderella Girl,* SE #640?), Lucy Gordon and Emilie Richards.

In each Silhouette **Special Edition** novel, we're dedicated to bringing you the romances that you dream about—stories that will delight as well as bring a tear to the eye. And that's what Silhouette **Special Edition** is all about—special books by special authors for special readers!

I hope you enjoy this book and all of the stories to come!

Sincerely,

Tara Gavin
Senior Editor
Silhouette Books

TRISHA ALEXANDER

When Somebody Loves You

America's Publisher of Contemporary Romance

To Barbara Lewis and Sharon Wright,
with thanks and love.

Special thanks to Sue Royer and Jennifer Zalud for medical expertise; Lt. Barry Wynne of the Baton Rouge Police Department, who patiently answered questions; Susan Brown for sharing her knowledge of Louisiana and Baton Rouge; and Alaina Richardson, Heather MacAllister, Elaine Kimberley and Betty Gyenes for their invaluable critique.

SILHOUETTE BOOKS
300 East 42nd St., New York, N.Y. 10017

WHEN SOMEBODY LOVES YOU

ISBN: 0-373-09748-4

First Silhouette Books printing June 1992

Printed in the U.S.A.

Books by Trisha Alexander

Silhouette Special Edition

Cinderella Girl #640
When Somebody Loves You #748

TRISHA ALEXANDER

has had a lifelong love affair with books and always wanted to be a writer. Now that she is, she can't imagine doing anything else. She also loves cats, movies, the ocean, music, Broadway shows, cooking, traveling, being with her family and friends, Cajun food and getting mail. Trisha and her husband have three grown children and live in Houston, Texas, with the real Pete and Phoebe.

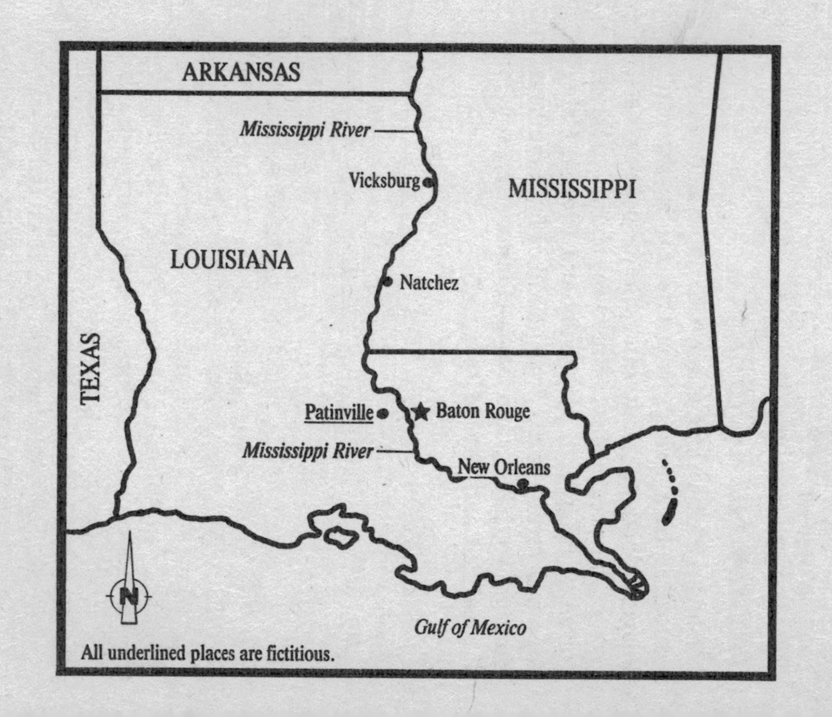
ARKANSAS
Mississippi River
Vicksburg
MISSISSIPPI
LOUISIANA
Natchez
TEXAS
Patinville
Baton Rouge
Mississippi River
New Orleans
N
Gulf of Mexico
All underlined places are fictitious.

Prologue

From *The Patinville Daily News* front page

Local Police Officer Killed In Baton Rouge Shoot-out

Sgt. James Edward Kendella, 31, was shot and killed last night during an undercover operation conducted by the Baton Rouge Police Department. Sgt. Kendella, a Patinville resident, had been a member of the Baton Rouge Police Force for ten years. Last night, during a stakeout, Kendella was killed by Tony Abruzzi, a notorious local gangster, who police have long tried to convict. Before dying, Kendella also shot and killed Abruzzi. Kendella's partner, ex-Patinville resident, Sgt. Neil Cantrelle, witnessed the shootings.

Kendella is survived by his wife, Alice, and their two children, James, Jr. and Lisa. Funeral services will be held at St. Anthony's Church on Friday at 10:00 a.m. See page four for complete story.

Chapter One

The dream is the same as all the others. He is running down a dark, rain-swept street. It is hot and muggy, just like it is every summer in Louisiana. His footsteps echo on the pavement and the street lamps cast long, eerie shadows that look like individual hurdles he must cross.

He rounds the corner, and for one awful moment he cannot believe his eyes. The tableau laid out before him is like a carefully staged scene from a police action movie: the muscular gangster standing in the doorway of the house, the cop on the other side of the street. And then, as if an unseen director has yelled "Action," the slow-motion movements of the players.

Everything happens at once. Jimmy shouts. Abruzzi whirls around. Gunshots erupt, spitting death. Jimmy folds over like a crumpled doll. Abruzzi staggers forward, then pitches face down across the concrete steps.

Abruzzi's girlfriend, wearing only a sheer nightgown, stands in the doorway. She stares at Abruzzi sprawled across her porch steps. Her high-pitched scream slices through the dark night. "Toneeeee, nooooo...."

The sound of the gunshots reverberate in the moist, thick air. Neil races toward Jimmy. A siren wails louder and louder. Neil's heart thunders in his chest, and his breath comes in shallow spurts.

No. No. No, his heart cries. His feet pound across the distance separating him from Jimmy Kendella, his partner, his best friend, the man he loves most in the world except for his father and brother.

No, he whispers, even as he kneels over Jimmy's motionless body, even as the siren whines to a stop, even as he hears the urgent voices and the clunk of car doors.

No. The word tears through his brain. Like a mechanical doll with jerky, stilted movements, he lifts Jimmy's head. His hands feel as if they belong to someone else.

No, please God. No, no. no. But even as he prays in desperation, even as his heart pushes into his throat, even as his hands shake in horror, he knows his denial is useless.

Jimmy is dead, shot through the middle of the chest. Blood puddles around his body, and his eyes are open and staring, their expression full of disbelief. Neil leans over him. He presses his ear against Jimmy's chest.

Hands clutch at Neil. He fights them away. "Jimmy!" he cries. "Jimmy!" More squad cars arrive, brakes squealing, sirens a cacophony of sound surrounding him.

"Come on, Cantrelle, there's nothing you can do," a gruff voice says. The hands pull him away, and he screams. "Jimmeeeee!"

"Jimmeeeee!" Neil screamed and sat up in bed. His head was pounding. No. Someone was pounding on the door. Still shaking, it took him a few seconds to distance himself from the dream. Someone really was outside, he thought, as he fumbled for his jeans in the milky moonlight.

"Neil!" a man's voice shouted. "Open up!"

Neil grimaced. That whiskey voice could only belong to Gastin Nesbitt, who owned the combination bait shop, gas station, grocery store right off Highway One, the overseas highway that linked the islands from mainland Florida over to Key Largo at its northeastern end to Key West at its southwestern end. Gastin, a Conch who had been born and raised on Cudjoe Key, was Neil's one friend on the island, the only friend he'd made since coming to the Keys three years earlier.

"Keep your shirt on," Neil grumbled as he padded across the bare wood floor to the door. He released the latch, and opened the door wide, letting the moonlight invade the room. Zoe, his black Labrador retriever, was suddenly at his side, a low growl rumbling in her throat. Gastin's wiry frame stood silhouetted through the screened door. The diamond-dusted gulf waters shone behind him, and Neil could see Gastin's rusted Ford pickup truck parked near the steps. Neil rubbed his eyes, trying to dispel the dream that still had him shaky.

"What are you doing here, Gastin? What the hell time is it, anyway?" He held the dog's collar. "It's okay, Zoe. It's just Gastin."

Zoe's body relaxed as Gastin said, "Your daddy called, Neil."

"Papa?" Alarm shot through him. His father had only phoned him once before, when his grandmother had died. René Cantrelle was not the kind of man who would roust Gastin out of bed in the middle of the night unless it was something important. "What's wrong?"

"It's your brother." Gastin opened the screened door and walked inside. The smell of fish that always clung to him drifted through the air.

"Norman! What happened?" Fear, thick and cloying, choked Neil's throat.

"He done had a automobile accident. Bad, from what your daddy said. They got 'im in the Mercy Hospital in

Baton Rouge, and it's plenty serious. They don't know if he's gonna make it. Your daddy said to tell you to come home as fast as you can. He said they need you."

Neil broke out in chills as the words hammered through his mind. Norman was seriously hurt. He could die. His father wanted him to come. He stared at Gastin. "What time is it? Maybe I can make the eight o'clock flight from Miami."

"It's three-thirty. You'd be cuttin' it close." Gastin switched on the nearest lamp. His right cheek bulged, and Neil knew he had a wad of chewing tobacco lodged inside his mouth. "You can come back to my place if you wanna call the airlines. You need money?"

"No, but thanks." Neil pulled a clean shirt from his makeshift closet, a broom handle laid across two pegs jutting from the wall. He stuffed underwear, a few T-shirts, two pairs of clean jeans, a couple of sweaters, a pair of sweats, and some toiletries into a nylon duffel bag, dressing as he packed. The duffel bag still had some room in it, so he added a couple of paperback books of poetry, and then, as an afterthought, a pair of dress pants and a blue long-sleeved dress shirt, both holdovers from his past.

"You need a ride to Miami?"

Neil shook his head. "No. I'll go on the bike." He'd bought a used Harley-Davidson when he first arrived in the Keys. He found it the perfect mode of transportation, using less gas and requiring a smaller place for storage when not in use. "Would you keep Zoe for me, though?"

"Yep." Gastin leaned down to pet the dog, and Zoe wagged her tail.

Neil knew the dog liked the old Conch. He also knew Gastin slipped Zoe tidbits from the table, something Neil didn't do. No wonder Zoe liked the old geezer. "And the boat? Will you keep an eye on *The Louisiana Lady,* too?" He was referring to his charter fishing boat, tied up at the dock outside Gastin Nesbitt's store.

"You know I will," Gastin said. He walked to the screened door and pushed it open, spitting tobacco juice in a perfect arch. Neil heard the splat as it landed on the hard-packed dirt surrounding the shack. "I won't let nobody touch that boat, no sirree." Zoe's tail thumped behind her as she watched the old man.

After pulling an old leather bomber jacket from the deep recesses of a storage chest, Neil lifted his duffel bag, and said, "I'm ready. Let's go." He yanked the chain on the ancient lamp, and the room was once more plunged into shadowy darkness.

Following Gastin and Zoe out the door, Neil drew it shut behind him. He didn't bother to lock it. There was nothing in the cottage worth stealing. If anyone wanted the beat-up footlocker he'd bought for ten dollars at an auction on Sugarloaf Key or the forty-five-dollar air mattress that served as his bed or the old stove that he'd picked up for less than a hundred bucks, they could have them. The only thing of value in the room was the small portable refrigerator Neil had bought new when he'd first come to the island. Even the shortwave radio was a relic.

Neil pulled the bike out from under the thick tarp he used to protect it from the sun and the salt spray.

Gastin opened the tailgate on the truck, and Zoe leaped into the bed of the pickup. Soon Neil, following behind the truck, was bouncing along the unpaved road that would take them to the highway and Gastin's place. Neil was only partly aware of the isolated landscape dotted with pine, buttonwood, and jacaranda trees as they barreled through the night. Unanswered questions churned through his mind as worry gnawed at him. Would Norman be all right? What kind of injuries did he have? How were their parents doing? His chest tightened. Their parents. They must be terrified.

As fear knotted into a lump in his gut, Neil wished he still believed in prayer.

* * *

"Hold that light steady for me, will you, Mrs. Peres?"

The voice sounded as if it were coming from far away. Laura Sebastian tried to speak, and a needle-sharp pain stabbed at her temples. When she breathed, her chest felt as if someone were sitting on it.

"Oh," she moaned.

"Laura? Can you hear me?"

"Umm..." Who was that?

"Laura?" The voice was insistent, and even though it hurt, she opened her eyes, trying to ignore the throbbing in her temples. Bright sunlight blinded her, and she lifted her right arm to shield herself. When she did, pain pounded her from every direction.

"Mmm..." Gradually her eyes adjusted to the brightness. A man with thick glasses and a dark brown mustache and beard stood over her. He was wearing a white coat and studying her intently. "Wh...what—?"

"—happened?" He frowned. "You've been in an accident. You're at Mercy Hospital. You were brought in last night. Do you remember anything?" His voice was impersonal and clipped, as if he were in a hurry.

An accident? Laura strained to remember, but the only images she could call forth were disjointed and fuzzy.

"I'm Dr. Dunado," he said. He was holding something that looked like a fat fountain pen in his left hand, but when he leaned over her and switched it on, she could see it was a small-beamed light. He shone it into her eyes, and she whimpered. The light hurt.

"Be still," he said, not unkindly, but brusque and matter-of-fact. After a few minutes, he switched the light off.

An accident.

He said she'd been in an accident.

Suddenly Laura's heart lurched as the events of the previous evening came rushing back, images tumbling through her mind.

The rain. The lightning and thunder. Norman shouting. Headlights. Another car. And then...oh, God. Then they'd crashed. Her heart pounded as terror flooded her body. "Nor...Norman," she cried. She tried to sit up, ignoring the pain that tore through her, but the doctor and someone else—someone standing on her other side—gently pushed her back against her pillows.

"Please, don't try to move, Laura," a female voice said. Wincing, Laura turned her head. A plump nurse with kind brown eyes smiled at her and said, "Hi. I'm Mrs. Peres."

"The...the accident. I...I remember now. Is...is Norman okay?"

"Mr. Cantrelle's doing fine," Dr. Dunado said, but when she looked at him he didn't meet her eyes.

The nurse lifted something and gently placed it in Laura's hand, closing her fingers around the cool, smooth plastic. "This is your call bell." She patted Laura's hand. "If you need me for anything, all you have to do is press this, okay?" With infinite care, she guided Laura's index finger and showed her where to push. "When you do that," the nurse continued, "a light goes on outside your door and at the nurses' station, too. We'll come right away."

Laura tried to concentrate on the nurse's instructions, but the effort was too great. Her head hurt too much. The only clear thought in her mind was Norman. Guilt mixed with fear engulfed her. Norman had reached for her hand. He had looked away from the road.

The accident was all her fault. If she hadn't been so stupid...if Norman had been paying attention to his driving... For a moment, tears blinded her. If only she had loved Norman the way any sensible woman would have, none of this would have happened.

Mrs. Peres tucked the blanket around her. "Now you just close your eyes and sleep. Don't you go worrying about anything. Your friend is going to be all right."

She walked out, leaving Laura with the doctor. Silently he lifted her wrist and checked her pulse.

Laura forced herself to speak calmly. "Where is Norman? Is he here?"

"Yes."

There it was again, his eyes skidding away from contact with hers. "T-tell me the truth, doctor. How badly is he hurt?"

Dunado frowned, and his eyes finally met hers. He gave her a long, considering look. "He's alive, but he's not in good shape," he said. "You were lucky. All you've got are a few cracked ribs, a nasty bump on the head, and a mild concussion." He released her hand. "I've ordered a painkiller for you."

"I don't need a painkiller." If she took a drug, she would be so dopey she wouldn't know what was happening around her. She shuddered as nameless fears clawed at her.

"I think you do," he said.

"I won't take it," she insisted.

His eyes narrowed. He shrugged. "Suit yourself. I'm not going to force you." He made another notation on her chart. "Get some rest. I'll see you later." Then, without looking at her again, he walked out.

Get some rest.

How could she rest when she was so worried? The accident was her fault! Norman had been badly hurt, and she was responsible. A vivid picture swept through her mind just as the blurred headlights of the oncoming car had swept across the windshield of Norman's Jeep seconds before the crash. Now Laura remembered everything.

Norman's large, square hands had gripped the steering wheel in fierce concentration. The windshield wipers, with their rapid whoosh-thunk, whoosh-thunk, had sounded as if they were keeping time with the drumrolls of thunder.

The weather had turned nasty late in the afternoon while Laura and Norman were visiting a roofing materials supplier near New Orleans. By the time they were on their way back to Patinville and home, they found themselves in the middle of a full-fledged storm.

But as worried as Laura was about the storm, she was even more worried about the confrontation ahead of her when they reached her apartment—a confrontation she could no longer avoid.

If only Norman hadn't asked her to marry him. If only she'd been able to keep their relationship one of friendship. If only he hadn't forced her to make a decision.

If only she loved him.

Why couldn't she be satisfied with Norman? Why weren't feelings of admiration and respect enough for her? Why did she hold on to her fantasy of a man who would understand her fears and insecurities? A man who would need her as much as she needed him?

She sighed heavily. In her mind, she'd been over and over the same questions; nothing had changed. She was not in love with Norman. She would never be in love with him. He had some wonderful qualities, but the things she needed from him most were missing. So no matter how much she loved his family, no matter how much she wanted to marry and have children, no matter how she longed to be part of that elusive circle—it simply wouldn't work.

She closed her eyes against the sudden longing that assailed her. From the time she was a little girl pretending the beat-up doll the woman from the social services agency had brought her was her very own baby, Laura had wanted a family. The kind of family she saw on television. Her daydreams were filled with images of fat, sweet-smelling babies she would cuddle and sing lullabies to; of warm kitchens filled with the aroma of cookies baking in the oven; of a tall, loving man who would open the door each night and gather her into his arms while their children shouted greetings at their feet.

Her eyes misted with tears—tears she fiercely rejected—as reality clutched her in its painful grip. Christmas was coming, and one little word—yes—would mean she wouldn't have to spend another Christmas as an outsider. Instead, she would be welcomed in the circle that included Norman and his parents and sisters and their huge, boisterous Cajun family.

Joie de vivre. A way of looking at things. A condition of the mind and heart. Full of the joy of living. Laura remembered the first time she'd heard the expression, only a few months after she'd arrived in Patinville. And that expression so perfectly described the Cantrelles it could have been coined with them in mind.

If she said yes to Norman, she would be a Cantrelle. She would share their love and unity. She would be a part of something good and desirable, instead of existing on the fringes—alone and set apart—as she had been for most of her life.

She loved Norman's family. Their lure was almost irresistible. They were everything she had always longed for. René, Norman's fun-loving and generous father; Arlette, his feisty, bossy mother; Denise and Desiree, his pretty, bright sisters. And although she'd never met him, she was sure she would also love Norman's older brother, Neil, who lived in the Florida Keys and ran a charter fishing business.

All this could be hers: this ready-made family that so closely matched the family of her dreams.

All she had to do was say she'd marry Norman.

And that was the one thing she knew she couldn't do.

And tonight she had promised to give him her answer.

Ever since he'd asked her over a week ago, she'd been dreading telling him. She knew that once she did, everything would change. He would be hurt. How could she continue going into the office every day? Even if he never said a word, his eyes would speak for him. The situation would be impossible—so uncomfortable Laura wouldn't be able to stand it.

She would have to quit her job. And if she quit her job as the bookkeeper/office manager of Cantrelle Roofing and Home Improvement Company, what would she do? Her dream of opening a day-care center would be set back for a long time, maybe even years. She guessed she could move to New Orleans, or back to California, but the idea was not appealing. Since coming to Patinville, she'd discovered how much she liked smaller towns. Besides, she'd made friends in Patinville, and for her, making friends had never been easy.

She shivered, a feeling of foreboding creeping through her, as her thoughts whirled around and around.

"Are you cold, honey?"

Laura started guiltily. *Honey. He's so sure I'm going to say yes. Oh, Norman, I'm sorry. If wishing could make it different, I'd feel everything you want me to feel.*

And then he reached for her hand, and Laura knew he sensed her worry. After that, things happened so fast, they were only a blur in Laura's mind. The headlights. The crash. The sickening sound of crunched metal and shattering glass. And then a black and empty silence.

Remembering all this, anxiety settled into Laura's chest like a dull ache. Norman. Poor Norman. The doctor had said he wasn't in good shape. Her fault. All her fault. Oh, God, what if he didn't make it? What if he died?

Bottom lip trembling, Laura began to pray.

Chapter Two

Neil paced the length of the waiting room. He felt the eyes of his parents and sisters watching him. He balled his fists, wishing he could do something concrete to help them—something other than offer platitudes. Damn, he felt helpless.

He stopped pacing; he wanted a cigarette desperately, even though he'd quit smoking two years earlier. The sound of footsteps alerted him to the doctor's approach. Neil waited silently as Dr. Dunado entered the waiting room. Dunado's face was impassive, but Neil saw the tension in the set of the man's shoulders. He nodded gravely, addressing his remarks to Neil's parents. "Mr. and Mrs. Cantrelle, I'm afraid I have some bad news."

At Dunado's words, Neil's father put his arm around his wife's shoulders. With his other arm he beckoned Denise and Desiree closer. Both women had frightened eyes. Neil stiffened, every sense in tune to the anxiety emanating from the doctor. In the few seconds before Dunado spoke again, the silence in the waiting room thickened, almost as if it were something you could reach out and touch. The phenomenon reminded Neil of those seconds between the time you saw a gun raised and pointed at you and the actual moment of firing. For one heartbeat he thought he was back on the force, staring down the black abyss of some drug dealer's gun.

"Your son has sustained some very serious injuries," Dunado said. He hesitated, then said bluntly, "As you know, he was pinned in the wreckage of his car. His right leg was mangled badly. We've done everything we can, but it can't be saved. We must amputate."

His father's face drained of color. Denise gasped, and Desiree's dark eyes widened in shock.

"Oh, sweet Jesus," Neil's mother said as she clutched her handkerchief to her mouth. Her hands trembled. Neil felt as if he'd been rammed in the stomach.

Dunado blurted out the rest. "His left leg was also severely injured. Both the femur and the tibia were crushed. We're going to do everything we can to save it."

The stark words reverberated in Neil's head.

"Oh, no, no. René," his mother wailed, turning into her husband's embrace. "René . . ."

"It's okay, Arlette," Neil's father soothed, patting her dark head ineffectually. "It's okay, everythin's go'n be okay. Please, *chère,* don't cry."

Desiree began to cry, too, and Neil, whose chest ached from his own grief, stood by impotently. A tidal wave of rage crashed over him at the thought of the tragedy that had befallen his baby brother. Because no matter what René said, Neil knew nothing would ever be okay again.

His father led his mother, who was still quietly weeping, back to the couch on the far side of the waiting room. His gaze met Neil's, and Neil wished desperately he could communicate some reassurance.

"Wh-what about Laura?" Denise said softly to the doctor. "No one's told us anything about her."

Neil frowned. Laura? Who was Laura?

"Miss Sebastian's going to be fine," Dunado said. "Her injuries are minor. I just left her room."

"Thank God," Denise said. Then she must have noticed Neil's consternation, for she said, "Didn't anyone tell you Norman wasn't alone? Laura Sebastian, who works in the office, was with him. Well, actually, she's more than an employee. She and Norman have been seeing each other for almost a year now."

Neil's curiosity was piqued by Denise's revelation, but the doctor had turned to leave, and there were still questions Neil wanted to ask him, so he abandoned the subject of Laura Sebastian. He walked after Dunado. "Can I talk to you for a few minutes?"

Dunado nodded, and Neil followed him to the other end of the hall, out of earshot of his family. "Tell me the truth," he said. "Is Norman going to make it?"

Dunado shrugged, his dark eyes like two bright pieces of glass behind the thick glasses. "I don't know. These first few days are critical. If he pulls through them, well...."

"What're his chances of pulling through?"

Dunado stared at him for a few seconds as if weighing how much truth Neil could handle, then said, "Look, he's young and strong. He was in good physical condition. That helps. But still... I'd say fifty-fifty."

"I see." Deep down in his gut, Neil had known the chances weren't great, a sixth sense born of years of dealing with crisis situations. "If there's anything else we can do, anybody else we can call in—"

"We're doing everything that can be done," Dunado said. "All we can do now is wait."

Neil stared at him. Bright images flashed through his mind: teaching Norman how to catch a football, chasing Norman through the woods behind his parents' home, wading barefoot through the creek that meandered across their grandparents' farm, the two of them dancing at the local Mardi Gras celebration. Neil was even the one Norman had come to when he'd had questions about sex. "How much of Norman's right leg will be taken?"

"We'll amputate just above the knee."

Neil's heart beat with slow, heavy thuds. The harsh reality of the situation was difficult to accept, but he knew he must. He couldn't afford to indulge in anger or pity or useless railing against the fates. His parents were going to need strength from him—strength and support and all the optimism he could muster.

"Well, if there's nothing else . . ." Dunado said, breaking into Neil's thoughts.

"Wait. There is one more thing. The woman who was with my brother, where is she?"

"Down on 2E."

"Can we see her?"

"Sure. And why don't you try to persuade your parents to go home? They look exhausted, and they've received a terrible shock. Right now there's nothing they can do here. Your brother will be in surgery and then in recovery for hours. Even after that, you won't be permitted to see him until he's conscious and able to handle visitors. As long as one of you stays here, you can call your parents if his condition changes."

Neil glanced down at the other end of the hall where his parents and sisters were huddled together. "I'll try."

Just then the singsong paging system hissed into life. *Dr. Dunado, call Extension 556. Dr. Dunado, call Extension 556.*

Emotions in turmoil, Neil walked back toward his family. Denise intercepted him before he reached his parents.

"What did the doctor tell you?" she asked softly.

"Only that he thinks Mama and Papa should go home and try to get some rest," Neil hedged. Then, to distract her, he said, "Norman never mentioned this Laura."

Denise shrugged. "You know Norman."

Yes, he did know Norman. Not much of a letter writer, his brother tended toward an occasional brief letter about his latest hunting trip or how many fish he'd caught the previous weekend, with an occasional golf score thrown in. Neil grimaced. No, Norman wasn't the type to talk about his feelings. He was active, physical, and relentlessly cheerful. He didn't take life seriously and never thought too deeply. He was the exact opposite of Neil. Neil had often wished he could be more like Norman.

"How'd he meet her? Is she from Patinville?"

"No. She moved here from California shortly after you left for Florida, as a matter of fact."

"Are they serious about each other?"

"Well, it's supposed to be a secret, but Norman told me a couple of days ago that he'd asked Laura to marry him."

"And?"

"I couldn't pin Norman down. Oh, you know how he is. When I asked him point-blank what she'd said, he just brushed me off. He said Laura hadn't given him a definite answer yet, but he knew what it would be. He wasn't worried." She frowned. "But I am."

Neil remembered how hard it had always been to hide anything from his older sister—how intuitive she was. Even when they were both kids she'd had an uncanny knack for knowing what he was thinking or feeling. She was the first person to guess when he'd fallen in love with Erica. She was also the first person to suspect that his marriage was falling apart. "Tell me," he urged. He trusted her instincts.

Denise's thoughtful eyes met his. "Now, remember, this is just a hunch. I have nothing concrete to base it on."

"I know."

"Well, I don't think Laura feels the same way about Norman as he feels about her."

Neil wanted to question her further, but Desiree was motioning to them. "We'll talk later," he said, and Denise nodded. They rejoined the rest of the family. Twenty minutes later he and Denise finally persuaded his mother to go home with Desiree. Desiree hugged Neil tightly before they left.

"Neil, I'm so glad you're here," she whispered, and Neil's chest tightened with a rush of love for his twenty-five-year-old sister. "We all need you." Her expressive brown eyes—Cantrelle eyes, his mother always called them—swam with tears.

His father refused to leave, and Denise insisted on staying, too.

"Jett's at home with the kids. There's no reason for me to go," she said, a stubborn tilt to her chin. "Besides, I want to see Laura."

After his mother left the hospital, the image of her swollen, haunted eyes preyed on Neil's mind. If only there was something he could do. Well, maybe there *was* something. He touched Denise's shoulder. "I know you're anxious to go down and see this Laura, but would you mind if I go first?"

She studied his face for a few moments, then said, "No, I don't mind."

He knew that Denise understood his desire to see for himself what the woman was like. "Will you stay with Papa?"

"Yes." They both looked at their father, who suddenly seemed much older than his sixty-eight years. His face was gray with exhaustion, and he twisted his hands helplessly as he stared out the window.

Neil squeezed Denise's hand, then walked toward the elevator. He was disturbed by what Denise had told him, and he hoped she was wrong. He hoped Laura Sebastian loved

Norman the way Norman loved her. He hoped she was planning to marry Norman, and that the news about Norman's leg wouldn't make any difference to her. He hoped she was a very strong woman and would be able to face the hard days ahead of them.

All I want is miracles, he thought wryly.

As he stepped off the elevator on the second floor, his concern for Norman was almost overridden by curiosity about the woman. A transplanted Californian. He'd bet money she was a bouncy blonde.

When he reached 2E, the duty nurse stopped him. "Are you one of the family?"

Neil shook his head. "No, but Miss Sebastian was with my brother when the accident happened."

"Well—"

"I won't stay long," Neil said quickly. "I just want to let her know we're here."

The plump nurse studied him for a few minutes, then lifted her shoulders. "I guess it'll be okay." She stood up. Her rubber-soled shoes squished as she walked rapidly down the hallway with Neil following closely behind. She stopped abruptly in front of a partially opened door at the end of the hall. "She's upset, so be careful what you say," she admonished. "And don't stay too long."

Neil nodded and pushed the door all the way open. The blinds had been partially closed against the bright afternoon sun, and the room was bathed in soft golden light. He walked to the bed.

The woman in the bed was asleep. Her chest rose and fell regularly. There was an angry-looking gash on her forehead, and her upper lip looked swollen. Neil studied her quietly.

For a minute he wondered if maybe they'd sent him to the wrong room. The woman in the bed didn't seem like Norman's type at all. Her face was pale and thin, with high cheekbones and a long, straight nose. Her body seemed thin, too. Norman had always liked women with some meat on their bones—curvy, feminine women—as Neil himself did. This woman was more angular than curvy.

Medium-length light brown hair framed her face. Her eyebrows were dark and well-defined, and long, curly eyelashes fanned her cheeks. Even though her upper lip was distorted, Neil could see that her mouth was wide with a generous lower lip.

She wasn't bad-looking. She had nice skin with a smattering of freckles across her nose and upper cheeks. He looked at her hands—long and slender with tapering fingers and short, unpainted nails. There was a simplicity about her that was appealing, although she certainly wasn't his type.

As Neil studied her, she whimpered in her sleep, the sound lonely and sad. Impatiently, he dismissed the thought. But she did look oddly defenseless lying there. She was nothing like Neil had pictured her. He grimaced. He'd jumped to conclusions. When Denise had described Laura Sebastian as an ex-Californian, Neil had immediately assumed she was one of the energetic beach bunny types with a toothpaste-ad smile and Farrah Fawcett hair. This woman looked more like...what? He didn't know. She was just an ordinary woman.

Idly, he wondered what color her eyes were.

Laura opened her eyes. There was a stranger staring down at her, but after a brief flutter of fear, she wasn't afraid.

His face was tough and darkly chiseled. A stubble of beard shadowed his narrow chin, and his black hair, thick but too long and wild-looking to be fashionable, fell forward over his forehead as if it resisted any kind of taming. His eyes were ebony, thoughtful, and still. His body looked sleekly muscled and taut under a close-fitting gray T-shirt.

Although Laura knew she'd never seen him before, he seemed oddly familiar and oddly disturbing.

"You're awake," he said. "Good. I was hoping we could talk."

He spoke in a low, clipped voice, with only the barest trace of a Southern accent. His words were pleasant enough, but the expression in his dark eyes was guarded.

She wet her lips and winced. Her top lip hurt. "Who are you?" she whispered.

Something flickered in the depths of his eyes. "Neil Cantrelle."

Laura stared. So this was Neil, the brother Norman talked about so often. The brother who had left Patinville because of some kind of trouble. The brother Norman practically worshipped.

Yes, now that she looked very closely, she could see the resemblance—an eerie similarity in the shape of their eyes and head, even in the shape of their mouths, but there the resemblance ended. Where Norman exuded an open friendliness, his brother's face was closed and watchful as if he were weighing you and finding you wanting.

"H-hello," she finally said. "Norman's talked about you so much." The effort to speak cost her, but she tried not to show it, strangely reluctant to let him see any weakness.

"Has he?" Now he smiled, a disarming smile that changed his entire face, making him look younger than the thirty-six years she knew him to be. The smile also dispelled some of the air of tension about him. "Knowing Norman, he probably described me as a cross between Clint Eastwood and Burt Reynolds." Then his face fell into serious lines once more. "How are you feeling? Everyone's worried about you."

Tears filled her eyes, tears she immediately blinked away, furious with herself.

"What's wrong?" Neil Cantrelle frowned over her, concern roughening his voice.

"Nothing, really. I just...well, it's so like your family to be concerned about me when Norman...how *is* Norman?" Her head was throbbing again, and she wished she could escape into sleep. The effort to talk had exhausted her.

Neil's jaw tightened, and a muscle jumped in his neck. "He's holding his own right now."

There was something he wasn't telling her. Laura didn't know how she knew it, but she did. "Please tell me the truth," she said. "I have to know the truth."

His dark eyes met hers. The sounds of the hospital surrounded them: the singsong voice of the paging system, the clink of metal, the muffled laughter of someone in the next room, the muted murmur of a television program.

"Please," she whispered. She had to know. Whatever it was, she had to know.

"They told me not to upset you."

"Please."

His face twisted, and he reached out to cover her hand with his own. "Are you sure you can take it?"

She nodded wordlessly.

"Norman's legs were pinned in the wreckage. He's in surgery right now." He hesitated, then said softly. "They're amputating his right leg."

Shock held Laura rigid for what seemed like eternity. Part of her was screaming inside; the other part of her was dispassionate, studying the hand that held hers—a hard, strong hand covered by a mat of crisp black hair, with a sturdy wrist wearing a no-nonsense stainless steel-banded wristwatch.

"Are you all right?" he said gruffly.

"Yes." But even as she said it, the tears came in a hot tide—down her cheeks—sliding into her ears. "No." She couldn't seem to stop the tears, and her hands clenched convulsively. His hand tightened over hers.

"I shouldn't have told you," he said.

Laura squeezed her eyes shut. Maybe she could squeeze out the pain, too.

"Miss Sebastian? You wanted something?"

Laura recognized the voice of Mrs. Peres.

"I called you," Neil said.

"What's going on here?" the nurse asked.

"I'm sorry. She wanted to know, and I—"

"You've upset her!"

At the nurse's reprimand, he moved his hand from Laura's, and she felt suddenly bereft. Mrs. Peres's face held undisguised fury as she glared at Neil. She extracted a tissue from the box on the side table and dabbed at Laura's eyes and cheeks.

"I'm sorry," he said again.

"Well, you should be!"

"It wasn't his fault," Laura said weakly.

"Whose fault was it then?" Mrs. Peres demanded. "He's the only one I see in here. I think you'd better leave."

Neil started to comply.

"Please," Laura begged. "Let him tell me the rest. I have to know the rest." She ignored the pain in her temples, in her lip, in her chest.

"There's time enough to worry about that," the nurse soothed, smoothing her hand across Laura's forehead. "You just get yourself well."

"Please..."

Mrs. Peres glared at Neil, while her hand continued soothing and comforting. Then she shrugged. "All right. I guess she won't rest until she knows."

Laura turned her head away from the angry nurse. She looked at Norman's brother. Neil's eyes were filled with disturbing glints, like shards of glass floating in a dark pool. "Is that all? Or is there more?"

"There's more."

"Tell me," she whispered.

Very softly, he said, "Now the problem is that several bones were crushed in his left leg. He may lose it, as well."

"Dear God," Laura whispered. She stared at Neil. Her heart thumped wildly. Norman. He was losing one leg. He might lose another. Her fault. It was all her fault.

"Okay, Mr. Cantrelle. You've done enough damage for one day," Mrs. Peres said firmly. "I want you to leave now." She pressed the call button at Laura's side. "I'm going to get the doctor to order a sedative for you. You need to rest so you can get well."

"Rest? How can I rest?" Laura tried to lift her head and roll over. Oh, if only she could turn the clock back.

"Can I—" Neil said.

"Please leave, Mr. Cantrelle," the nurse said. It sounded as if her teeth were gritted together.

They were taking Norman's leg. His leg. And they might take the other one.

"I'm sorry," he said again.

"Now!" Mrs. Peres ordered.

And then he was gone, leaving Laura with her chaotic thoughts, with misery and guilt churning around in her mind like a miniature tornado. Norman loved to hunt and fish. He loved to dance. He was the best roofer they had, the one with the surest step, the one who could clamber about for ten or twelve hours at a stretch. He had big, strong legs with thick thighs. He lived outdoors. He'd never liked sedentary activities like reading or listening to music or going to the movies.

This would change his life.

It would also change hers.

Chapter Three

"Neil! Wake up."

Neil jumped. "What? Something happen?" He shook his head to clear out the cobwebs. He must have fallen asleep.

"Nothing's happened," Denise said. "But the nurse wants to talk to us."

A skinny, redheaded nurse stood a couple of feet away. "I just came out to tell you that if you'd like to go home for a while, we'll call you if there's any change."

Neil rubbed his eyes as he tried to focus. His head throbbed. "What time is it?"

His father answered. "Almost eight o'clock."

Neil's stomach grumbled. No wonder, he thought. He hadn't eaten since breakfast on the flight in this morning.

"Why don't you give me a phone number where I can reach you?" the nurse offered. "That way, if your brother should regain consciousness before you come back, I can call you."

"What do you think, Papa?" His father looked exhausted. "Sounds like a good idea to go to the house for a while. We can get something to eat—you can rest a little. We can see how Mama's feeling."

His father wearily agreed.

"I'll take Papa in my car," Denise said.

"Okay. I shouldn't be much behind you," Neil agreed. Neil gave the nurse the phone number, then straightened his clothes and quickly ran a comb through his hair. His throat felt dry, and his mouth tasted like cotton. There was a kink in his neck, too. He must have been sleeping in an awkward position. He felt like hell.

He picked up his jacket and took off. He couldn't wait to shower and shave. Maybe then he'd feel more like a human being. But as he rode down on the elevator, he was smitten with the image of Laura Sebastian as she'd looked earlier, stricken by the news he'd had to give her. Impulsively, he stopped on the second floor.

The plump nurse who'd been on duty earlier was gone. In her place was a tall, rawboned woman with kinky gray hair. "Yes?" she said as he approached the nurses' station.

"I just wondered how Miss Sebastian is doing," Neil said.

"She's resting comfortably. Did you want to see her?"

"No. No, I just wanted to check on her." Neil walked away wondering why he'd felt compelled to ask about Laura. Guilty conscience, he told himself.

During the forty-minute drive to his parents' home in Patinville, Neil's thoughts centered on Laura Sebastian. He knew that if Norman were to survive this experience, the woman he loved would play a key role in that survival. Would Laura be up to it? Was she strong enough to face the arduous times ahead? Would she even want to?

From what Denise told him, Laura and Norman weren't officially engaged yet. Did Laura love Norman? Neil hoped for once Denise's instincts were wrong. How much bad luck could Norman stand at once?

But there were no answers to these questions. As soon as Laura was strong enough, though, Neil intended to ask her. If she *didn't* love Norman, if she wasn't going to stick by him, Neil would need to know. They'd all need to know. Because then they'd have to work doubly hard to help Norman.

Neil wished he knew more about Laura. That Norman had chosen her didn't necessarily mean she had the qualities Neil knew she'd need in these changed circumstances. As much as he loved his brother, he wasn't blind to his shortcomings. Norman tended toward the casual approach to life, rarely wasting any of his time worrying about anything. His attitude was that most problems would take care of themselves.

Neil wasn't sure what he thought of Laura. When he'd first seen her lying there with her eyes closed, she had looked so commonplace and unexceptional. She'd also looked pale and vulnerable—not at all like a woman who would be able to face much adversity.

But then she'd opened her eyes. Their color was the same startling shade of aquamarine as the water he gazed at each day from his porch, and they were filled with intelligence. And when she spoke, there had been a quiet strength in her soft voice. He'd had to revise his initial impression of her. How a woman could seem both vulnerable and strong at the same time, Neil wasn't sure, but Laura Sebastian did.

One point in her favor—she had certainly seemed to care about Norman. There had been shock and concern and real grief in her reaction to the news about his injuries.

As he drove down the narrow lane that dead-ended at the driveway leading to his parents' home, he put aside his thoughts about Laura. Parked haphazardly in front of the house and in the driveway were several cars. Neil recognized his father's pickup and his mother's old Plymouth station wagon. One he didn't know was a big, black Cadillac.

Disgust swept over him as he stared at the license plate of the Cadillac illuminated in his headlights.

Willis.

The car belonged to Willis Fontenot.

Neil grimaced. Good old Willis. His cousin and good buddy. The buddy who had testified against him to Internal Affairs. The buddy who had coveted not only Neil's wife but the position as a departmental supervisor he and Neil were both competing for.

Neil headed toward the back of the house. He was in no mood to see Willis or anybody else except the immediate family. What was Willis doing there, anyway? Had he continued to come around after Neil moved to the Keys? You'd think the opportunist would be too embarrassed to show his face.

The spotlight mounted over the back door was turned on. It bathed the backyard in artificial brightness. Neil took a deep breath of the cool December air and looked around at the familiar surroundings before climbing the steps to the back porch. There was a smell of wood smoke in the air, a smell that instantly transported him to his boyhood. A raccoon raced across the winter grass and disappeared into the woods at the back of the property. The woods looked dark and mysterious. Sadness rippled through him—sadness for the days that were gone and could never be recaptured. He and Norman...and Willis...had spent so many carefree summer days playing in those same woods. If he closed his eyes, he could still see their fresh young faces and hear their eager voices shouting and laughing.

Shaking off the memory, he opened the back door. Nothing would bring back yesterday. And he couldn't put off facing today any longer.

The smell of fresh coffee hit him the moment he stepped into the steamy kitchen. Angela DiCiccio, one of his mother's friends from the Altar Society, was removing a pan of corn bread from the oven. She looked up as he entered.

Her plump face creased into a smile. "Neil! It's been a long time!"

"Hello, Mrs. DiCiccio. How are you?"

"Oh, I'm doin' just fine. But oh, this is a terrible thing that's happened to your brother."

Neil's chest tightened. He nodded.

"You go on into the livin' room, Neil. They're waitin' for you. Do you want some coffee? How about somethin' to eat?" She gestured to a big pot of gumbo simmering on the stove.

"In a little while, Mrs. DiCiccio. I want to get cleaned up first." He mentally girded himself before he walked down the hall.

There were six people in the living room. His sisters Desiree and Denise; Denise's husband, Jett Hebert; his father; Willis Fontenot; and a blonde Neil did not recognize. Desiree's eyes were red-rimmed and puffy, and Jett, a nice down-to-earth hometown boy who Neil liked, looked sad as he sat with his arm around Denise. Neil's father stood staring out the big picture window, shoulders slumped. He turned at Neil's approach, and the others looked his way, too. Willis, a big-boned handsome man who looked older than his thirty-nine years—perhaps due to the fact that his brown hair had already started graying—had been sitting hunched forward in the armchair next to the fireplace. He stood, an uncertain smile on his face and a wary look in his dark eyes as he watched Neil's approach.

I'd look wary if I were you, too, thought Neil. He could feel his insides balling into a hard knot, and if he hadn't known how it would upset his parents, he would have told Willis he wasn't welcome there.

"Neil, it's been a long time," Willis said as he stepped forward, right hand extended.

Neil ignored the hand. "Willis," he acknowledged curtly. "I'm surprised to see you here."

Willis's face flushed.

No one said anything as the two men stared at each other.

Finally Neil's father said, "Willis, he came to pay his respects and ask about Norman."

"Really?" Neil said.

Willis made a visible effort to put a smile on his face, but the smile was strained. "This is my wife, Regina," he said. He gestured toward the blonde who was sitting in Neil's mother's favorite chair, an old porch rocker.

Regina Fontenot smiled slightly, a knowing look in her shrewd blue eyes. "I've heard a lot about you, Neil," she said, her voice smooth and silky as butter. "I understand you and Willis used to be real tight."

"Yeah, I guess you could say that." Neil extended his hand. "Nice to meet you." He had no quarrel with Willis's wife. After they shook hands, Neil turned to his sisters, saying, "Where's Mama?"

Desiree stood, pushing her thick, dark hair away from her face. "I forced her to go lie down." She smiled slightly. "She fought me all the way, but she finally gave in. She was exhausted. I hope she's asleep."

"Good." Neil addressed his father. "Papa, after I get cleaned up and eat something, I'm going to go back to the hospital. I want you to get some sleep before you come back."

"Now, you stop worryin' about me, you hear?" René sputtered. "I'm not dead yet, you know."

As tense and stressed out as Neil felt, he had to smother a smile. His father took such pride in his physical stamina. At family gatherings he'd outdance any of the men. His energy and enthusiasm were boundless. Norman was very like him. Had been very like him, Neil amended, sobering immediately.

"Regina, it's time for us to be going," Willis said. "These folks have things to do." His stiff stance told Neil exactly how offended he was by Neil's attitude toward him.

"Neil, I'm ashamed of you, the way you acted. Cain't you forget about what happened three years ago, no?" his father said as the front door closed on the Fontenots. "I know Willis, he wishes he never had to take no part in what happened."

"Papa, Willis took advantage of what happened to further his own career. Now if you want to pretend he only did what he had to do, that's your privilege."

No one said anything, but all eyes watched him.

Neil sighed wearily. "I don't blame Willis for what happened that night. After all, it was my wife and my responsibility. I know that. And believe me, I'll never forget it. I have to live with it the rest of my life—knowing that if Erica hadn't shown up that night, if I hadn't left, Jimmy would still be alive." He took a deep breath, willing himself to speak calmly, to force away the image of Jimmy lying in the street... "But what I *do* blame Willis for is the way he jumped at the chance to cast doubt on my ability as a cop, the way he twisted that argument we'd had into something more than a personal matter... used it to make it seem as if the only thing on my mind that night was Erica. *That's* what I can't forget. Or forgive."

"But Neil," Desiree said, "you were absolved of any wrongdoing."

"I know that, but it's no thanks to Willis." A wry smile twisted his mouth. "His strategy worked, too. Even though I was cleared, I was no longer any threat to him. He got his promotion." Neil laughed cynically. "But he didn't get the girl."

"I don' think his testifyin' like he did had anything to do with Erica, no," his father insisted. "He was just doin' his job. Why, Willis, he's fam'ly. You was friends all of your lives. How can you turn your back on that?"

"The same way he turned his back on me." As far as Neil was concerned, Willis Fontenot wasn't important enough to warrant any of his time or energy. Especially now, when all their efforts and thoughts should be concentrated on Norman.

"Son," his father said as he put his arm around Neil's shoulders. "It's not good to carry such bitterness around inside you. It's like a cancer, you know?"

"Neil..." Desiree said, hesitancy written all over her pretty face, "I...uh...think there's something you should know."

Neil tensed at her tone.

"I...I work for Willis's wife."

"What?" The question was like a gunshot in the quiet room. "You, what?"

Desiree cringed. "Please, Neil, don't look at me like that. She offered me a job as the receptionist for her real estate company. I...I couldn't refuse it. It's hard to find any kind of job here."

Jesus, he hated the idea of any of his family being obligated to Willis or his wife.

"There's nothin' wrong with Desiree workin' for Regina," his father said. "And I don' wan' to hear another word about it, okay?"

Neil recognized his father's tone of voice. It was the same one he'd used when Neil was a small boy and he'd pushed René too far. Even though part of him wanted to hammer his point home, force René to see Willis for what he was, Neil knew it would be a hollow victory if he upset his father any more than he was upset now. They *did* need all their energy for Norman.

"Willis was just elected mayor of Patinville, you know," Denise said, a wry smile on her face, her eyes communicating her understanding. "Quite an accomplishment, isn't it?"

Neil resisted the urge to say, "Who'd he step over this time?" Instead, he quietly met Denise's gaze. She always had been the sharper of his two sisters. Desiree rarely saw beneath the surface; she was very like Norman in that respect.

"Yep, Willis has come up in the world," Jett said in his quiet way.

Neil knew he had another ally in his family. His parents and sister meant well. They were just too naive. Willis had been a greedy boy who was jealous of Neil and everything Neil had ever had, and he had shucked their friendship at the first opportunity.

He wasn't worth wasting one more minute of Neil's time.

Laura couldn't believe she'd slept more than sixteen hours straight. She'd dreamed while she was sleeping—disjointed snatches that disturbed her: Norman crying in pain as he tried to walk with only one leg, and Neil Cantrelle pinning her with his dark, questioning eyes—eyes that seemed to look straight through into her soul for answers. Her heart skipped erratically as the memory of Neil's visit came tumbling back, and the realization of Norman's condition hit her full force.

Oh, if only Celeste were with her now. At times, Laura was sorry she'd left California, since her leaving had put so much distance between her and her oldest friend. She and Celeste Broussard had been as close as sisters. Even after Celeste entered the convent and became a nun, the two had remained close, although since Celeste had taken her final vows and been assigned to a hospital near the Oregon state border, Laura had had to be satisfied with letters and an occasional phone call.

If only she had someone she could talk to here. Someone who would understand how she felt and be nonjudgmental. Someone who could give her solid advice based on the realities of the situation and not on personal emotions.

Laura's only real confidante in Patinville was Denise Hebert, Norman's older sister. And Denise was involved, so how could she be impartial where it came to Norman's welfare?

Laura couldn't see herself telling Denise that she didn't love Norman and hadn't been planning on marrying him. That she had, in fact, planned to tell him so the night of the accident.

She sighed, the sound ragged with weariness and worry, then looked up as there was a soft rap on the door.

"Come in."

She tried to disguise her surprise as Denise Hebert, followed closely by Neil Cantrelle, walked into the room. For a moment Laura wondered if they'd somehow been able to read her mind. And her thoughts.

Denise grasped her hand. "Laura, I'm so glad you're okay."

Laura saw tears shimmering in Denise's eyes. Suddenly Laura felt her own defenses crumbling. She bit her lower lip to keep it from trembling and fought to control her emotions, which she knew were much too fragile and close to the surface due to her weakened physical condition.

I won't cry, she told herself. She hated to cry. This ability to control her emotions and present a picture of calm acceptance to the outside world had been her only defense during the years when everything in her life was so terrible; she would have been crying constantly if she'd allowed herself to. "Thanks for coming," she said.

Now Neil moved into her line of vision. He looked different today. Softer in some ways, probably due to the fact that it looked as if he had recently shaved, and his unkempt hair was combed and more or less neat. He was also dressed differently, which removed more of the hard edges. Today he wore clean jeans and a rich, rust-colored sweater, the perfect complement to his dark, rugged good looks.

But his eyes, which gleamed like polished onyx in the sunlight, were still guarded and full of questions. Her heart somersaulted crazily. *He knows. He knows the entire accident was my fault.*

She shivered involuntarily. She wanted to look away, but she couldn't. Her stomach jumped as they stared at each other. His eyes were relentlessly dogged in their determination to wrest her secrets from her. She licked her lips, and suddenly, his entire bearing changed. The rigidness fell from his shoulders, and he smiled, the smile catching her frazzled emotions and tossing them helter-skelter. Where first there had been mistrust, now his gaze seemed poignantly sad, and Laura had an almost irresistible urge to reach out and touch him.

"Hello, Laura," he said. His voice reminded her of rough velvet. "How do you feel today?" Sympathy was there in the gentleness of the question. Laura could feel it, could feel herself responding to it, even as she told herself that this man was dangerous to her own hard-fought equilibrium.

"Better," she murmured, still holding tightly to Denise's hands. She hurt everywhere, but for some reason, she didn't want to admit this to Neil Cantrelle, not in the face of what Norman was undergoing. "How...how is Norman? Have you seen him?"

"Not yet," Denise said. "We're going up to intensive care when we leave you. We wanted to check on you first." She smiled, her dark eyes filled with warmth. "Norman's sure to ask about you when he wakes up. We wanted to be able to tell him."

Laura looked away. Of course Denise was right. Norman *would* ask about her. After all, he loved her, didn't he? He had fully expected her to tell him she'd marry him.

Dear God. The knowledge that any decision regarding her future had been taken out of her hands by fate and a rainy night, thundered through her. If only he hadn't reached for her hand. None of this would have happened. None of it. *And I'd still be free.* The thought came unbidden even as she berated herself for her selfishness.

Then another thought hit her. "What happened to the people in the other car?" She had completely forgotten about them.

"There was only one person in the other car," Neil said. "And he was thrown free." Irony tinged his voice. "He fell asleep at the wheel. The accident was his fault."

"I—I thought—"

"You thought it was Norman's fault?" Neil interrupted. "No. The skid marks, the positions of the cars, everything points to the fact that the other guy swerved right in front of your car. There was nothing Norman could have done that he didn't do."

"No," Laura said, unable to keep from answering honestly. "I thought it was my fault."

"Your fault!" Denise exclaimed.

Neil frowned, a stillness settling over him. Laura could feel the tension in his body. There it was, that suspicion. Why was he so on edge, so defensive and guarded? she wondered. She could almost feel the wall he'd built around himself. *He's been hurt and now he's suspicious of everyone.* The thought came from nowhere, but she knew instinctively that she was right. He was like an animal who has been mistreated and who never quite trusts again. He would trust you a little bit, then he would retreat.

"I... was afraid," she explained haltingly. "And Norman turned toward me. I... I thought I'd caused the accident because he looked away from the road."

"No. Get that thought out of your mind. You had nothing to do with it!" Denise exclaimed. She turned toward her brother. "Tell her she's being silly, Neil."

"The accident wasn't your fault," he echoed, but the look of suspicion still hovered in his dark eyes. Or maybe it wasn't exactly suspicion. Maybe it was simply a holding back, an I'll-wait-and-see-before-I-decide look.

"Have you been worrying about this?" Denise demanded.

Laura nodded. "Norman's been so good to me. You've all been so good to me. I—"

"You're not to blame," As he reassured her, Neil's eyes softened, and some of the tension ebbed from his body.

Laura could feel her own muscles loosening, her heart slowing, as she relaxed against her pillow. Some of her anguish and guilt receded. "You'll let me know about Norman as soon as you know anything, won't you?" she asked, directing the question to both of them but unable to tear her gaze away from Neil Cantrelle's.

He nodded, his expression grave.

Denise squeezed her hand again, then bent to kiss her cheek, a flowery scent wafting over Laura. Laura felt her eyes fill again at the expression of kindness from Norman's sister. "Get well, honey. Don't worry about anything," Denise whispered. Then she straightened. "Jeannine's gone over to see the cats several times, and I've fed them and cleaned out the litter box."

Laura clasped her hand against her mouth, then flinched from the pain in her lip. How could she have forgotten her cats? They must be so bewildered by her absence. She hadn't left them alone overnight since she'd gotten them six months earlier. "Are you sure you don't mind taking care of them until I get home?" she asked Denise.

"No, of course not. Besides, you know how Jeannine adores them. She'll love helping out."

Laura did know. Jeannine, Denise's ten-year-old, came by each evening when Laura got home from work to play with Pete and Phoebe. Jeannine's visit was always the high point of Laura's day—spending thirty minutes or so with the bright-eyed charmer she'd grown to love.

Laura lived in one half of the duplex that Denise and her husband, Jett, owned. In fact, Denise was responsible for Laura's getting her job with Cantrelle Roofing and Home Improvement Company. The first day Laura had arrived in Patinville, she'd checked into the one small motel and been directed to Jett's for dinner by the motel's night clerk.

"Best Cajun food hereabouts," he said. "Just down the way a couple of blocks. You can't miss it."

Laura walked into Jett's, the restaurant Denise and her husband owned and worked in together, and Denise had waited on her. Laura had liked Denise immediately, her bright eyes, infectious smile, and easy manner impossible to resist. When Laura explained that she was new in town and looking for a place to live, Denise smiled.

"You've come to the right place."

Then later, after Laura moved into the duplex, she'd asked Denise for her advice on finding a job. When Denise discovered that Laura was a bookkeeper and experienced office manager, her dark eyes lit up with undisguised delight. "Norman is going to think he's died and gone to heaven when I bring you around. He's been looking for qualified help for weeks with no success."

Since jobs were scarce, Laura was puzzled, but Denise explained quickly.

"So many people have left this part of Louisiana since the oil business has gone into such a decline that there aren't many around to fill the few jobs there are. There're plenty of untrained, unskilled people, or people who only know the oil patch business, but the only person Norman could find with bookkeeping skills was a crabby old lady from Port Allen and Norman said he didn't want to have to look at her sour face all day." Denise grinned. "You'll be much nicer to look at."

And so it was settled, and Laura started to work for Norman the next day. She and Denise built on that initial liking for one another and soon became friends. Denise was the first real woman friend Laura'd made since Celeste. In fact, Laura thought, Denise had some of the same qualities that had attracted her to Celeste. The same quirky sense of humor, the same kindness and generosity, the same common sense. Denise also had a temper. It didn't flare often, but when it did, it was like a volcano in its fiery intensity. And then, also like a volcano, it would die down and lie dormant.

"Well, *chère,* we'd better go now. Let you get some sleep," Denise said. "Is there anything you want me to bring when we come back?"

"No, nothing." Her eyes met Neil's for one instant before brother and sister turned to leave the room. Her heart gave an odd little blip as he smiled.

"Hang tough," he murmured.

After they left, Laura sank back against her pillows. Doubts began to plague her again now that their reassuring presence was gone. What if they'd been lying to her, just telling her she had had nothing to do with the accident to make her feel better?

But, no. Denise might lie to her out of sympathy, Neil Cantrelle, on the other hand, would never lie to spare her feelings. She had an impression he said what he thought.

Once again, she wondered exactly what had happened when Neil left Patinville. She knew very little about the episode, even though Norman had talked about his brother often. And that was strange, because even though he'd told her many unimportant things, Norman had withheld certain information. The only thing he'd told her was that Neil had been accused of dereliction of duty but had been found innocent. He'd refused to talk further about the circumstances, one of the few times Norman had kept anything back concerning his family.

About Neil himself Norman had obviously been full of hero worship. He'd talked about Neil's quick intelligence, his strength and ability, and told her volumes about their childhood together. Obviously, the brothers had always been close. Neil had taught him to hunt and fish. Neil had taught him to whittle. Neil had watched over him, fought Norman's enemies fiercely. Neil had been a cop, a great cop. And Laura thought Neil had also been married, but now that she tried to dredge up the conversation when Norman had talked about the marriage, she couldn't remember much about it. Only the idea that the marriage had ended unhappily. She'd had the distinct feeling that the end of the marriage had been linked to Neil's quitting the police force and leaving Patinville, but Norman hadn't elaborated, and she hadn't probed.

Now, though, she wondered. She felt inexplicably drawn to Neil Cantrelle. There was that hint of sadness around his eyes—a longing she recognized, because she felt a similar longing deep within herself.

But there had been more than sadness and emptiness in his eyes tonight. There'd also been a question mark. Neil Cantrelle wanted something from her. Uneasily, she wondered what it could be.

Chapter Four

"Your brother's just regained consciousness." The same skinny redheaded nurse who'd been on duty the day before beckoned them from the doorway of intensive care.

Denise gave Neil a wide-eyed look. He squeezed her shoulder in a reassuring gesture. He felt the same apprehension he saw in her eyes.

"I'd better call Mama and Papa," she said.

The nurse waited with Neil. Once Denise had made the call, they headed for Norman's room. Pushing open the double doors that led into the unit, the nurse gestured them to follow. Inside, it was like being in a different world. The place hummed with activity, but it was a controlled, quiet activity. Neil glanced around, noticing with approval how each person moved with calm, but rapid, efficiency. The area smelled strongly of disinfectant and medication, and it was spotlessly clean.

The nurse led them to the second doorway on their left. "Wait here," she said. "I'll get Dr. Dunado."

She entered the room, and Neil and Denise looked at each other. Denise looked scared. Neil wished he could tell her there wasn't anything to be frightened of, but if he were honest with himself, he'd have to admit he was scared, too. Inside that room Norman was fighting for his life. Fighting for his life, and only thirty-four years old.

No one should die that young. Reluctantly, he remembered that Jimmy had only been thirty-one when he'd died. He shook off the thought. At the moment, he needed to focus all his energy on willing Norman to live. He couldn't even worry about the loss of Norman's leg. If Norman survived, they'd all have to deal with it, but right now, getting him past this crisis was the most important issue.

The nurse slipped through the door. "The doctor's coming out. He wants to tell you a few things before you go in to see your brother."

Neil nodded.

Within seconds, Dunado emerged from the room, a grave expression on his face. The thick lenses of his glasses looked almost opaque as he directed his remarks to Neil. "The two of you can go in for five minutes. No longer. Is that clear?"

"Yes," they both said at the same time.

"Your brother doesn't know about his leg," Dunado continued, "and I don't want you to tell him. I'll tell him when I think he's strong enough to withstand the shock."

Neil frowned. Wouldn't Norman be able to tell that his leg had been amputated?

"He's groggy and in a lot of pain. He's also restrained from much movement by the machines and tubes, so he's not likely to realize what's happened to him. By morning we'll probably have to tell him."

"I'd like to be with him when you do," Neil said. He'd rather be anywhere else, but he knew Norman would need him.

Denise's small hand slid into his, and Neil grasped it firmly. He could feel the tremor in her body.

"Okay, then, you two can go in. Whatever you do, don't upset him. He's probably aware enough to know he's been seriously injured—just don't give him any information he doesn't need."

After giving Denise's hand one more squeeze, Neil pushed open the door, and they entered the room. It was dimly lighted from a low-wattage fluorescent light attached to the wall over the top of the bed. A cardiac monitor bleeped next to the bed, and there was a pole with an intravenous bag and tubes everywhere. It seemed as if every available stretch of Norman's skin had something attached to it or stuck into it. Norman lay back against the pillows, swathed in bandages. His eyes were closed.

"Norman?" Neil said. He tried to control the shock radiating through his body at how suddenly helpless, even smaller, his brother looked. He'd thought he was prepared for this; he'd certainly seen enough injury and death during his twelve years on the force, but this was different. This was family. This was Norman.

Norman's eyes opened. "Neil?" he whispered.

The whisper was faint—so faint, Neil had to lean forward to hear him. He smiled. "I'm here, little brother." He touched Norman's hand, which was lying on top of the blanket. "Can't I trust you to stay out of trouble when I'm not around?" He forced himself not to look at the tented spot where Norman's right leg should have been. A lump formed in his throat, and his eyes burned. He hadn't cried since he was nine years old and the family dog had been hit by a car. But today, here, now, he wanted to bawl like a baby.

"I'm here too, Norman," Denise said, walking to the other side of the bed.

Norman slowly moved his head toward her. He made a visible attempt to smile, then closed his eyes wearily. "Denise," he whispered. "Hi."

"Hi," she answered, lower lip trembling. A tear slipped down her cheek, and she knuckled it away. Her dark eyes met Neil's gaze, and for a moment they stared at one another in silent agony.

Don't cry. Be strong. I know exactly how you feel, and you can cry when we leave this room, but not now. Neil concentrated on communicating his message, and Denise blinked. She took a deep breath and nodded slightly. Neil relaxed. She was going to be all right.

"Neil," Norman said, his voice weak but clear. "There was an accident, wasn't there?"

"Yes."

Norman closed his eyes, then opened them, frowning. "I...I think I re-remember." The frown deepened. "L-Laura." Now his voice grew agitated, and the monitor bleeped faster. "H-how is Laura? Is she okay?"

Neil covered Norman's hand with his. "Laura's fine. Denise and I were just downstairs talking to her."

"Are you...sure?"

His breathing was still too fast, Neil thought. "I'm sure. Now don't get excited. It's not good for you to get excited."

"Y-you wouldn't lie to me?"

"Norman," Denise interjected, "Laura is fine. She just has a few bruises, but otherwise she's doing great."

"I...I tried to save her," Norman said. "I saw that car come into our lane...and..."

"You don't have to explain," Neil said.

Ignoring Neil, Norman continued, and as he talked his voice became weaker. "I swerved so they wouldn't hit us head-on or on Laura's side...."

"Shh," Denise soothed. "Don't talk anymore. Just concentrate on getting well."

"My...my legs...hurt," Norman said.

Neil's heart hammered in his chest. Although he hadn't prayed much over the past years, he sent a silent prayer heavenward.

Denise bent over and kissed Norman on the cheek. "Try to sleep now," she murmured. "Neil and I were given strict instructions that we could only stay five minutes, so we'd better be going."

"Don't go—"

"We'll be right outside," Neil said. "In the waiting room, so if you need us, all you have to do is ask the nurse to call us."

"Wh-where are Mama and Papa?"

"They're coming. We made them go home last night. Mama was pretty tired," Denise said. "But they'll be here soon."

Five minutes later, as Denise and Neil stood together in the waiting room, Denise said, "Oh, God, Neil. It's so much worse than I imagined it would be." Her face crumpled, and Neil folded her into his arms. Her entire body shook as she cried, and he could feel the heat of her tears soaking through his sweater. His insides trembled, and he had to fight against his own despair. It wouldn't help anyone for him to break down. He'd be much better off—they'd *all* be much better off—if he became angry.

He clenched his teeth as he patted Denise's back. Her sobs had become quieter now. Damn it all, he *was* angry. He was furious that the fates had pulled such a cruel trick on Norman, who didn't deserve it. Having had firsthand experience with so many slimeballs in the world, Neil thought it was poor planning on somebody's part that so many of them seemed to prosper and thrive while people like Norman had gotten such a raw deal. The healthy spurt of anger gave him a needed injection of strength, and he said, "Come on, Denise. Pull yourself together. Crying won't help Norman. We've gotta be strong for him. He's going to need us."

Denise sniffed and pulled a handkerchief from the pocket of her jeans. She blew her nose. "I... I know you're right. I'm sorry, Neil. It's just that—"

"I know. It's okay. But now you've got it off your chest, so let's forget it."

She nodded.

"Let's go sit over there," Neil said. They walked to the couch in the corner and sat down. "Let's talk about something else while we're waiting for the folks. You were going to tell me more about Laura. What do you think of her, and why do you think she's not in love with Norman?"

Denise drew her legs up under her and settled more comfortably into the corner of the couch. "I really like her. She's thoughtful and intelligent, and when she lets her guard down, she's got a wonderful sense of humor. And she's fantastic with the kids. Jeannine adores her. And Jett likes her, too. He told me she was a very restful sort of person." Denise grinned, and Neil thought how pretty she was when she smiled. "I guess Jett was subtly trying to tell me that I'm often *not* a very restful sort of person."

"Did you tell him you're operating under a handicap?" Neil teased. "After all, you're a Cantrelle."

Denise chuckled. Then, suddenly, her face twisted. "Oh, Neil, here we are making jokes, and Norman—"

Neil reached over and grasped her hand. "I know, *chère*. But you can't be sad all the time. Just because we forget for a minute and laugh about something doesn't mean we don't care."

Her dark eyes slowly brightened, and she leaned over and kissed his cheek. "I love you, Neil," she said softly. "I'm glad you're home."

"I'm glad I'm here, too," he said, his heart full. "Now," he added briskly, "finish what you were saying about Laura."

"Well, she and I have gotten to be pretty good friends, although—"

"What?"

"Well, she's very private. She'll listen to me go on for hours, but she's told me very little about her own background. I don't know why, I mean, it's just a feeling—not based on fact or anything—but I think she comes from a background she's ashamed of. Or, if not ashamed, a bad situation she wants to forget. There's . . . there's a sadness in her eyes that she sometimes forgets to cover up." Denise looked up at him, her own eyes earnest. "It almost seems too pat, like armchair psychology or something, but Laura has always struck me as emotionally needy—like a woman who has never had love and comfort and desperately wants it."

It didn't seem too pat to Neil. He thought Denise was right. He'd seen something of the same thing in Laura Sebastian's eyes.

"You should see the way she reacts when Mama and Papa are around," Denise continued softly. "Her eyes follow them around like . . . well, like she just wants them to be *her* parents."

Neil couldn't condemn her for that. His parents were great.

"I also think she's got some problems, but since she's never confided in me, I haven't wanted to ask her."

"What kind of problems?"

"Well . . ."

"Come on, tell me," Neil urged. It wasn't like Denise to be reticent.

Denise frowned. "Well, I think she's terrified of the dark. Lights blaze in her part of the house all night long—"

"Her part of the house?"

"Didn't I tell you? She rents the other half of our house."

"No, you didn't."

"Anyway," Denise continued after explaining how Laura had come to be their tenant, "I asked Norman about my suspicion, and he just brushed it off. Said, well, yeah, Laura had kind of mentioned she was scared of the dark, but it wasn't a big deal. She'd get over it."

That sounded like Norman, Neil thought. He was reminded of the time the family had all gone to Gulf Shores on a vacation. Norman must have been about fifteen, so Desiree would have been eight. They were swimming, and Desiree wouldn't go into water deeper than her knees. Norman's solution to her fear was to pick her up, kicking and screaming, and take her into deeper water and throw her in. He hadn't meant to be mean, but he simply hadn't understood that her fear was real. He wasn't afraid. Why should she be? And when their parents berated him, he still hadn't understood. He was honestly bewildered by their anger.

"Neil," Denise said, breaking into his reverie, "Whatever happens, promise me something, will you?"

"Anything," he said with a smile.

"Be kind to Laura. I...I know your first loyalty is to Norman. Mine is, too. But Laura's hurting, I know she is. And she's going to need us, too."

Their eyes met. God, he'd missed her. How could he have stayed away for three years? "You've got yourself a deal."

When Laura awakened on Monday morning, she immediately knew she was better. For one thing, her head no longer hurt, and when she took a breath, although there was still some pain, it no longer tore through her like a rampaging lion.

"I'd like to go home today," she told Dr. Dunado when he made his rounds.

"Too soon." He listened to her chest.

"I really want to go home," she insisted. "I feel much better." She hated hospitals. And she missed her cats, her own things around her, and Jeannine. Especially Jeannine.

Dunado made a notation on her chart. He pushed his glasses up on his nose, then pursed his lips as he studied her. "You're doing quite well. You can probably go home tomorrow."

"Please let me go today," Laura persisted. "There's no one to do the payroll, and the men need their money."

"I said you can probably leave tomorrow. Now that's all I'm going to say." He turned to leave.

"Dr. Dunado! Is there any change in Norman's condition?"

He turned slowly. "He's conscious, but he's still in critical condition."

"Oh." Laura bit her lip. Conscious. Did that mean he knew about his leg? She wanted to ask, but she wasn't sure she wanted to know the answer. "Would... would you tell him I asked about him?"

He nodded, face softening for a minute, then he swung on his heel and left the room.

After he left, Laura wondered what Norman was doing right now. If his sisters and brother...

His brother.

Every time she thought about Neil Cantrelle she saw his eyes, dark, still, questioning eyes that seemed to be searching out all her secrets. Eyes that made her feel exposed and vulnerable. Eyes she couldn't forget.

Neil watched Norman's eyes as Dr. Dunado matter-of-factly explained what had happened during and after the accident. He saw the pain, then the shock, then the terror, then the panic. He felt Norman's hands begin to shake. The monitor bleeped louder and faster.

But the doctor seemed ready for this reaction because he soothed him until his heartbeat returned to normal. Then he walked around to the side of the bed where Neil stood.

"Will you stay with him?" he said in a low tone.

"For as long as he needs me."

"Good. He'll probably fall asleep soon. The medication keeps him pretty sleepy. In the meantime, I'll go out and talk to your parents."

Neil nodded, then sat by the bedside until Norman finally fell asleep. Only then did he rise and with a weary sigh, push open the door and escape to the hum of activity outside.

"Bad, huh?" a tiny nurse with big dimples asked.

Neil nodded. He was incapable of speech. Dreading facing his parents, he delayed the moment when he'd have to go out to the waiting area by kneeling to tie the laces on his running shoes.

Finally he could put off the moment no longer. He braced himself, then walked out the double doors.

"Neil!" His mother rushed to his side, her eyes anxious. His father followed more slowly. This morning Desiree had accompanied them, and Denise stayed home with her family. All three pairs of eyes sought his.

"How did he take the news?" his father asked.

"Is he okay?" This came from Desiree.

Neil shrugged. "He was shocked. And he's scared. But the doctor talked to him, even explained to him that with an artificial leg he'll be able to do just about anything he did before." Neil sighed. "I don't know if Norman believed the doctor, but at least he calmed down. He's asleep again."

"Blessed Mother," his mother whispered. "Please help him."

Just then one of the nurses strode out of the intensive care unit, looked down the hall, then beckoned to Neil.

"The duty nurse from two just called," she said. "Laura Sebastian is asking to see you or your sister."

Neil knew she meant Denise. He guessed he'd better go.

When he entered Laura's room a few minutes later, she was sitting propped up in bed, and she looked ten times better than she had the day before. Sunshine streamed in the window, and Neil noticed how the golden streaks in her hair glistened. Someone had obviously tried to freshen her appearance, because as he walked closer, he could see that her face was scrubbed and shining, and her hair had been brushed to the side. She had nice hair, he thought, straight and glossy and curling slightly toward her chin.

"Hi," she said softly. Then hesitantly, she smiled.

It wasn't much of a smile, as smiles go, but its impact went like an arrow straight through Neil's heart. There was something heartrending about the smile—crooked, tremulous, almost diffident. As if she were afraid of his reaction if she smiled at him. An apologetic smile.

Neil knew instinctively that she wasn't the kind of woman accustomed to having her wishes granted by bestowing a smile. Not like his ex-wife, who had expected people to jump through hoops when she smiled. Neil pushed the thought of Erica away. He'd promised himself long ago that he wouldn't waste another moment thinking about her.

"How are you doing today?" he said now.

"I feel much better, thanks."

"Good. Glad to hear it." He meant it. Even though he'd had twinges when he thought about Norman being so seriously hurt while Laura had emerged almost unscathed, he didn't really feel any animosity toward her. It wasn't her fault Norman had tried to protect her and probably was more critically hurt than he would have been if he hadn't swerved to take the brunt of the collision. That was just the breaks. Hell, Neil probably would have done the same thing. That was the way they'd been raised. A man always tried to protect a woman. Period. Women's lib didn't enter into the Cajun philosophy.

"The reason I wanted to see you is that the doctor says I can probably go home tomorrow, but I..." She hesitated, looking up at him squarely.

Whew, he thought. Those eyes are really something. The full force of their intense color hit him.

"But?" he prompted.

"I... I don't have a way home," she said in a rush. "Do you think you could ask Denise to pick me up in the morning?"

Denise was right, he thought. That apologetic tone and the wistful look in her eyes when she asked a simple favor said Laura Sebastian was a woman who had been taught to believe that she wasn't worth much so she shouldn't expect much.

Neil wondered who had done this to her. No wonder Norman had been attracted to her. He'd always been the kind of person who had taken in strays, both animals and people. Norman's approach to their problems was there was nothing a good, hot meal wouldn't fix. He would have latched on to Laura Sebastian no matter what she looked like, simply because he'd have to be completely blind not to see how much she needed someone to care about her.

But Neil was revising his opinion of her looks, too. Maybe she wasn't movie-star beautiful, but those eyes of hers combined with that nice skin—even that smattering of topaz freckles across her nose—and that shiny hair and sweet smile—well, there was definitely something about her that got under your skin.

"Sure," he said. He would do better than that. He would take her home himself.

At noon, after spending the morning with Norman, who drifted in and out of sleep, Neil pulled into the circular drive in front of the hospital. He got out and helped the orderly who had wheeled Laura downstairs in a wheelchair. Neil took her arm and helped her stand. She was taller than he'd imagined her to be. Neil was almost six feet tall, so she must be close to five feet nine. But tall or not, he still felt that odd protectiveness as he helped her into the front passenger seat. She fumbled with the seat belt, and he realized that she was still weak and shaky. He helped her fasten the belt, and their fingers brushed, sending a little jolt of electricity through him. Her gaze met his, and for a minute he felt disconcerted. Those eyes were enough to make a person forget his name. They had the clearest, most direct gaze he'd ever seen.

"Does the seat belt bother you?" he asked. He knew her ribs must hurt.

"No, it's okay."

He had a feeling she'd say it was okay no matter how it felt. He shut the door, then walked around to his side and got in. Within minutes they were on their way.

"Looking forward to getting home?"

"Yes." She looked out the window.

She sure wasn't a talker, he thought. He wasn't much of a talker himself, but for some reason, he felt uncomfortable with the silence between them.

"They told me you were allowed to see Norman last night."

"Yes." There was a little catch in her voice.

Neil slanted a look at her. Her hands trembled in her lap. He was suddenly ashamed of himself. She was upset, and he wasn't helping matters by questioning her. He, of all people, should have known that when life has dealt you something tough, you need time to adjust before you can face the world.

For the rest of the forty-minute drive Neil didn't attempt to make conversation. He thought about his conversation with Denise. The more time he spent with Laura, the more he realized how complex she was. He also felt a strong sense of foreboding, because Norman was basically a very simple person. Neil really couldn't imagine someone like Laura marrying someone like Norman, but then, he'd seen stranger matches. Maybe he was worrying for nothing. Maybe it would all work out.

Finally they arrived at the duplex, and he pulled into the driveway. Denise must have been watching for them, because she came bounding out of the house and down the front steps. She reached Laura's door before Neil did.

"Laura, honey!" She yanked the door open, and with Neil on one side, and her on the other, they helped Laura out and up the walk, then onto the porch. Dozens of wind chimes hanging on Laura's side of the porch jingled merrily in the breeze.

Denise unlocked Laura's door.

"I didn't expect you to be here. Shouldn't you be at the restaurant?" Laura asked.

"Elaine MacAllister's helping out for a couple of days."

The minute they walked through the door, two long-haired cats rubbed up against Laura. Neil wasn't crazy about cats, but he had to admit these two were beautiful. One she called Pete was gray and white with a bushy tail and clear green eyes. He was aggressive and friendly, abandoning Laura to come up to Neil. Neil couldn't resist kneeling to pet him, and he purred. Phoebe, the female, seemed shy but sweet.

"She's a snowshoe," Laura informed him. "Isn't she gorgeous?" The cat was a mixture of champagne, white, and deep brown with light blue eyes.

"Come on, Laura, you've got to sit down," Denise said.

Neil felt like excess baggage as Denise fussed over Laura, settling her onto the faded blue couch in the living room and covering her with an afghan. Pete hopped up on the back of the couch and hunkered down with his paws tucked under him. His alert eyes watched everything. Phoebe settled at Laura's feet, snuggling up against the afghan. Her eyes were more wary, less accepting. Like me, Neil thought. She's reserving her opinion.

"Are you hungry?" Denise asked. "I've got a casserole in the oven at home just waiting for someone to eat it."

Laura shook her head.

"I am," Neil said.

"You haven't changed," Denise said with a grimace. Then she turned back to Laura. "You've got to eat something. I'll go next door and get the food. Neil will stay here with you."

Neil couldn't help grinning. "Still bossy, I see."

Denise smiled back. She looked happier today, maybe because she was doing something concrete instead of sitting around worrying. "I'll be back in a minute."

Neil sat in a worn armchair. Laura looked at her hands, which were clasped loosely in her lap. Her head was bent, and her hair fell forward, hiding her face. A clock ticked loudly, and Neil looked away. The clock was an old-fashioned mantel clock that sat on top of a scarred maple buffet. It suddenly struck Neil that everything in the room had seen much better days, although the room wasn't depressing. Little homey touches were everywhere: in the gaily colored braided rugs that dotted the hardwood floor, in the healthy-looking plants that sat in clay pots on the windowsills and in the corners, in the bright hues of the pillows that adorned the couch, and especially in the big wicker basket of yarn that sat next to a maple rocking chair in the corner.

He noticed that she had filled the built-in bookshelves with hundreds of books, both paperback and hardbound. Most of them seemed to be mysteries, Agatha Christie type whodunits, which surprised Neil. Then he smiled. If he wasn't mistaken—he squinted to try to read the title—she had a duplicate of his volume of Keats's poetry. For some reason, this pleased him enormously.

When he looked toward her again, she was studying him. She quickly dropped her eyes, but pink stained her cheeks.

Embarrassed because I caught her, he thought. She seemed to be as nervous and on edge around him as he was around her. Well, they'd have to get it out in the open. This pussyfooting around wasn't Neil's style.

"Are you engaged to Norman?" he asked.

Her head jerked up. The flush on her face deepened, and her eyes were bright pinpoints of blue. She blinked. "I—"

"Tell me the truth," he said. He had no time to be subtle. He had to decide what to do if she wasn't going to be any help in the hard days ahead for Norman.

She bit her bottom lip, sighed, then met his gaze with a direct one of her own. "No."

"But he has asked you to marry him?"

"Yes."

"And?"

"And I had promised to give him an answer the night of the accident." Her voice was soft, but she didn't look away.

"Had you decided on an answer?" Neil said gently.

She picked at the afghan. "Yes." A look of weariness passed over her face. "I was going to turn him down."

"I see." Poor Norman.

Her eyes were filled with unhappiness. "I—I wished things could be different. It would have been perfect to be able to accept his offer. Norman's so nice, and he's been very good to me. But in the end, those are the very reasons I couldn't. I just couldn't lie to him. I'm not in love with him."

The words drummed through Neil's mind as he met her direct gaze. For one heartbeat, Neil knew exactly how Norman would feel when he knew the truth, how unbearable it would be to realize Laura wouldn't be his.

But Norman didn't know yet. He still thought there was a chance. He still had hope. Maybe...no. Neil immediately dismissed the thought. He would never ask her to lie.

But he *could* ask her to wait.

Chapter Five

"Please don't tell him until he's well."

Laura wasn't quick to anger, but Neil's assumption that she would even consider telling Norman now made her furious. Oh, she knew where Neil was coming from; he was very worried about Norman. Well, so was she.

Fighting to keep her anger from erupting, she said stiffly, "I didn't intend to." She was gratified to see a sheepish look pass over his face.

"I'm sorry," he said. "That was insensitive of me."

Laura didn't want to, but she felt a reluctant tug of admiration. It took guts to admit you were wrong. Lots of men had trouble doing it. "Yes, it was. I know you're only thinking of Norman's welfare," she said softly, "but—"

"But this is really none of my business." A lock of hair had fallen across his forehead, and he pushed it back in an impatient gesture. "I just feel so frustrated," he admitted.

The last of Laura's irritation with him vanished. He looked so tired.

"So what will you do?" he asked. "What are you going to say if he asks you for your answer? Try to put him off, or pretend you were going to accept?"

Laura had had plenty of time to think about this, but still she hesitated. She knew what her answer was, but she felt an odd reluctance to say it. "I'm going to tell him I had decided to accept his offer."

"Is that wise? Even though I don't want you to dash his hopes until he's stronger and able to take the disappointment, are you sure you want to lie to him?"

She bit her lip. "It won't be a lie."

For a long moment he didn't reply. Laura's heart thudded slowly as they stared at each other. Lord, she thought, I'd never be able to lie to *him*.

"Does that mean what I think it means?" he finally asked.

She sighed, stroking the thick fur on Phoebe's back as the cat inched closer. "Yes. If Norman still wants me, I'm going to marry him." Disquiet gripped her as she heard herself speak the words aloud. She didn't know if she was doing the right thing or not; she only knew she didn't seem to have any choice.

She'd always imagined when she was planning to marry she'd be filled with joy. She'd had all these romantic daydreams—daydreams fostered by her escape into movies and romantic novels during her growing-up years. But today all she felt was a weary acceptance. When Neil didn't comment, she glanced up. He opened his mouth, then closed it as they both turned in response to a loud thud against the front door. Laura could see Denise's face through the glass in the door.

"Open up! I've got my hands full," she shouted from outside.

Neil got up and opened the door, and in the flurry of helping his sister with the food, the subject of Norman was dropped. But Laura knew Neil hadn't forgotten about her revelation because while the three of them ate the spicy lasagna, salad, and rolls Denise brought, Laura caught him looking at her with a thoughtful expression in his eyes.

He made her feel so uneasy. How he could be Norman's brother was beyond her. There was none of Norman's open, easygoing manner about him. With Norman, she'd always felt nothing was hidden, what you saw was what you got. But Neil was an enigma. She never knew exactly what he was thinking. Every time he looked at her, she wondered if she had something smeared on her face.

What else does he want from me? she thought, meeting his look squarely, almost defiantly. I've told him I'm going to marry Norman. If he wants me to say I'm wildly in love with his brother, well, then he's asking too much. But even as she told herself not to let Neil's scrutiny bother her, she wished he'd leave.

Finally he finished his meal, wiped his mouth on the paper napkins Denise had provided, and stood. "I've got some things to take care of this afternoon. Thanks for the food, Denise."

"Are you going back to the hospital?" she asked.

"No, not today. Since Desiree and the folks are there now, I'm going to move my stuff over to Norman's place this afternoon."

Laura stiffened. Norman lived in the apartment over the company's office. The last thing she needed right now was to have Neil in such close proximity. She would never be able to relax with those eyes watching her every move.

"You're not staying with Mama and Papa?" Denise asked.

"I like my privacy."

"Well, I know Norman thinks you walk on water, so he won't mind."

"Got him fooled, don't I?"

"Yeah," Denise drawled, giving Laura a wink, "One of these days he's going to wise up. See you for what you *really* are." Then she grinned and pointed to her left cheek.

Wordlessly, Neil bent down and kissed her cheek, giving her a quick hug as well. "Why I put up with your lip," he said.

"Oh, you love it," Denise retorted.

He kissed her again, and Laura felt such a sharp yearning inside her, it was almost like a physical pain. Their loving relationship symbolized everything Laura had always longed for and never had.

When he turned to Laura his eyes were still twinkling, but the twinkle faded as his eyes met hers. "Well, I guess I'll see you again."

"Yes. Thanks for bringing me home, and...everything."

Now a quiet concern shadowed his eyes. "It was my pleasure."

After he left, Laura once again wished she knew what else it was he wanted from her.

Well, at least she wasn't a doormat, he thought as he got into Desiree's car. The sad-eyed Laura had some spunk. Good. She'd need spunk to get through the weeks ahead. He wished he felt better about what she was planning to do, and that surprised him. If someone had told him yesterday that he'd be concerned because Laura was going to accept Norman's offer of marriage, he'd have told them they were crazy. After all, that's what he'd been hoping for, wasn't it?

Neil frowned. Everything had changed in the last twenty-four hours. Norman was still his first priority, which was why he hadn't tried to talk Laura out of her decision, but Neil was afraid no good would come of it.

Still, was it any of his business if she wanted to sacrifice herself? Did he have any right to interfere in her life? In Norman's life?

Still struggling with these questions, he drove to his parents' home, gathered up his things, then made the short five-minute drive to the office. His father had given him Norman's keys, and Neil made short work of unlocking the outer gates, then Norman's apartment, reached by an outside stairway. It took him less than ten minutes to hang up or put away his few belongings. The place was neat, but comfortable, reflecting his brother's personality, Neil thought, as he looked around.

The apartment also brought back memories. Neil had lived there himself, when, as a twenty-year-old, he first tested his wings and left his parents' home. He smiled, remembering. His mother had protested, saying he was too young, but his father had backed him up.

"Neil is a man, Arlette," he said. "He don' need to be under his mama's eye all the time." He winked at Neil.

"Why? Is he going to do something he's ashamed for me to see?" she demanded, black eyes flashing with temper.

"That's his business," his father teased.

"Neil Cantrelle! You just remember, okay? If you do anything bad, you have to confess it to Father Richard, okay?" his mother warned.

Neil rolled his eyes, and his father laughed, slapping him on the back.

The next day, Neil moved into the apartment.

Now, as he remembered those exciting days when he was a rookie on the Baton Rouge Police Force and everything in his life seemed so new and full of promise, he sighed. He had lived in the apartment for four years, until he and Erica were married. He still hadn't wanted to move; he'd liked the apartment but Erica wouldn't hear of living over a roofing company office.

"No way," she said. She opted for a new, glitzy apartment complex in Baton Rouge. "I don't want to be under your mama's thumb."

Neil succumbed. When they were first married, he would have done anything to make her happy. It took him eight years to discover the truth, that he could never make her happy. Their marriage was a mistake from the beginning. Erica wanted different things from life than he did. He guessed on some level he'd always known that, but with the blindness of youth, he'd ignored the signs and plunged on, his desire for her overriding his good sense. He'd tried for a long time to make things work, hanging on to his illusions, and in the end, that refusal to face the truth had cost him dearly. It had also cost other people dearly.

Maybe it was time to right some of the wrongs he'd left behind.

Two hours later, he stood on a small rise overlooking Lake Verret near Napoleonville. Under the benevolent branches of a twisted cypress tree dripping with Spanish moss, a gray granite headstone rested. It was the first time Neil had visited the grave site since the day of the funeral, but it looked exactly the way he'd remembered it in countless dreams.

He stared at the words etched into the stone.

Kendella
Beloved Son
James Edward
Killed in the line of Duty

Dead leaves had gathered at the base of the headstone, and Neil bent to his knees to brush them away. His hand was shaking *Jimmy. I'm sorry. You'll never know how sorry. Please forgive me.*

As he knelt there, his chest felt so tight he could hardly breathe. Tears blinded him. He squeezed his eyes shut. All the anguish stored up over the past three years, all the regrets, came gushing forth. He leaned his head against the headstone. How long he knelt there on the cold, damp ground, he didn't know. But when he finally rose to his feet, brushing off the knees of his jeans and pulling his leather jacket closer around him, he felt better. He felt as if Jimmy understood.

Filled with new purpose, he turned and walked away. He didn't look back.

Laura spent a quiet afternoon with her cats and Denise, who popped back and forth between the two halves of the house. Laura usually preferred to be alone when she needed to think, but Denise's cheerful, bustling presence was comforting today. *Maybe I just don't want to think too deeply.* And it was nice to be coddled. She had had very little coddling in her life. Might as well make the most of it, she thought. She smiled gratefully as Denise brought her a steaming cup of Earl Gray tea.

"If it's not too much trouble, Denise," she said, "would you mind bringing me one of my pills, too?" Her head had begun its dull throbbing again.

"Sure. Do you feel up to Jeannine coming over for a few minutes? She's home from school and begging to see you."

Laura's spirits immediately lifted. "Oh, I'd love to have her come over," she said eagerly.

She spent a happy twenty minutes with the engaging ten-year-old. Jeannine, with her father's blue eyes and her mother's dark, curly hair, was a lively sprite with a wide grin and bubbly personality.

"I'm sorry you were hurt, Laura," she said. She sat on the end of the couch, holding Phoebe on her lap as Pete rubbed against her legs. "I missed you."

"I missed you, too, honey." Laura thought if she could have a child like Jeannine, she'd be the happiest woman in the world. Denise was so lucky. Jett adored her, and she had two great kids.

All too soon Denise was back, shooing Jeannine home. "Laura needs to rest," she said. "You can come over tomorrow."

After mother and daughter left, Laura slowly got up from the couch. She *was* tired. It would be good to take a nap. But first she walked around the apartment, turning on all the lamps. Only then did she feel secure enough to go back to the couch and lie down again.

She hated this weakness in herself, but the thought of waking in the dark terrified her. The cats, sensing her anxiety, tensed, too. Pete's ears were up, as if he heard something, and Phoebe's tail twitched rapidly as her blue eyes stared with unblinking observation of Laura.

Laura knew she should get professional help. She'd known that for years. And she wanted to; she was tired of being a freak. But she also knew if she sought help she would have to talk about the reasons for her fear, and she still wasn't sure if she could. That was one of the things that really bothered her about her plans to marry Norman. He knew about her fear; they couldn't work together every day without him finding out. But he'd dismissed it, telling her not to worry about it.

"It'll go away," he'd said, "if you quit thinking about it."

But Laura knew it *wouldn't* go away. And Norman's airy unconcern disturbed her, because it was so typical of the way he dealt with problems. But Norman had good qualities, too. He was gentle, tolerant, and undemanding. He would be comfortable to live with, not expecting much from her.

Unlike his brother. Very unlike his brother. There was nothing comfortable about Neil Cantrelle. The way he looked at her, the things he said to her—everything about him was unsettling. She had a feeling he would never be undemanding, whether it was in his everyday relationships or as a lover.

Now, where did that come from?

Carefully, she explored the thought. Remembering the dark, questing look in his eyes, those eyes that hinted of sadness and disillusion, and the curve of his sensual mouth, she could feel herself blushing. Blushing, for God's sake. *What's wrong with you? This is a totally unsuitable train of thought, so get it out of your mind. Neil Cantrelle is your future fiancé's brother, and you'd better not think about him any other way. Ever.*

But her disturbing thoughts refused to go away, and even as she slipped into sleep, she was seeing the shape of Neil Cantrelle's mouth and wondering what it would feel like pressed against her own.

"Neil!"

Alice Kendella's gray eyes widened in shock as she stared at Neil through the screened door.

"Hello, Alice," he said quietly, his manner belying the tension in his body.

She put her hand to her mouth, and he could see how it trembled. "Oh, Neil," she breathed.

"Aren't you going to ask me in? Or am I persona non grata?"

"Don't be crazy! Of course, you can come in!" She flung the screened door wide and opened her arms.

Heart full, Neil gathered the diminutive blonde in his arms. She smelled like talcum powder and soap, and he hugged her hard. When they broke apart, she had tears in her eyes.

"Neil, I'm so happy to see you." She took his hand. "Come in. Let's shut this door. It's cold out there."

Drawing him forward, she pulled him into a cluttered living room. The room was as familiar to Neil as the rooms in his family's home. He'd been here so many times.

"Let's go back into the kitchen. I was feeding the kids an early supper," Alice said in her breathy voice. He had always teased Jimmy that Alice sounded like Marilyn Monroe.

"That sexy little voice must be a real turn-on," he would say, laughing when Jimmy would blush.

His heart turned over as they entered the warm kitchen and he saw Jimmy, Jr., a good-looking ten-year-old with carroty hair who had his father's coloring and his mother's features; and Lisa, a smaller version of her mother, whose five-year-old eyes showed no recognition of him.

"Hey, Jimmy, how's it going?" Neil ruffled the boy's hair, and Jimmy smiled happily. Neil's heart warmed. The kid remembered him and seemed happy to see him.

"How about some coffee? Do you want some soup?" Alice said.

Neil glanced at the kids' bowls. Vegetable soup. "Is it homemade?" He remembered her homemade soups and how good they always were.

Alice nodded.

"I shouldn't. I ate a big plate of lasagna not three hours ago." He grinned. "But I will anyway."

While she dished up his soup, he glanced around. He'd always loved this homey kitchen. It was so unlike the sterile whiteness of the one in his and Erica's apartment. Of course, Erica never cooked, and the kitchen was too small to hold a table, so he told himself it didn't matter.

Instead, he spent as much time as he could in Jimmy's kitchen, surrounded by Jimmy's wife and kids. With or without Erica. He touched the table, smiling at the grooves in the soft wood—grooves made by kids' spoons and kids' pencils. Grooves made with love.

As Alice seated herself opposite him, her quiet gray eyes met his, and she smiled.

There had been a thick knot inside him ever since he'd said goodbye to Jimmy that sweltering August day when they'd lowered the bronze coffin into the ground. The first part of the knot unraveled today when he knelt over Jimmy's grave. Now the last part came undone at the sight of Alice's loving smile and the lack of blame he saw in her eyes. Warmth and something that almost resembled happiness crept through him.

"I've missed you," Alice said.

"I've missed you, too."

"I've thought about you a lot."

"Me, too." He tasted the soup. Wonderful. Just like he remembered it. "Good soup," he said, trying to dispel the heavy atmosphere. He could only handle so much drama right now. "You always were a good cook."

"I try."

"Mommy, can I have some ice cream?" piped Lisa.

"Me, too," added Jimmy, Jr. with a shy smile in Neil's direction.

Alice rose to get the ice cream out of the freezer. "You're looking good, Neil," she said as she brought the filled bowls to the kids.

He shrugged.

"'Course, you always did," she added with a teasing grin. "I remember how jealous of you Jimmy always was."

"Jimmy! He was never jealous of me." *It was always the other way around.*

"Yes, he was. He told me once that women looked at you in a different way than they looked at him." Then she chuckled. "Of course, I was delighted they *weren't* looking at him, and I said so!"

"It wouldn't have mattered," Neil said softly. "He never had eyes for anyone but you."

"I know." Once more tears misted her eyes. "I miss him," she whispered.

"I know you do. I do, too." Neil thought how proud Jimmy would be if he could see how well she and the kids looked. "Has it been rough?"

Now it was her turn to shrug. "Not as rough as it could have been. People have been so kind."

"Good."

"I've never had a chance to thank you for the money."

"I don't want thanks."

"I know you can't have that much yourself, and sending me a check every month . . . well . . ."

"I have plenty." He really *didn't* want her thanks. He shifted uncomfortably, wishing she'd drop the subject. "I don't need much."

"Still . . . one or the other would have been more than enough. I mean, after you sent the ten thousand dollars, I never expected to get the checks each month. . . ."

Neil frowned. "Ten thousand dollars? What are you talking about?"

Now Alice frowned, too. "You know. The check you left for me the night you left town. I—"

"I never left you a check." He put his soup spoon down, and gave her a quizzical look.

"You didn't?"

He shook his head. "No. It wasn't until I got to Florida that I realized I'd meant to ask you about money. That was when I got the idea that I'd just send you some each month." So who had given her a check for ten thousand? "Wasn't the check signed?"

"Well, yes, but it was a cashier's check, drawn on the First National Bank."

Neil nodded. First National had been his bank. But that wasn't unusual. There were only two banks in Patinville, and the other one, the Patinville Savings and Loan, didn't have checking account facilities, so almost everyone, even if they saved money or borrowed money through the savings and loan, still carried an account with First National. "Did you ask the bank who had sent the check?"

"No. I never thought to. I just assumed it was you."

Neil could see how she would think he'd sent the money. She'd probably thought it was guilt money. A stillness settled over him at the thought. No, that was ridiculous. Why would anyone feel guilty about that night? No one else was involved except Abruzzi and Neil. And Erica, he thought. Still . . . the anonymity of the check bothered him.

"Alice," he said slowly, "didn't the Department have some sort of collection for you?"

She nodded.

"Who handled that?"

"Uh, they did it through the Survivor's Club."

"That's what I thought. Did you by any chance keep the stub from the ten thousand dollar check?"

Her eyes reminded him of shiny pewter as she stared at him, wide-eyed. "I don't remember," she said slowly.

"If you had kept it, where would it be?"

"Buried somewhere in Jimmy's desk, I guess. . . ." Her voice trailed off, and she bit her bottom lip. Neil could see her thinking hard. "Do you think it's important for us to find out who sent me that money?"

"I don't know," Neil said honestly. It might have been sent by a good samaritan who didn't want to be thanked and had a perfectly good reason for not just donating the money to the Survivor's Club. On the other hand, it might have some other, darker, connotation. All Neil knew for sure was that he was mighty curious. He smiled at Alice. "But I'd sure like to know. Wouldn't you?"

She nodded, then stood up. "I'll look for the stub. But right now if I don't get hopping, Jimmy will be late to his Boy Scout meeting." She turned to the boy. "You'd better hurry, honey. Go get your uniform on."

After Jimmy left the room, Neil said, "I'm going to the hospital. Do you want me to drop him somewhere on my way?"

"Oh, Neil! I completely forgot to ask about Norman. I heard about the accident." She hit her forehead. "God! What's wrong with me?"

It didn't surprise him that she'd heard. News traveled fast in Patinville.

"How is he?" she asked, concern etched into her face.

"Holding his own as of this morning." He quickly told her about the loss of Norman's leg and brought her up to date on his prognosis.

"Oh, Neil. Your poor parents. Is there anything I can do to help?"

Neil put his arm around her shoulders and hugged her close for a minute. "No. But thanks for offering."

"Is he allowed to have visitors?"

"Only family right now."

"Well, I'll keep checking on him, and when he's up to it, I'll go see him." She smiled sadly. "I've always liked Norman."

He dropped a kiss on her cheek. "You're a pretty special lady, you know that? I was afraid you wouldn't even let me in the door today."

"I've never blamed you, Neil."

"You had every right to."

"That's crazy, and you know it. What happened to Jimmy was his own fault."

"I wish I knew what made Jimmy leave the apartment that night. I'll never understand it."

"Well, Jimmy was impulsive. You know that."

"I know, but he was also a good cop. He knew better." Neil sighed wearily. "No, I should never have left the stakeout."

"Neil," she said, exasperation now evident in her voice, "What choice did you have? When Erica showed up, you had to get her out of there. And you *told* Jimmy to call for backup."

"Yes, but I should have had some control over my personal life," Neil said stubbornly. He'd been over this so many times.

"The Department knew you were having some serious problems with Erica. According to the testimony, even Lt. Richardson knew Erica had called several times with emergencies that turned out to be false alarms. They should have pulled you off that stakeout, made sure you got your home life straightened out. They *knew* she was unstable where you were concerned. If I blame anyone, I blame them."

God knows that's what he wanted to think. Thinking like that would go a long way toward making him feel better, but was it realistic? The fact remained that he *had* left the stakeout when he wasn't supposed to. That Jimmy had urged him to go, said he'd call for backup, didn't lessen the guilt he would always have to shoulder.

"Come on," Alice said softly. "Let's not talk about this anymore tonight. Here's Jimmy, ready to go. And if you were serious, I'd love for you to drop him off at the Scout Hut."

So twenty minutes later Neil was pulling up in front of the small frame building that housed Patinville's Boy Scout troops.

"'Bye, Neil," Jimmy said as he scrambled from the car.

"'Bye, sport."

"Will you be back to see us?"

The boy's eager face smote Neil. "You can count on it," he promised.

Chapter Six

Laura stared at the closed door to Norman's room, heart pounding and mouth dry. For the past four days, ever since she'd told Neil she intended to marry Norman, she'd worried that she wouldn't be able to put on a convincing performance when she told him. Would he see through her?

In just a few minutes, she'd find out.

Taking a deep breath, she pushed open the door and, clutching her purse tightly under her left arm, walked slowly toward the bed. The room looked cheerful and bright, but smelled like all hospital rooms—of antiseptic, medicine, and sickness. But at least Norman was no longer in intensive care. Yesterday he'd been taken off the critical list and moved to this private room.

The doctor told the family the worst was over, even though Norman still had a long road ahead of him. And—Laura sent a grateful prayer heavenward—there was no longer any threat to his other leg. Dr. Dunado also emphasized that Norman's emotional well-being was the most important factor in his recovery.

"Don't say or do anything to upset him," he warned, and Neil had given Laura a meaningful look. "We must all try to keep him happy and optimistic about his future."

Well, here goes, Laura thought. She touched Norman's shoulder softly. "Hi, Norman."

"Laura?" He turned toward her.

His voice still sounded weak to her. "How are you feeling today?" she said, determinedly cheerful.

"Better," he murmured, "now that you're here." His eyes, dark like all the Cantrelles', raked her face.

Laura's stomach muscles were jumping from nerves. She hoped it didn't show. She studiously avoided looking at the flat space on the bed where his leg should have been. She hadn't looked the other times she'd seen him, either. She wasn't sure if she could handle looking, and even without the doctor's admonition, Laura wouldn't have wanted to go to pieces on Norman.

"It sure is good to see you," he said. "The other night when you were here, I was out of it."

"I know. But I understood."

He reached for her hand, clutching it tightly. His hand felt clammy and cool but surprisingly strong. She smiled, striving to make the smile bright and happy, but she knew her effort fell short.

"How are *you* feeling?" he asked. "Your face still looks black and blue."

"You should talk. Yours looks terrible," she teased.

He grimaced. "I know." He touched his left cheek, which was horribly bruised and swollen. "You never answered my question."

"Oh, I'm fine. Most of the soreness is gone. I even managed to work all day yesterday."

"Yeah, Neil was here a little while ago, and he told me."

She nodded. "I know. We rode over here together."

Norman tried to smile, but obviously his face still hurt, for he winced. "What do you think of my brother? Are you in love with him yet?"

Laura's heart skittered, and even though she knew Norman was teasing her, she flinched.

"I was only kidding," he said.

"Oh, I know that." She struggled to compose her face into nonchalant lines. "I like your brother a lot. He's been very thoughtful. He's not you, of course, but he's nice."

Her answer must have pleased him, because his eyes glowed warmly. Then they clouded up.

Laura's insides felt as if someone were using a hand mixer on them. She knew without being told that Norman was thinking about the loss of his leg, comparing himself to Neil. *Tell him. Tell him now. Get it over with.* "Norman..."

"What?" The dark eyes were full of pain.

"Norman, I've been doing a lot of thinking this past week."

"Yeah, me, too." He looked away from her.

Her heart twisted inside her. Before he could say anything else, she rushed on. "I've been so scared that you wouldn't make it, and I've come to realize just how that would make me feel."

Now she had his attention. His dark eyes gleamed as they fastened on her face.

She hesitated. *Say it!* "Nearly losing you really opened my eyes to what matters in life. Norman, as soon as you're well, I want us to get married." There. That hadn't been so bad.

For a minute his eyes shone with happiness, but then the happiness slowly faded. "No."

"No? Well, that's a funny thing to say." Even to her own ears, her voice sounded brittle, the words false. "I thought you'd be happy! Don't tell me you've changed your mind about me." She laughed, and the laugh sounded hollow. Oh, she was making a mess of this.

"Laura—"

"I hope you don't mind if we have a big wedding. I've always dreamed of a big wedding. I was thinking I could ask both Denise and Desiree to be my bridesmaids, and Jeannine and Justin could be the flower girl and ring bearer." She was babbling; she sounded stupid. But the look in his eyes told her he didn't believe her. "Maybe—" She faltered, doubt assailing her. But she pushed it aside and plunged on. "Maybe Celeste could even come for the wedding."

"Laura—"

"Yes, I'm sure Celeste would come." She *had* to do this. She owed Norman this much. If anyone was going to sever their relationship, it had to be him. Not her. Never her. "Let's tell your parents today. I think they're coming to see you tonight. They might even be outside right now. Let's call them and your brother in—"

"Laura, please shut up!"

Laura felt like a balloon that had been stuck with a pin—all her forced cheerfulness hissing out of her in one great whoosh. Despair was a heavy hand pushing against her chest. She'd failed. He hadn't believed her for one minute. What would Neil say? She shuddered. What would his family think of her?

"Laura..." Norman squeezed her hand tighter, and although Laura wanted nothing more than to escape the direct gaze of Norman's clear, dark eyes, she told herself not to be a coward and returned the pressure. "I appreciate your offer, but we both know you didn't want to marry me before the accident, so there's no reason for you to want to marry me now."

Laura wanted to deny this statement, but honesty forbade her telling a direct lie. "Nor—"

"You know I'm right. I'm not gonna pretend that I'm not tempted. I... I still love you..." His face twisted, and Laura felt a corresponding knot form in her stomach. His gaze finally left hers, his eyes fastening on their intertwined hands. "But I won't let you be a martyr because you feel sorry for me."

"Norman—"

"Please, Laura, let me finish, okay?"

Laura swallowed. She felt like a worm, because even though she didn't want to hurt him, had never wanted to hurt him, relief had begun to crawl through her.

"Before the accident, if you'd said yes, you'd marry me, I would have been overjoyed. But everything's different now. The accident changed things."

He sighed again, releasing her hand as he did. He looked down, and when he spoke, the words were so soft, she had to lean over him to hear. "Look, Laura, I know you think I'm a little dense at times, and maybe I am. I usually don't think about things I don't want to think about. But I know you don't love me the way you should. You never have. It didn't matter before, because I knew I could make you love me once we were married, but now it *does* matter."

A tear slipped down Laura's cheek, and she had to bite her lower lip to keep from crying harder. "Norman," she whispered, clasping his hand once more, "we could make it work." *Oh, God, please help me to say the right thing.* She fought to control the tears that now flooded her eyes. "The loss of your leg makes no difference to me."

He wouldn't look at her. "Maybe it makes no difference to you, but it does to me." He pulled his hand from her grasp, and she could see the effort caused him pain.

Laura knew that whatever she said now was crucial. Knowing what she had to do, she purposely made her voice hard. "I never thought I'd see the day when Norman Cantrelle would feel sorry for himself." She gave a little bitter laugh, cringing inside at the cruel words. "I thought you were a fighter. I didn't think you'd ever let anything get you down."

His head jerked up; his jaw hardened. Angry glints appeared in the depths of his eyes.

They stared at each other for a long moment. Laura's heart pounded in her chest, but she didn't drop her gaze.

When he finally spoke, his voice was expressionless. "I'm tired, Laura. I want you to leave." He picked up his call bell.

"Norman, you know—"

"I *said* I want you to leave. End of discussion."

Laura opened her mouth to say something else, but the door opened, and a nurse walked in. "Did you need me, Mr. Cantrelle?"

"Yes. I..." His shoulders sagged; the angry glints in his eyes faded. He didn't look at Laura. "Is it time for my pill?" Weariness was etched into his face.

Guilt consumed Laura. Guilt because down deep, she felt so relieved. Guilt because she hadn't been hurt in the accident, and Norman had. Guilt because she knew Norman was right. Perhaps, in time, if the accident hadn't happened, if she hadn't met... Her mind refused to conclude the thought.

"I think you'd better go now," the nurse said to her.

"Goodbye, Norman. I'll come tomorrow."

He closed his eyes. "Goodbye, Laura."

Dazed, Laura walked out of the room. When she emerged into the brightly lighted waiting room, she blinked. Neil was sitting on the couch in the corner leafing through a magazine. He looked up as she approached.

"What's wrong?" He dropped the magazine, jumped up and strode toward her. When she didn't answer, he grabbed her arm. "Dammit! What happened? What's wrong?"

She trembled, all her bravado gone now that she no longer had to keep up any kind of pretense. Her eyes filled with tears.

"Laura! Talk to me. Why are you crying?" Neil's hand tightened on her arm.

"Let go, Neil. You're hurting me."

He dropped his hand. "I'm sorry."

She sniffed, dug a tissue out of the pocket of her jacket, and wiped her eyes. "I...oh, damn! I've made such a mess of things!" Suddenly she felt completely exhausted, and she staggered as she walked toward the couch.

His hand shot out, and he steadied her. "Whoa," he said softly. "Are you sure you're all right?"

She nodded. "I...I think so." She allowed him to ease her down onto the couch, and she laid her head back, closing her eyes until she felt she had her careening emotions under control. When she finally opened her eyes, Neil was still standing over her, a troubled look etched on his face. She took a shaky breath. "Sit down. I'm okay now. I guess I'm not as strong as I thought I was."

"Do you want a cup of coffee or a soft drink?"

"A diet soft drink would be wonderful."

"Okay. I'll be right back. Don't move."

Within minutes, he returned, handing her an ice-cold can of the soda, which she drank gratefully.

Neil sat across from her, in one of the leather chairs, hunched forward with his elbows resting on his knees. "I didn't mean to get rough with you before."

"I know you didn't. It's okay."

"It's just that I thought something had happened to Norman. Your face was so white, you scared me."

"No, nothing's happened to Norman." She grimaced. "Not while I was in the room, anyway."

"What *did* happen?"

"Oh, nothing much. He just doesn't want to marry me, that's all." Laura felt so guilty. She sank back against the cushions of the couch, hung her head, and blinked back tears. For someone who never cried, she had certainly done her share of it lately. "He said he wouldn't marry me, period, end of discussion."

When Neil didn't answer, she looked up. He sat staring into space, worry lines furrowing his brow. He looks tired, she thought. This is hard on him.

"I was afraid of this," he said. "Norman's proud. All the Cantrelles are proud." He turned toward her, and once again, his dark eyes were full of some unfathomable emotion as his gaze bored into hers. "And he's probably guessed that you feel sorry for him."

Laura forgot about feeling guilty. Everything in her rebelled at his assumption that he knew why she had decided to accept Norman's proposal. Whether she'd been motivated by pity or not, Neil hardly knew her. He had no right to judge her. But even as she felt herself bristling, her senses were stirred by the heat in his eyes. She stood, knocking her can over in the process and spilling soda on her skirt. She ignored the spill, saying heatedly, "You don't know anything about me."

Neil's eyes narrowed. "Look, Laura, it's not going to do anybody any good for you and me to argue about this. Hell, you told me yourself that you don't love him!"

"I never said I didn't love him! I said I wasn't *in* love with him. There's a big difference!"

"What are you getting so mad about? What damn difference does it make? Love, in love, who cares? Norman's the only important one here."

"I know that. Don't you think I know that?" Anger had driven her tears away. "I knew you'd blame me. Probably everybody's going to blame me."

"Nobody's going to blame you." But there was no conviction in his voice. "Damn. I had my doubts about what you planned to do, and it looks as if I was right."

"Then why didn't you say something? Why didn't you stop me?"

"As you pointed out the other day, it really wasn't any of my business, was it?"

She knew she was being irrational, because he was perfectly right. She glared at him, then righted the can of soda and without saying another word, stalked off. She could hear him coming after her. Laura didn't turn around, she just kept heading toward the elevator. Why didn't he leave her alone?

"Laura!"

She ignored him.

"Dammit, Laura!" He grabbed her arm from behind, bringing her to a halt.

She wrenched her arm from his grasp, gasping from the new onslaught of pain and whirled to face him. Her breath came in short spurts as she looked up. They were standing so close they were almost touching. She could see the tiny bristles of beard on his chin, the fine lines at the corners of his eyes, the dark furrows under his cheekbones. "Leave me alone!" she muttered through clenched teeth. "Don't you think I feel guilty enough? I don't need you to tell me how stupid I am."

"Look, I'm sorry," he said. "I don't know what it is about you, but I always seem to say the wrong thing when we're together."

The elevator dinged its arrival, and when the doors glided open, several people walked off. One woman looked at them curiously as she walked past. Laura stared at her, and the woman's gaze slid away.

Laura wanted to get on the elevator. She wanted to get away from this disturbing man who always caused her emotions to rush full throttle in a direction she'd rather they didn't go. She stepped forward, but the elevator was empty. No matter how much she wanted to escape, she couldn't get on an empty elevator. The moment the doors closed she would start to hyperventilate. Her claustrophobia was at its peak on elevators, and the only way she'd ever been able to ride in one was if other people were with her.

Neil touched her arm again.

"Go away. I have nothing more to say to you." She moved toward the elevator, the need to get away from him almost stronger than her fear of the small, empty enclosure.

"Even if I wanted to go away, I can't," he said in exasperation.

"What do you mean?"

"I drove you here, remember? And I'm not going to just leave you stranded."

Belatedly Laura realized she had no car. She'd made the seventeen-mile trip to Baton Rouge with Neil in a truck that belonged to the company.

"Come on," he said gently, leading her into the elevator. "Have you had dinner yet?"

"No."

"Why don't we call a truce, let me buy you a hamburger? I'm starving. While we're eating we can talk about this situation calmly."

"I'm very calm," she said.

"You have an odd way of showing it." Suddenly he chuckled, and at the warm sound, she glanced up. His dark eyes were fired with amusement, and most of the tension eased from his body. "Come on," he urged softly. "We're both tired. We've both been under a strain. We're both worried about Norman. Hell, we're both on the same side. We have no reason to fight."

Laura wanted to stay angry. Angry was the safest emotion she could think of where Neil was concerned. But he was right. So she gave him a reluctant smile and nodded her acquiescence.

"That's much better," he said as the elevator reached the ground floor and the doors opened.

Thirty minutes later the two of them were sitting in a booth at a roadside café about ten miles from Patinville. Clint Black's voice drifted from a jukebox in the far corner of the room, and smells of frying onions and grilled burgers filled the air, mingling with the muted voices of the other diners.

"Have you decided yet?" a peppy dark-haired waitress said, giving Neil the eye and blatantly flirting as she smiled down at him. Laura wondered if the woman knew she had lipstick on her teeth.

"Give us a minute, okay?" Neil said.

"Anything you want, sugar."

Laura couldn't help comparing the waitress's reaction to Neil to the way women reacted to Norman. When they smiled at him, the smiles were friendly but casual. The smile this woman was giving Neil was anything but casual. It fairly reeked of unspoken invitation.

"Do you know what you want?" Neil asked.

Laura nodded. "I'll have the bacon burger and hot tea."

"Same for me," he said. "Except I'll have coffee. And how about a basket of curly fries?"

"Like I said, anything *you* want," the waitress said, giving Neil one more coy smile. When she walked away, her fanny twitched.

Laura grinned.

"Glad to see you're feeling better," Neil said.

"Do you always have this effect on women?"

"What effect?"

"Don't play dumb. You surely saw the way that waitress looked at you."

He shrugged. "Overactive hormones, that's all." But his eyes twinkled. "Most women can't stand me. Think I'm impossible."

Something curled in Laura's stomach as their eyes locked. If she hadn't known better, she'd think he was flirting with her. To cover her reaction, she said, "No wonder. You think you know everything."

"I apologized, remember. Do you want blood, too?"

"Yes."

He grinned. When he forgot himself and smiled, he seemed almost carefree. He was a very attractive man. Too attractive, she thought. "I aim to please." He picked up the butter knife lying on his side of the table, pretended to saw at his hand.

"Could you please wait until after we eat?" she said, another smile tugging at her lips. "I can't handle blood on an empty stomach."

He laid the knife down, his eyes filled with a warmth that made her feel good inside for the first time that day. "Like the little waitress said, anything you want." When Laura laughed, he added, "It's good to hear you laugh."

"There hasn't been much to laugh about the past week."

"No, there hasn't."

Laura started to respond, but the waitress reappeared, so Laura waited until Neil's coffee and her tea had been put on the table and the waitress was gone before saying, "I'm sorry I got so mad before."

"Forget it. We were both overreacting. Now, can we talk about what happened tonight?"

"Okay." She squeezed lemon into her tea. "What do you want to know?"

"Was Norman upset when you left?"

She shrugged. "I'm not sure. He was very tired, but I don't know if the tiredness was brought on by our conversation or simply because he's still so weak."

Neil stirred sugar into his coffee. Steam floated from the cup. The sounds of clinking silverware and the zing of the cash register mingled with the strains of Dusty Mitchell singing "My Cinderella Girl," one of Laura's old favorites.

She took a deep breath. "Neil..."

He looked up.

Her heart skipped. She wet her lips. "Neil, I haven't told you everything."

His hands stilled.

"I...I purposely tried to make Norman mad before I left his room."

"What!" He dropped the spoon, and it clattered on the Formica tabletop.

"I accused him of feeling sorry for himself, of being a coward." She watched the play of emotions cross his face. First shock, then anger, then a dawning approval, and for the first time that evening Laura began to think maybe, just maybe, she'd done something right.

He smiled, and a warm feeling spread through her. "Smart girl," he said softly. "Very smart girl." Then his face once more fell into sober lines. "Do you think he's going to be all right?"

"I hope so."

"What you did—trying to make him mad—that was a good thing to do. Norman's always been a fighter."

"I know." Their eyes met again, and the warmth curled around in the pit of her stomach. His next words were as soft as a caress. "I can see why Norman's crazy about you."

Oh, God, why was he looking at her like that? Laura wanted to look away, but like a magnet, her gaze remained locked with his. More and more uncomfortable by the look in his dark eyes, Laura strove to speak lightly. "Well, I can't. I'm a very ordinary person."

Just then, the waitress walked up with their orders. By the time she'd plopped their burgers in front of them, given Neil a few more bats of her eyelashes, and tucked the check under the little china container filled with packets of sugar and sweetener, the awkward moment passed. When Laura looked at Neil again, his face had settled into its impersonal grooves once more.

"My father has asked me to help out at the office," he said a few minutes later. "There's a bid that needs to be finished. Something about a new school?"

"Yes, Norman was working on it the day before the accident. I'd forgotten about it."

"I thought I'd come in on Monday."

"Okay." She hesitated. "Do you know anything about the business?"

"I used to work for my father every summer. The three years after high school before I enrolled at the Police Academy in Baton Rouge, I worked part-time for him and went to college part-time."

"How long were you a cop?"

"Twelve years."

Twelve years. She wished she had nerve enough to ask him what had happened to make him quit the way he did.

He was silent for a long time. Then, as if he'd read her mind, he said, "Did Norman tell you what happened?"

"No. All he said was that there was some trouble."

Neil finished the last two bites of his hamburger, wiped his mouth on his napkin, then leaned back against the back of the booth.

She studied his face, saw the darkness that shadowed his eyes. "Would you like to tell me about it?"

He sighed heavily, picked up his discarded fork and tapped it against the Formica tabletop. In a low voice, he said, "I was what's known as an up-and-comer in the department. I was idealistic and eager."

As he talked, Laura watched the play of emotions over his face.

"I was promoted steadily, and when I took the exam to make sergeant, I passed it easily. Eventually, I was transferred into Narcotics, which was where I met Jimmy." He stopped, looked at her, his eyes sad. "Jimmy Kendella was another eager-beaver type. When they made us partners, the two of us became really tight."

He began to shred his napkin. Laura motioned to the waitress. When the girl came over, Neil stopped. "Can I have more tea?" Laura asked.

"You want more coffee?" the girl said to Neil.

After she left, he continued, "I'd never had a friend like Jimmy before. I could tell him anything...."

Laura wondered what he was thinking as his brows knit and his voice trailed off. "Go on," she prompted.

"Jimmy and I, well, we were as close as two people can be." He gave her a halfhearted smile. "A good partnership is like a good marriage, I suppose. You know without being told that the other person will always be there for you." His face clouded and he stared at the steamy windows.

"The department had been working on a big drug bust for months. But when it finally came down, the big boy, the man in charge—a well-known mobster named Tony Abruzzi—got away and went into hiding. But we had somebody in the tank who agreed to testify against Abruzzi. It was our chance to put him away for a long time. Stakeouts were set up at all his known haunts. This whole operation was a big deal, given number-one priority. Jimmy and I were assigned to the graveyard shift watching his girlfriend's house."

Laura sat quietly. The waitress brought their coffee and tea, then left. It amused Laura that even though Neil paid no attention to her, the waitress couldn't seem to stop herself from trying to catch his interest.

"At the time I was having some serious problems with my marriage. My wife was real unhappy. She hated me being a cop. She'd wanted me to quit for years." He stared down at his cup. "She especially hated it when I was gone at night. She kept calling the department, saying she had to talk to me. Twice during the stakeout someone had to come and replace me, and I went home. Both times there wasn't anything wrong."

He sighed, the sound full of weariness and regret. "Anyway, this night, for some reason, she took it into her head to follow me when I left the house. I still don't know why. But when I'd only been at the stakeout for about five minutes, she showed up."

His eyes met Laura's, and her heart went out to him. "I couldn't believe it. A cab pulled up in front of the apartment, and Erica got out. She marched up to the door and banged on it, yelling my name. I had to get her out of there. Jesus, she could have blown the entire job. She was practically hysterical, demanding to see the woman I was with. When she saw Jimmy inside she quieted down, but the damage was done. She was there, and she'd made so much noise, no telling who'd heard her."

Laura cupped her hands around her warm mug, her eyes never leaving Neil's face.

"Anyway, I told Jimmy to call for backup. I rushed her out the door and around the corner to the street where I'd left my car. I gave her my keys and ordered her to leave. I was so mad at her I felt like strangling her."

"Then I ran back. When I was at the end of the street, I saw Jimmy race out of the apartment where we'd been hiding. Across the street, on the porch of the house we'd been watching, a man was standing at the door. He turned out to be Tony Abruzzi. Jimmy yelled something—whether he was yelling at me or Abruzzi, I guess I'll never know. Abruzzi whirled around, they both fired, and they both went down."

He gulped some coffee, his eyes filled with pain as they stared at her over the rim of his cup. Something stirred deep in her belly. "God, I couldn't believe it. For a minute, I couldn't move. Then I ran. When I reached Jimmy, he was dead."

Laura shivered. She could imagine his pain. She ached to comfort him.

"The whole thing was a fiasco. There were so many unanswered questions. And the only people who knew the answers were dead!" He bowed his head. "I can't forget it. I dream about that night all the time. It was my fault."

She reached across the table to touch his hand. "It was an awful thing that happened, but you've got to stop blaming yourself for what can't be changed."

He turned his hand palm up and closed his fingers around hers. The feel of his warm hand wrapped around hers filled Laura with something queerly like happiness. "I know you're trying to make me feel better, but I can't help what I feel," he said quietly, his thumb rubbing against the back of her hand, sending a shivery trail up Laura's arm. "If only Erica hadn't shown up. That's what I keep telling myself."

"You had no control over your wife's actions."

He released her hand. "Maybe not. But I had control over mine. And there's something else I haven't told you..."

She waited.

"Jimmy was a little impulsive, and I knew it. I'd always been the one to keep him straight. I depended on him for some things, and he depended on me for others. He never let me down. But the one time he really needed me to be there, I wasn't."

"I don't see what you could have done differently," she said reasonably. "You didn't know your wife was going to show up like that. And you *did* tell your partner to call for backup."

"He *did* call. He just didn't wait for them to show up."

"But why not?"

"That's one of the things I'll never know."

"Neil, can't you see that you're being unreasonable? There were lots of things at work here. Lots of people have to share the so-called blame. Okay, so maybe you feel you shouldn't have left, but your partner shouldn't have run outside like that, and your wife shouldn't have followed you, and lots of things shouldn't have happened that did. None of that can be changed. You've got to let go of it, Neil. You can't let this affect the rest of your life. Your partner wouldn't have wanted that."

He grimaced. "Easier said than done." He drained the last of the coffee from his cup. "Well, that's enough about me. Are you ready to go?"

They drove the rest of the way home in silence, and Laura wondered what he was thinking. She knew talking about what had happened had been painful for him, but she also knew he had to work out his feelings by himself. No one else could make him come to terms with what he viewed as his failure. She already knew enough about him to know he was a very honorable man, so his belief that he'd let Jimmy down must be extremely hard to accept. She hoped he wasn't angry with her though. She *had* said an awful lot in the restaurant. Maybe he resented it.

When he pulled into the driveway of the duplex, he turned off the ignition, then turned slowly to face her. He reached for her hand, squeezing it gently. "Thanks for listening."

He wasn't mad. Thank goodness. Then, taking her completely offguard, he leaned over just as she turned toward him, and the kiss that he'd probably meant for her cheek landed at the corner of her mouth. Every nerve ending leaped at the touch of his lips. She could feel the heat of his hand covering hers, his warm breath against her skin, smell the faint hint of spice from his after-shave and the heady scent of male emanating from his skin and clothes and hair. Her heart thrummed up into her throat as her startled eyes met his.

"Laura..." His voice sounded gruff.

She held her breath. She knew she should open the door of the truck and get away. Get away fast.

Because what she wanted most in the world right now was for him to put his arms around her and *really* kiss her.

Chapter Seven

He wanted to kiss her.

He wanted to kiss her more than he'd wanted anything in a long time.

The knowledge slammed into him like a bullet slamming against a shooting-range target. He clenched his teeth and called on all his self-control to keep himself from reaching for her. He wondered if his breathing sounded as loud and ragged to her as it did to him.

Did she know what he was feeling?

He could see her eyes shining in the darkness. Then, so quietly it was more like a sigh than spoken words, she said, "Good night, Neil." She opened the door, slid out of the cab, and walked carefully up the steps to her front door. He trembled from the sheer effort of controlling his chaotic emotions as he watched her disappear inside.

Neil had always been proud of his self-control—a control honed to a fine edge—first by his years on the force, then by the past three years. He was a master at submerging his feelings. But tonight, his feelings tumbled unchecked. In a daze, he started the truck, drove to Norman's apartment, climbed the steps, opened the door. All the while he was remembering the concern in her brilliant blue eyes when she listened to him tell his story. He was reliving the warm feeling her quiet laughter had evoked, the easy camaraderie they'd shared at the café. And he was telling himself that all he'd felt there in the cab was a healthy surge of desire because he'd been without a woman for so long, and because she had been so sympathetic. No big deal. Right?

Hands not quite steady, Neil poured himself a strong drink and got ready for bed. He could still feel the dark intimacy of the cab, the softness of Laura's hand when he held it, the faint scent of flowers clinging to her skin—a scent that had filled his senses when he kissed her cheek.

His pulses raced as he remembered the rush of longing that tore through him, how badly he'd wanted to haul her up against him and cover those soft-looking lips with his. A deep shudder ran through him as his body, even now, responded to the dangerous desire that he hadn't been able to banish.

Sinking onto the side of the bed, he raised his glass and took a long swallow. The whiskey burned its way down his throat, firing his belly. Neil closed his eyes.

What in God's name had happened tonight? What was wrong with him? Laura was the woman his brother loved! Off-limits. He drained his glass and set it on the bedside table. Switching off the lights, he lay in the moonlit room and stared at the ceiling.

The whiskey hadn't helped. He'd thought it would dull the edges and help him sleep. Instead he lay there with his eyes wide open.

Hours later, he was still awake. He couldn't get Laura out of his mind. His body ached with need. His soul ached with loneliness. His heart ached with guilt.

He wanted her.

Something in Laura had called out to him, and he had responded. The knowledge reverberated through him—stark and undeniable.

He wanted Laura Sebastian, the woman his brother loved.

Disturbing images filled Laura's dreams and flickered through her subconscious. When she finally opened her eyes in the predawn hours of Sunday morning, she knew she wouldn't get back to sleep. Tossing aside the comforter, she picked up her quilted robe, shoved her feet into her furry slippers, and padded out of the bedroom and into the bathroom.

Fifteen minutes later she set the teakettle on the stove and put fresh water in the cats' water bowl and shook some dry cat food into the food dish. She shivered as she waited for the water to boil and decided to turn the heat up. The apartment was cold. It felt as if the temperature had dropped in the night, and she could hear tentative raindrops pattering on the roof.

More rain. Wouldn't you know it?

After the water boiled, she took the mug of tea into the living room and curled up on the couch with the afghan around her, the mug warming her cold hands. She heard the furnace kick on.

It was very quiet in the room, only the sound of the sighing wind and the steadily increasing rain penetrating the walls of the duplex. She could hear the mantel clock ticking and the wail of a siren somewhere in the far distance.

Phoebe hopped up onto the couch, settling down beside Laura. The cat's purr sounded like the steady drone of a motor and was comforting. Laura absently scratched behind Phoebe's ears, the feel of the cat's thick fur soothing and familiar.

You can't put it off forever. The thought pushed its way into Laura's brain, and she trembled, squeezing her eyes tightly shut. She could almost always bury her unwanted memories. But tonight they were too close to the surface. She felt raw and very fragile. She felt as if it wouldn't take much for her carefully constructed outer veneer to crumble to bits, leaving her totally exposed.

What had brought on these feelings wasn't clear in her mind. The accident? Neil's confidences about his own guilty feelings and his past? Or her potent and unwelcome sexual awareness of him? Or was it a combination of everything that had happened over the past week?

She didn't know. All she knew was that her old wounds had reopened, and her dreams had been filled with a kaleidoscope of images: Neil, Norman, Ginger.

A deep shudder ran through Laura as her mother's face flickered through her mind. Ginger had always hated her. Laura had known it from the time she was a small child and able to recognize the expression in her mother's eyes for what it was. For a long time Laura tried to be good, to make Ginger love her, but it didn't work. No matter what Laura did, it wasn't right. Ginger's red lips would curl up in disdain, her aquamarine eyes would glitter, and she'd toss her platinum hair. "Why are you so stupid, Laura?" she'd say. "How'd I get to have such a stupid kid?" She would turn away, muttering over her shoulder. "And such an ugly, skinny one at that?"

Laura withstood the verbal slings. She learned to tune out Ginger's hurtful words, to live in a pretend world made up of the characters she read about in books or saw on television. Withstanding the physical abuse wasn't as easy. Because Ginger Sebastian—whenever she got tired of looking at Laura's face, or whenever Laura had committed some unforgivable crime, and most especially, whenever Ginger wanted to go out for the evening—would shove Laura into the bedroom closet and lock the door. The first time she did it, Laura panicked at the dark, stuffy enclosure. She screamed and beat on the door, sobbing and begging her mother to let her out.

"I'll be good, Mommy. I'll be good. Please open the door." But Ginger didn't open the door, and hours later, exhausted and sick to her stomach, Laura tumbled out when her mother finally relented.

"That'll teach you," Ginger snarled. "And the next time, if you cry and scream like that, I'll make you stay in there overnight!"

It hadn't taken many times for Laura to learn that she mustn't make any noise at all. So she'd forced herself to be completely silent, to curl up into a small ball and pretend to be somewhere else. To ignore the creepy, crawly feeling and the suffocating darkness. To close her mind to the fear that threatened to overwhelm her and send her into hysteria.

But she couldn't close off her hearing the way she closed off her brain. There were times when Ginger brought a man home with her. The sounds coming from outside the dark closet were indelibly stamped in Laura's mind and they had shaped her view of sex and sexual attraction to the point where Laura wondered if she would ever feel the kind of physical desire she read about or saw in the movies, especially because none of her own experiences had been satisfactory. They didn't come close to matching her dreams of love and belonging.

At the back of her mind, she wondered if she were normal. Last night had shown her she was. Because last night she'd wanted Neil Cantrelle with a razor-sharp longing that shook her down deep inside. Neil, with his dark intensity, had touched her in a way she'd never been touched before. He'd awakened reactions and physical and emotional needs she didn't know she was capable of feeling.

On one level, she was happy to know she could respond to a man the way she'd responded to Neil. But on another level, she knew she was flirting with disaster, because Neil was forbidden territory.

Neil came racing down the steps and into the office only moments after Laura arrived for work.

"Good morning," he said, shaking water from his hair.

Laura looked up, heart skipping as she gazed into his eyes. "Good morning."

"This rain is really getting to me," he said as he stamped into the office. His voice was friendly but impersonal.

Laura nodded. "I know." She wondered if he felt as uncomfortable as she did. She also wondered by what law it had been decreed that some men should have the kind of animal magnetism Neil Cantrelle had and others should not? It wasn't fair, she mused, as he shed his dripping jacket and slicked back his hair. Her stomach tightened as she watched the muscles in his arms and chest flex and ripple with his movements. His jeans molded his thighs in a way that set her pulses racing.

Steady, girl, she told herself, looking away before she betrayed her fascination. "I got the papers out that I thought you'd need," she said. "They're all there, on top of Norman's desk."

He smiled. "Great, but I just came down to get a cup of coffee, then I'm picking up my mother and we're going in to the hospital. I probably won't work on that bid until later this afternoon. What time do you usually leave?"

"At five." She wondered if he had any idea how much his smile changed his face.

"Maybe we could go over the stuff now? That way, if I don't get back here until after you leave, I can still work on it."

Laura was disappointed and relieved all at the same time. It was probably better for her if she didn't have to deal with his presence all day long. She wasn't sure she could maintain this casual façade. Quickly, she explained which forms needed to be filled out and where he could find the information he needed in the files.

"I'll just sit here—" he gestured toward Norman's desk "—and look through these before I go."

"Okay." She sat at her desk and reached toward the adding machine, but she couldn't concentrate on the figures before her. She was all too aware of Neil as he moved around the enclosed space, pouring himself a cup of coffee, opening the filing cabinet, settling himself at Norman's desk. The rustle of the papers he handled, the steady pattering of rain on the windows, the brush of branches against the roof: all interfered with her ability to focus on her work. She felt like a rubber band that someone was stretching taut. Her nerves hummed with the knowledge that all she had to do was turn her head and Neil would fill her vision.

Finally, he stood. "Well, I guess I'll be on my way."

Laura tried not to watch as he reached for his jacket and put it on, but she couldn't help it. Everything about him fascinated her, even the smallest, most mundane action.

Five minutes later, she was alone again. Her hand trembled as she reached for her cup of tea. She closed her eyes. It was worse than she'd thought. If his presence for thirty minutes could rattle her like this, how was she going to handle all the times she'd be around him in the future? *Dear God. What am I going to do?*

For the rest of the day she managed to keep thoughts of him at bay. She worked diligently, keeping an eye on the weather, which got steadily worse as the day wore on. By four-thirty, the wind was gusting up to 35 mph, according to the radio, and the rain was so heavy she could hardly see out. It was also as dark as midnight outside, and although she had been hoping Neil wouldn't make it back to the office before she left, now she wished he would come. She wondered about the advisability of trying to drive home in this downpour. Sometimes Patinville's streets flooded, and she had no wish to get stranded. Maybe she should just stay put.

At five o'clock, she cleared her desk and prepared to leave. Walking over to the clothes tree in the corner, she lifted her tan raincoat. Just then she saw the yellow glow of headlights sweeping across the parking lot. When Neil pushed open the door minutes later, dripping water everywhere, she was relieved.

"It's terrible out there," he said. "I didn't think I'd ever get back from Baton Rouge."

"How was Norman today?" she asked, trying not to think about how glad she was to see Norman's brother.

"A little depressed, but that's not surprising, is it?"

Was he trying to make her feel guilty? "I went by to see him last night, you know." She couldn't keep the trace of defensiveness out of her voice.

He nodded. "He told me." He noticed her holding her raincoat. "Are you leaving?"

"Yes, I thought I would."

"It's really bad out there. Be careful driving."

Just then, a bolt of lightning streaked across the sky, and the lights in the office flickered. Laura's heart leaped in alarm. "I'd better be going," she said, hearing the tremor in her voice and hating it.

"Here, let me help you." Neil reached out, holding the coat for her. Just as she put her right arm into the sleeve, lightning cracked again, the sound like a cannon shot, and she jumped. Without warning, the lights went out, and the office was plunged into darkness.

Terror welled into Laura's throat, mindless and suffocating. *No, no!* She twisted away from Neil's hands and ran blindly toward the door.

"Laura!"

She flung the door open and plunged into the pelting rain. Shaking, she huddled under the small overhang outside. She tried to control her rapid breathing and pounding heartbeat.

"Laura, it's okay. You're okay." Neil tried to pull her back inside, but she fought off his hands.

"No! I...I can't go back in there. Please, Neil!" She couldn't seem to stop shaking.

"Come on, it was just lightning." Now he was beside her, and he reached for her. He put his arms around her, and she huddled against his comforting warmth. "My God, Laura, you're shaking like a leaf. Here..." He opened his jacket, folding the open sides around her so that they were sharing its protection.

"I...I..." She could hardly talk. She closed her eyes and took a long, shuddering breath. Her body refused to stop its trembling. All she could think about was the darkness. Never again. She would never allow herself to be shut up in the darkness again. He lifted her chin, and she raised her eyes. She could feel her bottom lip quivering as his gaze raked her face. How could she tell him?

"Laura..."

Uncontrollable tremors racked her body as rain blew under the meager shelter. His hand, which had been holding her chin up, brushed over her cheek and cupped the back of her head, drawing her close again. He stroked her head, whispering words of comfort, while his other hand rubbed her back.

Laura kept her eyes closed, absorbing his warmth and strength, oblivious to the storm raging around them. His right hand settled against the back of her neck, under her hair, and now another kind of shiver raced along her spine as his fingers kneaded the sensitive hollow. Without conscious thought, she strained against him, her own arms snaking around his waist, under the jacket. He smelled of wet leather and the faint remnants of a spicy cologne. She could feel his heart beating against hers.

Because she was nearly as tall as he, her face was pressed up against his neck, and when he spoke again, she could feel his warm breath against her cheek. "You're all right now. Everything's okay. You're here with me." He nuzzled his face against hers. Instinctively, she turned her face toward his, and when their lips met, she trembled. His lips were cool and wet from the rain as they settled softly against hers.

At first the kiss was just a sweet mingling of breaths. Their lips met for an instant, clung, then drew apart. Met again, lingered a moment longer, then drew apart. Then, as if they belonged there, his lips settled against hers with more urgency. Laura's heart hammered against her chest as his arms tightened around her. Now she could feel every line of his body against hers, and need spiraled through her. She strained against him in mute appeal, her mouth opening under his. Neil responded instantly, and a hot, dark desire flooded Laura as she felt the insistent touch of his tongue against hers.

Everything else receded from her thoughts: the rain, the noise of the thunder rolling around them, Norman, her fears, and her good sense. The only thing that mattered to her was Neil: his smell, his touch, his mouth, and his kiss, which could have come from the depths of hell with its searing possession, its devilish torment, its fire that fueled her deepest needs.

She kissed him with all the pent-up desperation of years of being alone, of years of wanting so many things she was afraid she'd never have. She kissed him with all the greedy intensity of a person who has been starving and is suddenly presented with more bounty than she could ever have imagined. She clung to him, opening her mouth and her heart, pouring all of herself into her response.

Only the lights flaring back on caused Laura to realize where she was, who she was, and what she was doing. Even then, it took everything in her, all the strength she possessed, to drag her mouth away from Neil's. He seemed to recover his own senses at the same time, and they suddenly staggered apart. Laura felt as if she were in shock. She couldn't think, and she didn't know where to look or what to say. She shuddered.

"Let's go back inside. You're soaked," he said, his voice thick.

She let him take her elbow and propel her through the door. Her own limbs felt lifeless. The knowledge that she'd thrown herself at him pulsed through her. She stumbled.

He steadied her. "Laura...Laura," he said, "look at me."

I can't. She was afraid of what she'd see in his eyes. He was probably embarrassed. Or worse, he was disgusted by the way she'd acted when all he'd intended was comfort in the face of her panic attack. *Oh, God.* How could she ever face him again? She'd been all over him. And he was Norman's *brother,* for God's sake. But no matter how much she berated herself, she knew, deep down where only her darkest secrets lay, that if he were to kiss her again, she would respond exactly the same way. Where Neil Cantrelle was concerned, her scruples and principles didn't seem to matter.

All that really mattered was Neil. The knowledge stunned her. It changed every perception she'd ever had of herself. It frightened her and repulsed her and fascinated her. One part of her wanted to scream a denial. The other part of her was chillingly accepting. *Look at him, you idiot. Don't let him see how this has affected you. Brazen it out.*

Neil touched her shoulder, and she turned. Slowly, she raised her eyes. But when she met his dark gaze, what she saw wasn't disgust or embarrassment but a look of wistfulness mixed with regret. He didn't smile, but his voice was gentle. "That should never have happened. I'm very sorry it did."

"It wasn't your fault." A tiny seed of hope began to replace her own embarrassment, a hope she knew she had no right to feel.

"Yes, it was. It won't happen again."

But even as he said the words, Laura knew that whatever this thing was between them, it wasn't going to go away.

Chapter Eight

Neil could see she was still shaking, and her white blouse and navy blue skirt were both plastered to her. Even as he told himself he had to minimize the importance of their kiss, he couldn't help noticing how the cotton fabric of her blouse clung to her, molding against her breasts and slender torso. The wet material was now transparent, and through it, her lacy bra and what it covered were clearly visible.

She's freezing, he thought, disgusted with himself, and he was standing there staring at her breasts like he'd never seen any before.

"Let's get you dry." He took her by the arm, and she let him lead her to the bathroom, where he snatched a towel from the rack. "You should get those wet clothes off. You're soaked through."

She didn't meet his eyes as she took the towel and began drying her face and hair. "I'll be okay."

"I'm going to get you one of my sweatshirts to put on."

"That's not necessary—"

"I'll only be a few minutes," he said, cutting off her protest. "Go on into the bathroom and take off that wet blouse. Get yourself dry."

While he was gone he berated himself. What the hell was wrong with him? Why had he kissed her? Neil tried to tell himself his reaction was natural, just a way of comforting her when she was upset and afraid. But he was too honest not to know the truth.

Don't lie to yourself. You wanted to kiss her. You've been thinking about her ever since Saturday night. You took advantage of the situation—and her.

Disgust flooded him. *You're a real jerk. All you had to do was pat her back in a friendly, brotherly way. Instead you couldn't keep your hands off her.*

Brotherly. The word pummeled him. It kept pummeling him as he yanked a thick sweatshirt out of the dresser and raced back down to the office. Laura took the sweatshirt and disappeared into the bathroom.

He was still grappling with the fact that he'd betrayed his brother in the worst kind of way when Laura emerged wearing his dark blue sweatshirt. She'd toweled her hair dry and now it was neatly combed. Her face was composed.

"Feeling better?" he asked.

"Yes, thanks."

He could see she was trying hard to act as if everything were normal between them. But she didn't meet his eyes. He had to say something. "Laura, we can't pretend nothing happened. We have to talk about this."

Now she looked at him. Color stained her cheeks, and her eyes were bright. Too bright. "I'm so embarrassed," she admitted. "You must think I'm—"

"I don't think you're anything. What happened wasn't your fault. You were frightened and upset, and I...I just..." *Listen to you. You can't even explain it so that it makes sense.* "There's nothing for you to be embarrassed about. It was my fault, I'm sorry, and it won't happen again. I promise you."

She swallowed, then bit her lower lip. The gesture touched something deep inside Neil. She looked so defenseless standing there. He desperately wanted to go to her and hold her in his arms again, tuck her head under his chin and bury his face in her shiny, sweet-smelling hair. Tell her they'd done nothing wrong.

"I just feel so stupid," she said.

"Why?"

She grimaced. "Oh, come on. You know it's not normal to act the way I did. You must think I'm a basket case."

"No, I don't." Belatedly, he'd remembered what Denise had told him about Laura's fear of the dark. That fear must be what had triggered her actions.

The full brilliance of her eyes met his, and now it was Neil's turn to swallow. Those eyes were enough to make a man forget his own name. No woman should have eyes like hers, eyes that you could drown in, eyes that made you want to protect her and take care of her, eyes that were so beautiful they made you ache inside.

"I hate being a freak," she said.

"Laura, don't be so hard on yourself. We all have weaknesses. Hell, I told you about mine the other night."

"That's different."

He sighed. "Listen, why don't you sit down? Let's have a cup of coffee and talk. It's so bad out there now, I don't think you should try to go home until it clears up some."

As if to emphasize his point, the windows rattled as the wind whistled around the building, and thunder rolled overhead.

Five minutes later they were sitting facing each other, each behind a desk. Laura held a mug of tea in her hands.

"Want to tell me about it?" Neil suggested softly.

She didn't pretend not to know what he was talking about. She stared down into her mug as if fascinated with the steam curling up and into the air. After a few minutes, she raised her eyes and looked directly at him. "I've never talked about this before. I...I've always been too ashamed."

Her eyes seemed to be asking him if she could trust him. Without words, he tried to tell her she could. She sighed deeply, then said, "The reason I'm so afraid of being closed up in a dark place is that my mother used to shut me up in the bedroom closet for hours at a time. Sometimes even all day...or all night. She'd tell me I was stupid, that she hated me, and then she'd lock me up."

The stark words hung in the air. Neil didn't know what he'd been expecting, but it was nothing like this. Sure, he'd sensed that Laura had suffered, that something had given her the idea that she wasn't worth a hell of a lot, but this...this was worse than anything he could have imagined. "Jeez," he whispered softly. "Why?"

Her shoulders lifted. "Who knows? I always thought it was because I wasn't good. For years I tried and tried to be good, to be the daughter she wanted. But it never worked. She couldn't stand me. Now I realize it probably had nothing to do with me. She...she was just terribly unhappy." Laura took a sip of her tea and looked away from him.

Neil thought about his mother. How good she was. How much she had always loved him and his brother and sisters. How she would gladly lay herself down in front of a truck if she could prevent one of her children coming to harm. Cold anger seeped into him like a slow-moving poison. "How old were you the first time this happened?" he finally managed to ask. He was no psychologist, but he thought it might do her good to get it all out in the open.

"I'm not sure. Two or three, I guess."

Neil balled his fists. A baby.

"My father abandoned my mother when I was about eighteen months old. I don't know why, maybe he just couldn't take the responsibility of a wife and child. I'm not really sure what happened, because Ginger—my mother—never had anything good to say about him. It's hard for me to know what was fact and what was fiction as far as she's concerned."

"This was where? In California?"

"Yes. My mother was an actress." She laughed, the sound brittle and hollow. "Well, let's put it this way. She *wanted* to be an actress. The closest she ever came was a small part in a teen scream horror movie. My dad was a burlesque show comic. We lived in ratty apartments in run-down sections of Hollywood. I really hated my life."

Neil remembered what Denise had said about Laura loving his family. No wonder, he thought. Compared to what she was describing, his family must have appeared idyllic.

"From the time I was old enough to realize that not everyone lived the way I did, I wanted to get away from her. I dreamed about having a family like the kind I read about and saw on TV shows..." She laughed again, this time one tinged with embarrassment. "You know—families like Beaver's."

He smiled. "Yeah, June and Ward Cleaver *did* make life seem ideal. But that's not the way real life is. All families have their problems."

"That might be true, but to me it never seemed that way. I had a wonderful friend—actually, we're still friends—and I used to go to her house, and it was so perfect. Sitting around her kitchen table. Having her mother fuss over me. Feed me cookies she'd baked herself..." Her voice trailed off wistfully. "I used to go back to our apartment and think about what I was leaving behind."

Her voice was filled with yearning, and once again, Neil wished he had the right to go to her. "My entire life I've felt like the rest of the world—the normal world—existed inside a huge golden circle of love with families that cared about each other—and I was on the outside of the circle, always looking in, always wanting to be a part of all that but knowing I never would be."

He couldn't stand it another minute. He got up, walked over to her desk and knelt in front of her. He took the mug away from her trembling hands and set it on the top of the desk. Then he took her hands into his. She didn't look at him, but she didn't resist him. Her head was bowed, and her hair fell like a shining curtain around her face. Her gold-tipped lashes lay against her pale skin, shielding her eyes from his view. Her lower lip stuck out, vulnerable and soft-looking. It was all Neil could do to hold her hands quietly when what he wanted to do was gather her close and never let anyone hurt her again.

No wonder Norman had fallen in love with her. Neil knew if he wasn't careful, he would fall in love with her, too. He picked his words carefully. "Laura, I know you think I couldn't understand, but I do. Although I never thought of it in just that way, I've had some of the same feelings."

Her startled blue eyes met his. "You!" She pulled her hands away, and Neil reluctantly got to his feet. "How could you possibly understand? You've got the most wonderful family in the world. It's obvious to anyone how close you all are, how much you care about each other."

He heard the disbelief in her voice. "Yes, well, sometimes family isn't enough."

"I'd give anything to have a family like yours, Neil. You should be grateful for them."

"I *am* grateful for them. All I'm saying is that sometimes a person needs something different. I..." *Go ahead, say it.* "I had a marriage that wasn't exactly storybook, and I used to feel the same way you did. I'd go over to my partner's house and sit in his kitchen and see what a great family life he had, and I'd be jealous. I wanted the same kind of relationship. So I know what you mean when you talk about being on the outside looking in. You're not alone in those feelings."

Forehead knitted, she considered what he'd said. He could see her struggling to accept the idea that she wasn't unique. That she wasn't a freak.

Pressing his advantage, he said, "Listen. Your childhood was rotten, so you idealized everyone else's, but believe me, the rest of the world is just as screwed up. In fact, I don't know anyone who hasn't got some kind of skeleton in the closet." He stopped. "Uh, that was a bad metaphor, wasn't it?"

He knew he was making headway when he saw the tiny smile tipping her lips. "Laura, you're tough. Tougher than you think. Yeah, you got a raw deal, but you survived it. You're not hiding out feeling sorry for yourself." As soon as he said the words, he thought, like you did for three years. Laura really *was* strong. Stronger than he was. He'd run away from the things he didn't want to face, but she was coping. Trying to cope, anyway.

He smiled at her. "Now, why don't you go the rest of the way? Have you ever thought about getting professional help?"

She nodded. "Yes, I've been thinking about it a lot lately."

"Good. That's the best thing you can do for yourself." He stood, leaned against her desk. "Tell me a little more about your fear. Are you just afraid of the dark, or do you have claustrophobia, too?"

She studied her hands. "I have some claustrophobia. As long as I'm in well-lighted places, I'm okay. But I don't handle small, enclosed places well. Some I can't handle at all."

"But just a little while ago I saw you go into the bathroom and close the door."

She grimaced. "I know. But it's still a struggle." She gave him a wry smile. "When I'm here alone, I leave the door open."

"And cars don't bother you?"

"No, thank goodness. There's something about the movement of the car and being outdoors that makes it okay." She sighed. "I know. I'm weird. The whole thing's weird."

He grinned. "We're all weird." Striving to lighten the atmosphere, he added, "Now, I don't know about you, but all this talking has made me hungry. Want to go get a pizza or something?"

"Thanks, but I think I'm going to go home and build a fire in the fireplace and heat up some soup."

He knew she was being more sensible than he was because the more time he spent with her, the harder it was going to be to pretend that all he felt for her was friendship. And the last thing she needed right now was more turmoil in her life, more guilt heaped on her.

He helped her with her raincoat, taking care not to touch her. She tied a scarf around her head, and Neil couldn't help thinking how much she looked like a waif, with her pale face sprinkled with freckles and her big, sad eyes.

She picked up her umbrella and just before she turned to go, she said softly, "Thanks, Neil. Thanks for listening."

"Anytime."

Laura hardly remembered driving home. All she could think about was Neil and how kind and understanding he had been when she'd told him about her mother, how easy it had been to talk to him, how much she trusted him. When had this happened? When had she gone from feeling uncomfortable and tense around him to feeling as if she could tell him anything?

What a difference from the way she felt about Norman. Although she had been comfortable with him, she had never been able to talk to him. Because she worked with him every day, she'd had to tell him about her fear of the dark and closed-in places, but she would never have been able to tell him the things she had told Neil because Norman didn't want to hear them. He refused to look beneath the surface. He told her she was making too much of her fears.

"If you don't think about them, they'll go away," he said, as if that easy answer were really possible.

Laura sighed. His attitude about her problem was typical of his attitude about everything. He saw only what he wanted to see. He hadn't known her at all. She'd realized long ago that they weren't right for each other, but still she'd delayed breaking off their relationship because of her growing love for his family and for what he represented.

She'd been crazy to think she could marry him. Thank God Norman had refused her impulsive gesture. A marriage between them wouldn't have worked. It was bad enough they didn't really communicate, but she'd also never felt any physical desire for Norman. She'd certainly never wanted to feel his arms around her, never wanted his kisses, never ached to have him touch her and make love with her.

Like Neil.

The knowledge throbbed inside like a toothache. Something that wouldn't go away, wouldn't let you forget about it. The feelings she had for Neil weren't casual, weren't brotherly, weren't wise.

She wanted him. She wanted him as a lover as well as a friend. She wanted to feel his hands on her naked skin, warming and caressing her. She wanted his mouth taking hers the way it had taken it today: hungry, demanding, possessive. She wanted him to fill her up, all the empty spaces and places that craved filling.

She was in deep trouble.

She wished she'd never met him.

* * *

Neil didn't finish the roofing bid until after ten o'clock that night. He spent so much time thinking about Laura, reliving everything that had happened and everything they'd said, that it took him much longer than it should have.

About eight the rain slacked off, and he sent out for a pizza. Then he forced himself to concentrate. When he was done, he put the finished bid on Laura's desk so she would see it first thing in the morning. Then he put on his jacket and left, locking up behind him. He started up the stairs to the apartment, then remembered that he needed shampoo and a couple of other things. He'd meant to stop on his way back from the hospital, but had forgotten.

Better go now, he thought.

Ten minutes later he drove through downtown Patinville, turning onto Main Street. Maybe the drugstore would still be open. Sure enough, Bradley's Drug Store blazed with light.

Neil parked in a vacant slot across from the store. He was glad the rain had stopped, but it was chilly out, and he zipped up his jacket, then sprinted across the street. Entering the store, he quickly scanned the signs over the aisles, then headed for the one where he should find shampoo. After selecting a bottle and grabbing some shaving cream and toothpaste, he headed toward the front of the store.

He put his purchases on the counter and looked for a clerk. He could see the top of William Bradley's bald head behind the pharmacy counter in back, but no clerk. Just as he was about to pick up his purchases and walk toward the rear, a woman's voice said, "May I help you?"

He looked up and met the green-eyed gaze of Margaret Chase, his ex-wife's mother. He saw recognition flash across her fleshy face, then the narrowing of her eyes, and the clenching of her jaw. Animosity was evident in her very stance. Well, it was mutual, he thought. He'd never liked Margaret because he felt she fed Erica's dissatisfaction with life by leading her to believe she was better than other people. That she deserved more than she was getting.

"Hello, Margaret."

"Neil." She inclined her head. "Wondered if you'd come home. Heard about Norman."

There it was again, that small town network that sped news with more efficiency than any newspaper or telegraph.

"How are you?" he said. He'd be civil if it killed him.

"Oh, I'm just *fine.*" She smirked. "How about you? You find your fortune down there, wherever it is you went when you left here?" She didn't say, *with your tail between your legs,* but Neil knew she wanted to.

"I'm doing okay." He kept his tone neutral.

"That'll be $7.14," she said. She dropped his purchases into a plastic bag.

He handed her a ten-dollar bill and waited for his change. She started to count the change out, mouthing the numbers under her breath. Then she stopped. A sly smile slid across her face. "I guess you're wondering how Erica is doing, aren't you?"

He had been, but he would never have given her the satisfaction of hearing him ask.

"Well, she's doing just great. She went out to Hollywood, you know, and she married her a rich producer. Yes, sirree, she's living high on the hog now. They got them a huge house in Bel Air. You should see it. She's even got a heart-shaped swimming pool. Johnny—that's her *new* husband—he's loaded, and he had it built 'specially for her." The smile on her face was one of glee. "I go out to see her two, three times a year. Johnny treats me real good."

Neil didn't begrudge Erica her new-found wealth with her successful husband. If that's what it took to make her happy, so be it. The knowledge that this was so made him smile with genuine warmth. "I'm delighted to hear it," he said. "Give her my best, will you?" He couldn't help the additional feeling of satisfaction from seeing Margaret's face fall in disappointment. What a witch. No wonder Erica had such skewed values.

What made people like that? he wondered as he climbed into the truck. She was actually disappointed that he wasn't jealous. He was still shaking his head when he got back to the apartment, but by the time he got inside, turned on some lights, and put his purchases away, Margaret Chase and her nasty little digs had disappeared and he was once more thinking about Laura.

He wondered what she was doing now. He eyed the phone. What would she think if he called her? He took two steps toward the phone, then stopped. He couldn't call her.

Remember your brother, he thought as he headed for the kitchen and the bottle of J&B. In the middle of pouring himself a hefty drink, he stopped, the second time in less than five minutes that he'd halted an action. What was he trying to do? Drown his sorrows?

Then he laughed at himself. Melodrama didn't suit him. He finished pouring his drink and carried it into the living room. He was making too much of all this.

When he saw Laura tomorrow, he probably wouldn't feel anything at all.

Chapter Nine

On Wednesday morning, Neil was coming down the steps from the apartment when Laura pulled into the parking lot. He took one look at her and knew all his rationalizations were so much garbage. She gave him a shy smile as she walked toward him, and he felt just like he'd felt when he was a freshman in high school and Susan Traylor, who was a senior and had been homecoming queen that year, winked at him.

"My father asked me to help out with the Port Allen job today," he said.

She looked up at the sky. "I hope it doesn't rain again. We've lost a lot of time on that job."

"Yeah, I know."

That was all they said, but it was enough to keep her in Neil's thoughts all day. And it was enough to prove to him that if he hoped to handle this impossible attraction he felt for her, he'd better keep his distance.

And for the most part, he did. He kept himself busy helping the crews on the days it didn't rain; the other days he spent at the hospital with Norman. But there were times when he couldn't stop himself from doing something for her. He knew it would be much better for everyone concerned if Laura thought their kiss was only a gesture of comfort, that it really meant nothing to him, so he tried.

But one day he was on his way out of the supermarket and he saw a display of fresh flowers. Impulsively, he picked up a bunch of red and white carnations and gave them to Laura that afternoon. The spark of happiness he saw in her eyes when she realized the flowers were for her made him ache to have the right to lavish gifts on her.

Another day he stopped in the local used bookstore to pick up something else to read besides the books of poetry he'd brought from Florida, and he saw a new mystery that had already hit the bestseller lists. He picked it up, wondering if Laura would like it. Knowing he shouldn't, he bought it anyway. By the time he reached Norman's apartment, Laura was gone for the day, and he knew the most sensible thing to do would be leave the book on her desk with a note. Instead he waited until the next morning and delivered the book in person. Her obvious pleasure warmed his heart for days.

He told himself there was nothing wrong in what he'd done. He was just being nice to someone who had had too little kindness in her life. And, after all, hadn't he promised Denise he'd keep an eye on Laura? Be kind to her?

Two days before Christmas, Dr. Dunado told Neil and his parents that Norman was completely out of danger. "His left leg is coming along nicely, and the stump is clear of infection. If he keeps up this pace, we might move him over to physical therapy by the middle of January. It all depends on how fast he can walk on that left leg."

"That's good, isn't it?" Arlette asked.

"Yes, that's very good." Dunado rubbed his nose where his glasses had made little indentations. "Surprising, too. For a while he was exhibiting signs of depression, as if he didn't care about getting well, but now he's fighting."

Neil had noticed this change, too. He'd been worried about Norman's depression and was grateful for the change. He wondered if the change had anything to do with what Laura had said to Norman. He'd been meaning to feel Norman out on the subject, but the right opportunity hadn't presented itself.

"Well, my Norman, he never was one to give up, you know?" Arlette said. "My children aren't quitters."

She didn't look at Neil, but Neil knew her remark was meant for him as much as for the doctor. Obviously, if she was back to her old feisty self, she was feeling better about everything. She was an amazing woman. Also a determined woman. She had been dropping hints for days now—hints that perhaps Neil should think about staying in Louisiana. And if it hadn't been for Laura, he probably would have considered it.

"When will he get his prosthesis?" Neil asked Dunado.

"Once he goes to physical therapy, the first thing they'll do is put on a shrinker. That's a thick, stretchy type of knee hose that shapes the stump and prepares it for the artificial limb. That'll stay on about a week or so, then they'll fit the prosthesis."

Neil hadn't known things would move this fast. He'd had some vague idea that Norman might have to wait six months or so before getting his new leg. "And then what?"

"Once we get him fitted, he'll have to remain in rehab for anywhere from one week to a month. It just all depends. He'll have physical therapy twice a day until he's able to function on his own and has regained most of his strength."

Encouraged by this news, Neil walked with his parents to their car. The sky was heavy with dark clouds, and a fitful wind scattered dead leaves and small bits of debris across the parking lot. Even the air smelled of rain. Neil was sick of the wet, cold weather, but the forecasters were predicting more on the way. He zipped up his jacket against the chill and shoved his hands in his pockets.

"I'm so happy about Norman," his mother said.

"Me, I wonder how long it will be before he can go back to work," his father said, forehead furrowed.

"Who cares when he goes back to work? We should just be thankful he's alive!"

Neil grinned at his mother's show of spunk. She was definitely back to her old self.

René looked wounded as he answered. "I know, Arlette. I *am* thankful. I thank God every day that he let Norman live, okay? But I can't help worryin' about the business."

Neil's father had only expressed a concern that had been gnawing at Neil for days. The business was important, not only because it was the family's livelihood, but because it was an integral part of all their lives.

When René had graduated from high school, he had gone to work for a roofing and home improvement company in Baton Rouge. After working there for five years, he had decided to strike out on his own and started Cantrelle Roofing and Home Improvement Company in Patinville, borrowing money wherever he could. That first year he worked long hours seven days a week to build it up. Gradually, over the years, he had hired several other men to work for him. Both Neil and Norman had grown up working for their father, and although Neil wanted to be a cop and joined the Baton Rouge police force, Norman had never seemed to want anything else. When René retired two years ago, Norman took over and had been running the business ever since.

"It's been slow because of the holidays and the rain, but soon business will pick up again," René said. He eyed Neil's mother. "Me, I'll pro'bly have to go back to work."

"René Cantrelle! You sure won't! You're sixty-eight years old. You're retired. There are lots of employees to take care of the work! Besides, you'll be coming to Baton Rouge with me every day, okay? Norman's going to need us."

Neil suppressed another grin. His mother was working herself into a state. But she was right about Norman needing them.

"Employees don' feel the same way about the business as we do," his father said mildly. He looked at Neil, a question in his eyes.

Neil evaded his gaze. He knew what his father wanted. Normally Neil wouldn't have hesitated. He'd have volunteered to help out with the business for as long as it took. There was nothing in Florida that couldn't wait for him. But with this dangerous attraction he felt for Laura, he knew he would be asking for trouble if he worked with her on a daily basis.

"Neil will help out until Norman is well again, okay?" his mother said, her voice firm, her dark eyes meeting Neil's.

"I don't think that's—"

"It's perfect," she continued as if Neil hadn't spoken. "You don' have no reason to hurry back to Florida." She smiled happily. "In fact, now that you're home again—where you belong—there's no reason to go back to Florida at all. Okay?"

"Mama—"

"Cantrelles, they don' run away from their problems."

"Mama, you know as well as I do—"

"This is where you belong."

Neil sighed in defeat. There was no talking to her. "Mama, this isn't the time or the place to discuss this."

"No better time," she said stubbornly.

"You're too emotional just now."

"Who's emotional? I'm not emotional. I'm just stating the truth, okay?"

"Can we discuss this some other time? It's starting to rain." As if to emphasize his point, a fat raindrop splattered on the roof of his mother's Plymouth wagon.

After René helped her into the car, he turned to Neil again. "You're a grown man, Neil. You gotta make your own decisions. If you want to go back to Florida, me, I won't try to stop you. But, you know, I feel I must tell you that I agree with your mama. We both think you should stay. We both *want* you to stay."

Neil felt torn between his love for them and his good sense. "Thanks, Papa," he said.

"But, me, I need you right now. Will you promise to stay at least until Norman is well enough to go back to work?"

How could he say no? He owed them. He owed them for all the years they'd loved him and supported him. "Of course."

A big grin split his father's face, and he hugged Neil.

As Neil waved them on their way, he knew he'd had no other choice.

Laura's soreness had finally disappeared. It was nice to be able to lift her arm to blow dry her hair without feeling pain. As she shut off the blow-dryer, Phoebe hopped up onto the vanity. "Myup," she said as she watched Laura fluff her hair.

"Myup, yourself." Laura gave the cat an affectionate head rub, then stooped to nuzzle her face in the thick fur. "You know I'm going out, don't you?" She was spending the evening with the Cantrelles, first going with them to the hospital to see Norman, then going back to René and Arlette's home for a late supper, then on to midnight mass. Laura knew she should try to avoid Neil's company but Denise had insisted, saying Christmas Eve was no time to be alone.

"Norman would have brought you along if he wasn't in the hospital, you know that," Denise said, a stubborn tilt to her chin. "Of course you'll be with us. And you'll be with us Christmas Day, too!"

Laura knew that look, and since she couldn't tell Denise the real reason she'd offered resistance to the invitation, she gave in. *And if you're honest with yourself, you'll admit that's exactly what you wanted to do, anyway. You want to be around Neil. Even though you know it's not very smart.*

The cat purred and Laura, sighing, lifted her and placed her gently on the floor. She only hoped she could keep her emotions safely controlled tonight. She thought she'd managed fairly well the few times she'd seen Neil since the kiss they'd shared, but each of those times they'd been alone. She hadn't had to deal with the presence of others.

She pressed her hands against her stomach. Just thinking about him made her insides flutter alarmingly. *Oh, Laura. You're a mess.* Why had this happened? Why, of all the people in the world, did she have to feel this hopeless longing for Neil Cantrelle?

She wondered about him. How did he feel? Was he half as confused as she was? That he felt something for her, she was sure of. She thought about the flowers he'd bought her, and the book. She thought about how she'd felt the other morning when she accidentally ran into him. If she'd entertained any notion that she could handle her feelings for him, that meeting had squashed it. The minute she saw him, running lightly down the steps with surefooted grace, dressed in jeans and a black turtleneck sweater under his bomber jacket, she'd known she was lost. Her heart beat faster, and her stomach curled, and all she could think about was the way she felt when he kissed her.

And now here she was, getting ready to spend Christmas Eve with him and his family. How would she keep her equilibrium surrounded by the love and warmth and intimacy of their family circle, a circle she could now never be a part of? She'd have to keep telling herself that she was the outsider, that if Norman's family guessed how she felt about Neil, they'd close ranks very quickly.

But even as she told herself these hard truths, she couldn't prevent herself from trying to look as attractive as possible, and she carefully applied makeup and took pains with her hair. Then she looked at her image in her full-length mirror. She was wearing one of her few dresses, a soft cranberry wool with a high neck and long sleeves and gently flaring skirt. The color gave her skin a rosy glow, and the simple lines of the dress were flattering.

Sighing again, she turned away from the mirror.

Ten minutes later, she was sitting in the back seat of Denise and Jett's car, on her way to Baton Rouge and the hospital. When they arrived, Laura was grateful to find they were the first of the family to get there. Somehow she knew it would be easier for her if she were already in Norman's room, their first awkward greetings behind them, when Neil and his parents arrived.

The hospital rules had been bent for the holidays, and all of them were allowed into Norman's room at once. The hospital staff had decorated each room with a wreath on the door and a red bow at the foot of the bed. In addition, Norman had a small Christmas tree that Laura knew his parents had brought, the poinsettia she'd sent to him, and an arrangement of red and white carnations and greenery with a red Christmas candle in the middle. The flowers immediately reminded Laura of the ones Neil had given her, but she pushed the thought aside. Someone had sprayed pine scent in the room, for the room smelled Christmasy.

"Well," Denise said brightly as the three of them trooped in, "your room certainly looks festive." She bent over the bed to kiss Norman's cheek. "Merry Christmas, Norman."

"Merry Christmas," he said. Over the top of Denise's head, his eyes met Laura's, and they contained a spark of joy he didn't try to hide.

There was a lump in her throat as she too bent over him. She clasped his hand and squeezed it. "Merry Christmas, Norman," she whispered. She kissed his cheek.

"You, too." His hand gripped hers tightly. "Thanks for coming."

The emotional moment passed as Jett greeted Norman, and Laura and Denise sat down—Denise on the bottom edge of the bed and Laura against the windowsill.

Norman looked much better than he had a week ago, Laura thought, with more color in his face. But he was much thinner.

"How are you feeling?" Denise asked.

Just as Norman started to answer, Desiree, followed by René and Arlette, with Neil bringing up the rear, entered the room. During the flurry of greetings, Laura steeled herself. When Neil said, "Hello, Laura. Merry Christmas," she was proud of herself for her light response and the elaborately casual way she delivered it. "Hi! Merry Christmas!"

Neil stood by Norman's bed, facing her, so that she couldn't look at Norman without looking at him. She also couldn't help but see how happy it made Norman to have Neil there. It was obvious to everyone how much they cared about each other.

"You'll never guess who came to see me today," Norman said, looking up at Neil.

"Who?"

"Alice Kendella."

Neil smiled.

"Jimmy's wife?" Denise asked.

Laura looked at Neil. Jimmy. That was the partner he had told her about. The one who had died.

"Yeah. We were in the same class in high school," Norman said. "She said you'd been over to see her, Neil, that you'd told her about me."

"Yes. I've been there a couple of times."

"She's sure a nice person," Norman said. "She brought me those flowers." He gestured toward the arrangement of carnations. "And a couple of books to read."

"Yes, she's terrific," Neil agreed.

"Pretty, too," Jett said. "She comes into the restaurant every now and then with those two kids of hers."

"Hey," Denise said, "you're not supposed to notice things like that. You're a married man."

"Married, but not dead," Jett said, laughing as Denise punched him playfully on the arm. Then, with a sly smile on his face, he added, "She's got a sexy voice, too. Reminds me of Marilyn Monroe. Come to think of it, she even looks a little like Marilyn."

Both Neil and Norman grinned at Denise's indignant, "Hmph!" but Laura couldn't help the sharp stab of jealousy she felt over the unknown Alice Kendella, who had managed to produce such a look of admiration on Neil's face.

For the rest of their visit with Norman, Laura was sunk into depression. She had no right to feel jealous over anyone, she knew that. She would never have that right, so she might as well get used to it, for if Neil stayed in Louisiana, she was bound to see him with other women. Unhappiness, like a giant wave, engulfed her at this dismal prospect.

Finally their visit was over. Everyone kissed or hugged Norman goodbye and then they were all walking out together.

"Laura, *chère,*" Arlette said. "You'll ride back with us, okay?"

"Oh, no. I came with Denise and Jett," Laura protested. That's all she'd need, sitting for more than a half hour in the back seat of the car with Neil. "I'll ride back with them, too."

"They're going to pick up the children at Jett's mother's house," Arlette said.

"Yes," Denise piped in. "There's no sense in you having to ride over there with us. Plus, knowing Mama Hebert, she'll want us to stay awhile. You go on with Mama and Papa."

Cornered, Laura didn't argue. And, of course, as if everything and everyone were conspiring against her, Desiree slid into the front seat between her parents, and Laura found herself in the back with Neil. The ride to Patinville was pure torment. She was acutely aware of Neil, only inches away, and the intimacy and warmth of the car only intensified that awareness. She was conscious of every movement he made and had to force herself not to look at him. They were so close she could smell his after-shave, something spicy and clean. Her heart refused to beat calmly, like it was supposed to, and instead skipped around like a crazy thing.

I can't take this. I can't. I can't stand being around him like this. But even as this thought swirled through her mind, she knew she really had no choice.

I could leave Patinville. Quit my job and go away. But could she? Norman needed her. All anyone had to do was look at his face tonight when she'd walked into his hospital room to know how he felt about her. Could she just walk out on him, walk out on his family? Aside from Norman personally, there was the business. Laura knew more about the office than anyone else. How could she leave? As a responsible adult and an honorable person, how could she let both Norman and his family down?

Laura bit her lip and stared out the window the rest of the way to Patinville.

* * *

The smell of incense and burning candles was the first thing Neil noticed as he walked behind Laura and his family into St. Anthony's. Although he hadn't been inside a church in years, the sounds and smells were as familiar to him as his boyhood home, and he could feel the years slipping away as memories came flooding back.

He'd spent countless Sundays here. Sundays filled with sunshine and the hot, still air of summer that floated through the open windows, and the whirring sound of the fans that were ineffectual in attempts to cool the church. He remembered how, as a small boy, he'd been restless and noisy, fidgeting through the service, and how his mother would glare at him with narrowed eyes that told him to be still or else. Then, as a teenager, how he'd doze through the homily and yawn his way through the rest of the Mass.

As a child he had spent more time at St. Anthony's than he'd spent anywhere else, except his own home. Father Richard, dead for years now, had been an ex-basketball player, and he'd encouraged the boys in the parish to hang around the school yard where he could easily be persuaded to join them in a pickup game at any time of the day or evening.

Neil had been an altar boy, too, and for a while, when he was about ten, he fantasized about becoming a priest, but the idea faded as he grew older and finally disappeared altogether. Neil smiled wryly. He would have been a terrible priest, doubting everything.

The church was only about half-full, but they were early. It was only eleven-thirty. By midnight, Neil knew, St. Anthony's would be packed. His father stopped at the first empty pew and motioned Desiree in, then he went next, followed by Neil's mother, then Laura, and finally Neil. It didn't surprise him that he'd ended up next to her. That seemed to be the way the entire evening had gone, and he had no doubt that nothing would be different tomorrow.

He was very aware of her as they sat shoulder to shoulder and listened to the choir sing "The Little Drummer Boy." When they began, "It Came Upon a Midnight Clear," Laura joined in, and Neil was struck by the sweetness of her voice, pure and clear and light as the bells of her brass wind chimes, as it lifted into the air and mingled with the voices of the other worshipers.

He slanted a glance at her as she sang. She looked very lovely tonight, he thought, in her rosy wool dress and single strand of pearls. She'd done something to her hair, too. It was fuller and fluffier, as if she'd curled it a little, but the sides still curved around and under her jawline like a soft caress. Tenderness tugged at Neil as he studied the slender line of her throat, the vulnerable curve of her full lower lip, the faint dusting of freckles across her cheeks and nose, the thick gold-tipped eyelashes framing her vivid eyes. She looked so fragile right now, so defenseless, so in need of love and protection.

For Neil, as Mass began and the priest intoned the words of the liturgy, the night took on an unreal quality, as if he were a player on a stage, with lines and actions that were predestined, only waiting for him to say them or do them. He stood and knelt and said the responses, the words awkward at first, then more sure as the service proceeded. Around him, in the flickering candlelight, the faces of the other worshipers receded into the background, and there was only Laura beside him.

As the congregation joined hands to say the Lord's Prayer, Neil felt the warmth and softness of Laura's hand as it slid into his, and when his fingers closed around hers, he was filled with a fierce longing. And later, when he turned to her to wish her peace, their eyes met as they shook hands, and when he gazed down into those bottomless blue depths, he knew that the next few weeks would be the hardest weeks of his life, and that he would need all the strength he possessed to get through them.

* * *

On Christmas Day, all the Cantrelles had been invited to a celebration being given by René's brother, Leon, and once again, they invited Laura to spend the day with them. After the strain of spending Christmas Eve in Neil's company, having to watch everything she said or did, Laura told Denise she was feeling a bit under the weather, and really preferred to stay at home. But Denise wouldn't hear of it.

"You'll do no such thing! Why, Mama would have a fit! You can't be alone for Christmas."

"Really, Denise, I don't want to go with you," Laura insisted. "And I won't be alone. I'll spend the afternoon at the hospital with Norman."

"We're going to the hospital, too."

"I know. But I'll stay on. Really," Laura added as she saw the stubborn glint in Denise's eyes. "I'll enjoy a quiet afternoon with him more than a noisy party. Besides, they're your family, not mine."

Denise gave her a knowing look. "Come on, Laura. You don't have to pretend with me. I know Norman has asked you to marry him, so we're practically your family, too."

Laura couldn't stop her sound of dismay.

Denise looked stricken. "Oh, I'm sorry. I wasn't thinking when I said that." Then she put her arms around Laura and hugged her. "No matter what happens, we'll always be friends."

Laura closed her eyes as she hugged Denise back. The urge to confide in her was strong. It would be so wonderful to have someone she could discuss her feelings with. Keeping everything bottled up inside, especially the way she felt about Neil, was really getting her down. Having to put on a face every time she was around him was so hard. And it would be nice to assure Denise that only Neil's presence was stopping her from accepting the invitation, because Laura *would* enjoy being around the exuberant Cantrelles and sharing in the closeness of their Christmas.

"It's sweet of you to ask me," she said. "It means a lot to me."

They hugged again and Denise turned to leave. "See you at the hospital, then?"

That afternoon, as Laura stepped off the elevator onto the fourth floor, she didn't notice Neil right away because several other people had exited the elevator at the same time and were blocking her view. But as she walked down the hall toward Norman's room, she saw Neil standing outside the door. When he saw her, he walked toward her.

Her stupid heart immediately started beating erratically, maddening her. For the thousandth time, she wondered exactly what it was about this man that made her react this way.

Only good looks, charm, kindness, intelligence, and sex appeal, her inner voice chided. Laura couldn't help smiling. Neil certainly possessed all of that, and more. Today he looked particularly attractive, wearing khaki dress pants and a bright red cable-knit sweater. The sweater looked new, and she wondered if it had been a Christmas present.

"Laura," he said in a low, urgent voice, "before you go in to see Norman, there's something I have to tell you. Let's go down there." He motioned to the other end of the hall.

"What is it? Has something happened?" Alarm jolted through her. Had Norman taken a turn for the worse?

As they walked quickly down the hall, Laura slanted a look at Neil. His face was set in pensive lines. Anxiety gnawed at her.

When they reached the end of the hall, he turned to her and said, "Don't look so worried. It's nothing terrible, it's just that I came to the hospital early today, and Norman and I had a long talk. About you."

"Me?"

Neil nodded. "When I mentioned that Dunado was really pleased by his progress, especially his positive attitude—which I'm sure you've noticed—"

"Yes, of course I've noticed." They'd all wondered about the change in him. Laura had hoped that maybe the change was due to her challenge when she told him she hadn't realized he was a quitter.

"You know what he told me?"

"I have no idea." Neil's dark eyes held her gaze for a long moment. Her heart gave another little flip.

He watched her face intently. "He told me he'd thought everything over, especially the things you said to him, and that he finally realized all he had to do was get well. He said once he learned to walk with his artificial leg as well as he'd walked with his own leg, then he was sure everything would work out the way he wanted it to. Then he told me he still hoped to marry you. He told me the whole story, how he'd asked you, what you'd said, what he'd said, and I pretended I didn't know anything about it."

The longer Neil talked the more alarmed Laura became. "But Neil, when I told Norman I'd marry him, I really thought it would work out. But I know better now." Her eyes locked with his. "Things are different now."

Something like pain flashed across his face. "I'm sorry, but I thought you needed to know how he feels."

"This isn't fair."

"I know it's not." Now there was real anguish in the dark gaze that pinned hers. "But as long as he has something to fight for, he'll fight. And isn't Norman's recovery more important than anything else right now?"

Laura felt as if someone were pressing down on her chest. She didn't want this kind of responsibility. It had been such a relief to stop pretending. It was hard enough that she had to watch herself around Neil. But now she'd have to be doubly careful. She'd be walking on eggs all of the time. She wasn't sure she could.

Five minutes later she stood in Norman's room with a bright smile pasted across her face. He was in high spirits. The entire family was already there, and because it was

Christmas, even Jett's and Denise's children had been allowed to come. When Laura walked into Norman's room, Jeannine was sitting on the side of the bed and Norman was holding her hand. They were laughing and giggling. Justin, her six-year-old brother, was standing on the other side of bed.

Norman looked Laura's way, a big grin on his face. She kissed him on the cheek, noticing the blush of pleasure he didn't try to hide. Everyone greeted her happily, and for the next hour, they all laughed and talked and watched Norman open the presents they'd brought.

But the whole time, Laura could feel Neil's presence, even though they avoided eye contact. Each time Norman said something to her and she answered, she knew Neil was listening to every word and every nuance of her reply. She wondered if anyone else felt the tension in the air. She'd have given anything to just be herself, to be completely honest with all of them.

But she knew if she did anything to cause Norman to have any kind of relapse, Neil would never forgive her.

And she would never forgive herself.

Chapter Ten

A storm front was moving in from Texas, and the weather forecasters were predicting possible major flooding. Laura considered calling Norman to tell him she wasn't coming to see him that evening, but she hadn't been to the hospital for three days.

After what Neil had told her, she hated to disappoint Norman. Even though she knew she couldn't marry him, Neil had made it very clear she was his touchstone, and she was resigned to the part she was playing. She just kept telling herself it wouldn't be long before she could stop the pretense. Norman was doing better all the time.

So despite her reservations about the weather, when she locked up the office that night, she decided she'd go home, make a quick sandwich, change into warmer, more sturdy clothes, and head for Baton Rouge and the hospital.

An hour later she was on her way. It was already raining, a steady downpour from leaden skies. As she drove cautiously toward Baton Rouge, keeping her speed moderate and two hands on the wheel, the wind picked up, rocking the small Honda, and lightning streaked the sky. Now Laura wished she'd followed her instincts and stayed home, but she'd come so far, it seemed silly to turn back now.

When she finally reached the hospital, a trip that took her more than an hour instead of the usual forty or forty-five minutes, she was so tense her shoulders ached. She wasn't all that fond of driving at night under any circumstances, and driving in this weather, especially so soon after the accident, had been a nerve-racking experience.

But she'd made it, she thought in triumph, as she entered the brightly lighted lobby of the rehab wing and nodded to the guard on duty.

"Terrible night, isn't it?" he said, smiling and lowering his magazine, a dog-eared copy of *Field and Stream.* He was an older man, middle fifties, Laura thought, with thinning gray hair and kind eyes.

"Yes, it's awful." She removed her coat, shaking some of the water off. Then she turned it inside out so she wouldn't get the rest of her clothes wet, and folded it over her arm.

"Not many people here tonight," the guard said. "Been real quiet."

Just then, there was a tremendous clap of thunder, and Laura jumped. She laughed shakily. "Sounds like it's getting worse, doesn't it?"

The guard nodded. "Yep. You pro'bly should've stayed home. Do you live far from here?"

Laura grimaced. "Yes. I've come over from Patinville."

The guard raised his eyebrows. "If I was you, I'd think about stayin' here tonight. Mebbe gettin' a hotel room, or somethin'."

He had given voice to her own uneasy feeling that it had been foolhardy to come out tonight. The ride back to Patinville would probably be a nightmare. But there was nothing to be done about it now. She was here.

Trying not to think about the drive home, she walked over to the elevators. Both were in use, so she pressed the Up button. A few seconds later, the one on the left descended, pinged its arrival, then opened, disgorging two nurses who were laughing and talking. They smiled at Laura, and she smiled back.

As they walked away, Laura eyed the yawning empty space of the waiting elevator. Trying to act nonchalant, she looked around. There was no one else in sight. The nurses had disappeared in the direction of the cafeteria, and there was only the guard, who was once more reading his magazine.

He looked up, idly curious. "What's the matter?"

"Uh...nothing." He must think she was crazy. Biting her lip, she moved toward the empty elevator, but her feet felt like two concrete blocks, and her heart pounded against her chest wall. *Boom. Boom. Boom.* It sounded so loud, she was afraid the guard would hear it.

No. She couldn't do it. She knew she couldn't do it. Stomach jumping, she stopped, looking around again. Her face must have reflected her growing panic, because the guard frowned, pale blue eyes now containing a glimmer of concern.

She would have to say something. Do something. "I—"

At that moment, the front door opened, letting in an explosive gust of wind and rain as well as a sodden-looking Neil.

A tidal wave of relief swept her. She felt weak with it. She had never been so glad to see anyone in her entire life.

Neil, shaking himself like a dog, spraying droplets of water everywhere, swore softly. "Damn, it's bad out there." He looked up, surprise firing his dark eyes. "Laura! You drove over here tonight?"

"Yes." Her heart was pumping madly, which she told herself was the aftermath of her panic attack and had nothing to do with seeing Neil.

"I wish I'd known you were coming. I would've tried to talk you out of it." He shrugged out of his wet leather jacket. Underneath he wore a pale blue sweatshirt and jeans. His cheeks were reddened from the cold, and his dark hair looked windblown and wet.

She smiled gratefully as he walked toward her. "It took me longer than usual, but I didn't have any real trouble getting here. I *am* a bit worried about driving back, though."

Now that he was here, her fear had disappeared. With no hesitation, she stepped into the open elevator with him, and Neil pushed the button for five, the top floor of the wing. "I don't think it's a good idea for you to drive back on your own," he said. "Maybe you should ride back with me."

The elevator doors slid shut, and the car started its ascent.

"But I have my car—"

She broke off the sentence as lightning, sounding like the boom of a cannon, struck somewhere near. The lights in the elevator flickered, and Laura froze. A split second later, the elevator was plunged into darkness and rocked to a stop.

She couldn't breathe. The air was all gone. She tried to take a breath. The darkness closed in on her. Terror, unreasoning and wild, exploded inside her. A scream bubbled into her throat. *No, no, no, no.* The thought raged through her like a maddened bull, terrified and out of control.

The scream ricocheted off the walls and filled the darkness. Kept filling the darkness as it went on and on.

Strong hands gripped her arms, but she fought against them, screaming and sobbing at the same time.

"Laura, Laura, it's all right! It's just the electricity. Calm down." The hands tried to subdue her. "You're safe. You're here with me."

She couldn't stop screaming. The blackness closed in on her. It was suffocating her. She couldn't get any air. She kept trying to beat the hands away, but they only held her tighter.

"Laura, it's okay. I'm here. You're all right. Please, Laura. Please, *chère,* please stop."

"No, no!" The words were ripped from her throat. She squeezed her eyes shut, trying to escape the panic and hysteria and unreasoning terror, shaking violently and hitting out against Neil. The darkness, the terror, was everywhere, surrounding her, suffocating her, pressing in on her from all sides. "No! No!" She flailed at Neil, sobbing and gasping, her nails connecting with his face as one arm tore free from his grasp.

"Laura, stop it! Stop it! You're okay. It's okay. You're safe. I'm here. I won't let anything happen to you." His arms pinned hers to her sides, and he pulled her close to him. "Shh. Calm down. Calm down, *chère.*" He whispered against her ear, his voice soft and steady.

"Neil, Neil," she cried, grasping at him.

"Shh, shh, it's okay."

She clutched at him, tears streaming down her face, and he held her tightly, gently kneading her back, all the while speaking softly and soothingly. "I can't stand this. I can't stand it." She could hear her breath coming in ragged gasps, hear the hysteria in her voice. She squeezed her eyes shut, the self-induced darkness more bearable than the inky blackness of the motionless elevator, with unknown horrors waiting to pounce.

She buried her face against Neil's neck, unable to stop crying, and he stroked her hair and her face, murmuring words meant to be comforting. She couldn't seem to stop shaking, and she could feel another scream building and she jerked her face free.

"Neeeeillllll..."

As the scream echoed around them, he grasped her face in his two hands, and his mouth covered hers, smothering the scream in her throat. At first she fought him, pushing against his chest, but her efforts were useless and ineffectual.

Her heart pounded like a mad thing, and her strength slowly ebbed away. As soon as she stopped fighting him, he released her mouth, and she collapsed against him.

"Neil," she whimpered, the sound like the mewling of a kitten. There was no strength left in her body. Tears streamed down her face.

"Shh, baby, don't cry." He brushed the wetness from her cheeks. "Don't cry. It's all right. I'm here."

"Neil..."

She slid her arms around him and turned her face into his neck, burrowing into his warmth, feeling as weak as if she'd just survived a long illness. She took a deep breath, and he stroked her hair and nuzzled her face. He smelled like rain, and soap, and his spicy after-shave—all comforting, ordinary, everyday smells.

She was still shaking, but now she could feel the heat of his body, its hard length pressed against her, and she could feel the strong beat of his heart. His hand slid under her hair, stroking her neck. The other caressed her face, lifted her chin, and brought her mouth slowly back to his. He murmured soft words, his breath mingling with hers, and he kissed her again and again, coaxing, comforting, tender, openmouthed kisses that slowly changed the tempo of her breathing and the cadence of her heart.

"Laura, Laura," he murmured. "So sweet. You're so sweet." He kissed her eyes, her cheeks, brushed his lips over her nose and down the side of her neck. His breath was moist and heated, and now her shiver wasn't caused by fear, but by a dawning awareness of the sensations he was causing by his kisses.

Laura moaned. "Neil..." Her body arched and she leaned her head back as his lips brushed over her sensitive skin. Her fists clutched handfuls of his sweatshirt and she pressed herself closer. Need pulsed through her.

With a sound that was half moan, half grunt, his mouth captured hers once again. His tongue swirled inside, and a fine trembling raced through her body as his hands abandoned her face and moved over the rest of her body, stroking and caressing, kneading and demanding, igniting nerve endings wherever they touched, fueling the need that was building rapidly.

Now she was touching him, too, and as his hands pushed her sweater up, and his mouth dropped to the hollow between her breasts, she buried her face in his hair, breathing him in, taking his strength and the safety and warmth he offered, drawing it into herself. She could feel the coiled strength of his body as her hands slid under his sweatshirt, curling into the crisp mat of hair on his chest, then sliding around against the taut muscles of his back.

"Laura," he whispered, the sound ragged and uneven. With fumbling fingers, he found the hooks of her bra, and when his hands cupped the bare skin of her breasts, his thumbs rolling back and forth against the nubs, something tight and painful burst within her, and all thought, all reason, all sanity, disappeared. Laura strained toward him, tightening her arms around him, fitting her body against his. A primitive need poured through her, consuming her like wildfire consumed a forest.

His hands molded and shaped, moving roughly over her body, and Laura responded to the strength and raw desire in the fierce caresses, the need inside her so intense it was the only thing in the world that mattered. The only sounds were the rasp of their breathing and Laura's moans as they kissed greedily. Without even realizing it had happened,

Laura found herself on the floor and Neil had covered her body with his own.

Every part of Laura—her body, her mind, her heart—was aware of what was happening between them, but she wasn't experiencing it with her brain or with rational thought. She was feeling it with her emotions and her senses. She was filled with a throbbing awareness of this great aching void inside her, a void that had been a part of her from earliest childhood, a void that she had always known existed and she knew Neil was the only person in the world who could ever fill it.

He kept kissing her as his hands stroked her bare skin—demanding, bruising kisses—and she moaned and cried, the sounds incoherent and beseeching. She needed him. She needed him. The kisses weren't enough. She wanted him inside her. She wanted him to fill her up. She wanted him to take her. She didn't want him to be gentle. She wanted to feel his strength. She needed his power, his force, his dominance. Now. She needed it now.

"Laura, my God, Laura," he said, as her body writhed under his hands and tongue.

Laura felt as if she were coming apart, as if she were made out of glue and papier-mâché and Neil was peeling off the layers, exposing the empty core inside. Tears slid out of her eyes, and she couldn't stop them. "I need you, Neil. I need you." She dug her fingers into his back.

She heard the rasp of his zipper. He yanked her skirt up and pushed her underwear down. "Now!" she insisted, lifting herself to meet him.

And then he was thrusting himself into her.

Suddenly, all her desperation and frenzy and fear were over. As soon as she felt his heat, and the throbbing life within her, she wound her legs around him, and drew him in as far as she could, knowing everything really was okay, that as long as she had Neil, here, part of her, nothing could hurt her.

A radiance spread through her, and with it, a sense of peace and homecoming. She no longer felt empty. She no longer felt alone. She no longer felt as if she were standing on the outside of the circle watching the people within.

And as he began to move inside her, she felt warm and good and protected, safe, and loved.

"Neil," she murmured. "Neil." His name was like an incantation or a sigh, and she said it again. "Neil." She drew his head down, and savored the taste of him. Straining against him, she matched her movements to his. *Yes,* she thought. *Yes. Take me. Take me.* Nothing in her life had ever felt as good as having this man—this man who was her universe—inside her. All she wanted was to give him as much as he'd already given her. She tightened her legs around him, concentrating on helping him.

"Laura!" he cried as his hot seed burst within her. Pride and happiness filled her, and she gripped him tightly, while he shuddered from the aftermath of their union. As they clung together their breathing finally slowed. Laura could feel his heart beating against her own, and she had never felt so close to another human being, never known that anything could feel so right. She could still feel him inside her, and she wanted him to stay there forever. For the first time in her life she understood how the whole can be better and stronger than the sum of its parts.

Together, she and Neil could be invincible. They belonged together, and nothing and no one could ever change that.

Oh, my God. What had he done? In the aftermath of their chaotic lovemaking, reality crept slowly back, chilling and sobering. Neil had only meant to comfort her and calm her down. Instead, he'd lost all control and practically attacked her. What had happened to him? Where had his reason gone?

Very gently—he didn't want to hurt her—he moved away from her, rolling off her and sitting up. When she tried to stop him, he took her hands and said, "Look, Laura, we've got to talk about this."

He couldn't see her at all in the darkness, but he knew her eyes would be big and luminous as they stared at him. He could see how her lower lip would jut out, and how vulnerable she would be. Part of him wanted to gather her back up into his arms and kiss her eyes and cheeks and reassure her, tell her he would always take care of her, that nothing would ever hurt her again.

The other part—the part that even now was cringing away from the cold truth that he had broken a code of honor so old and so ingrained that he had never known any other—was trying to figure out how they were going to live with what they'd done. How they were going to face each other. How they were going to face Norman.

"Neil—"

"Come on, Laura, let's get ourselves straightened up, okay? The lights could go on at any minute. You don't want anyone to see us like this, do you?" He tried to make his voice gentle and calm even though he felt anything but calm.

"No." The word was a whisper in the darkness.

Jesus, what was he going to do? Mind spinning, Neil zipped up his jeans, smoothed back his hair, and tried to regain his composure. After a few minutes, he could hear her moving around.

"Here," she said. "Here's my comb. Do you want to comb your hair?" She sounded okay.

But when he handed the comb back to her, he felt her hand tremble. He reached for her, and she came into his arms without any resistance. He closed his eyes as he held her close, one hand stroking her silky hair, the other splayed across the firm muscles of her back.

She put her arms around him, and they didn't talk at all, just held each other. Neil finally let himself think about her—not what they were going to do or the rightness or wrongness of what they'd done together—but Laura herself. How he felt about her, and how he'd felt when they were making love.

The experience had been like nothing he'd ever known before. Knowing how much she needed him, feeling her desperation and emptiness as he held her and comforted her, and then the tortured sweetness of her kisses and the way she clung to him, he had been assaulted by feelings and emotions that he'd kept buried for years. All the aching loneliness and yearning that had been a part of him for a long time began to splinter and fall away, and when he finally felt Laura take him in, all warm and loving and welcoming, he no longer felt as if he belonged to himself. Somehow, in the space of minutes, he had become a part of Laura, and she had become a part of him.

And now, as his fingers delved in her hair, and he listened to her even breathing and felt the warm, firm contours of her body, and breathed in her clean, feminine scent, he knew he loved her. And the knowledge tore at him, because he also knew his love for her wouldn't change anything.

"Laura, we have to talk," he said again, and even to his own ears, his voice sounded strained.

She lifted her head and he felt her warm breath feathering his skin. "I know we do."

He brushed a kiss against her forehead. "Let's sit down, okay?"

"All right."

They sat on the floor, up against the back wall of the elevator, and Neil took her hand. It felt warm and smooth and fragile as her fingers closed around his.

"I don't know where to begin," he admitted.

"I love you, Neil," she said quietly. "Why don't we begin there?"

Neil closed his eyes. A flame of happiness burst inside him, but it was no good. He knew that. "Laura, please don't say things like that."

"But why? It's the truth. I think I loved you from the first day I saw you." There was a tremor in her voice. "Don't you love me?"

He couldn't stand it. He wanted so much, so much he could never have. "Oh, God. I...I don't want to hurt you. I never wanted to hurt you."

She went still. He could feel her stillness in the way her hand relaxed its grip. "What does that mean, Neil?"

"It means how I feel isn't important. It means I'm not free to love you."

She was silent for a long time. Then she said, "Neil, I understand how you feel. You feel guilty. You think we've betrayed Norman. And I... I know we have to talk about Norman. But first we have to settle things between us, then we can decide what to do about Norman."

He closed his eyes against the weakness in him, the part that wanted to say the world was well lost for love, but Neil knew he couldn't do that. He had to live with himself.

"Laura, *chère,*" he said, "there can never be an *us.*"

"Neil, don't say that. How can you say that after what's happened tonight? How can we go on as if it didn't happen?"

He heard the desperation in her voice, but he couldn't allow himself to give in to it. Their situation was hopeless, and she would have to face it. But he also knew how vulnerable she was, and he couldn't stand to hurt her any more than was necessary. "We *must* go on as if tonight never happened. We have no other choice."

"Neil, just tell me one thing..."

He tensed.

"Do you love me?"

Closing his eyes, he drew on all his strength. Then he took a deep breath. "I can't answer that, Laura."

"Can't, or won't?" Her voice was thick with tears.

Knowing how she'd interpret his answer, he braced himself and said, "Won't." He waited one heartbeat. "Because I don't want to hurt you and I don't want to lie to you."

Chapter Eleven

On the drive back to Patinville, Neil was very quiet. Earlier, after the electricity came back on, and the elevator jolted to life, he had seemed to take it for granted that they would skip the visit to Norman and just go home. Emotions in turmoil, Laura gave him no argument. Neither could have carried on a normal conversation with Norman—not tonight. Not after what had happened between them. Norman wasn't stupid; he would have sensed something was wrong.

When Neil insisted that she ride back with him in the company truck and leave her car at the hospital, she agreed to that, too. She was in no shape to drive herself home.

So she climbed into the cab of the truck, mind and heart numbed by Neil's silence, by the almost impersonal way he helped her into the truck, by the set lines of his jaw and the distant expression in his eyes. A great tiredness seeped through her, the trauma of the night's events finally catching up with her. As they headed west toward Patinville, she stared out the window. It was still raining, but the wind had died down, and there were only occasional flashes of lightning streaking across the sky. Laura pressed her forehead against the window glass and closed her eyes. She shivered, pulling her coat closer around her. She was so cold.

"I'm sorry. I know it's cold in here. It'll just take a few minutes for the heater to warm up," Neil said.

But will it warm up my heart? If only he would tell her he loved her. She knew there would be problems. She knew it would be hard to face Norman. But together, if they loved each other, they could overcome anything.

Only, Neil hadn't said he loved her.

He'd said he was sorry. He'd said he didn't want to hurt her. And he'd said he didn't want to lie to her. *Lie to her.* Every time she thought about those three words, she felt sick. What had he meant? She shivered again. What else could he mean except that he couldn't say he loved her because it would be a lie?

She sat in the dark cab watching the rivulets of rain snake across her window, the darkness outside relieved only by an occasional watery light in the distance, and she couldn't evade the harsh reality any longer.

Neil didn't love her.

He just felt sorry for her. What they'd shared hadn't meant the same things to him as they had to her. And he was a caring person, so he hadn't wanted to hurt her by telling her.

An icy coldness wrapped around her heart and an emptiness settled into her stomach like a dull ache.

She was suddenly afraid. So terribly, terribly afraid.

On the long drive home, Neil was all too aware of Laura sitting huddled against her door, face turned toward the window. The knowledge of what he'd done hammered at him.

Her misery was all his fault. Tonight was all his fault. He couldn't place any of the blame for tonight on Laura. Jesus, he'd made such a mess of things. From their first meeting he'd sensed her vulnerability. Even Denise had told him Laura needed kindness and friendship. And instead of being her friend, he'd taken advantage of her and then hurt her even more by turning her away.

He slanted a look at her. His heart squeezed painfully as he saw the dejected slump to her shoulders. She looked so unhappy and so alone. Only inches separated them but it might have been thousands of miles. He ached to hold her and make everything right.

It had almost killed him to imply that she meant nothing to him. But what else could he do? What purpose would be served by telling her he loved her? They couldn't be together, so in the end Laura would be hurt even more. She was much better off without him. He couldn't even be sure his motives for making love to her were as pure as he'd like to think they were. Hell, he could tell himself thousands of times that he had only reacted to her anguish and fear, but the truth was that he had wanted her ever since he'd met her. She'd been on his mind more and more; each time he saw her his feelings had gotten stronger.

If he'd really loved her, he would have stayed away from her knowing all he could ever give her was heartache. If he'd been strong, he would have done the right thing. Instead, he'd been weak, and he'd hurt Laura, betrayed his brother, and dishonored himself.

The best thing he could do for Laura right now was make her hate him so she'd get over him quickly. But how he was going to accomplish that without making her hate herself, too, he didn't know.

The cats were both sleeping on the couch in the living room, and they slowly stretched and yawned as Laura entered her apartment, Neil following behind her.

He walked toward her fireplace, leaned his hands against the mantel, and looked down at the floor. His stance reminded her of the way cops in the movies made people stand when they wanted to frisk them. He didn't speak.

Laura hugged herself. They were together, in the same room, but she felt as if there were a Plexiglas barrier between them. She could see him and hear him but she couldn't reach him.

Finally he turned around. His voice was strained as he spoke. "Laura, I can't ever tell you how sorry I am about tonight. Someday I hope you'll forgive me."

"There's nothing to forgive," she said. She felt numb.

"But now we've got to try to forget about it."

Forget about it. Laura rarely lied to herself, but obviously Neil did. There was no way she could pretend nothing had happened tonight, and she wasn't sure he could, either, despite what he said.

"If anyone guessed about tonight, it would rip the family apart," he continued. "I can't allow that to happen."

"I see."

"We both know that under normal circumstances it would never have happened."

How could eyes that had looked at her with a rich, warm softness suddenly look so cold and hard? She stared at him. The room was very quiet. Even the cats were still, and Laura could feel the heavy beat of her heart. "So you think what happened was just a natural reaction to the emotion of the moment? That it wasn't very important, and we can easily forget it? Is that what you're saying?"

He met her gaze squarely. "I never meant to hurt you, but you have to understand the way things are."

A good healthy jolt of anger replaced the numbness that had kept her almost paralyzed with fear for the past hour. "The way things are? Oh, I think I understand the way things are!" She hated herself for the betraying quiver she heard in her voice.

His face softened. "Laura, please. You're just making this harder for both of us. You know the situation. We *have* to put this behind us. We can't do anything to jeopardize Norman's health. If he knew about this..." he ran his hands through his hair in a gesture of defeat "...Jesus, if anybody knew about this...."

"So you're ashamed, right?"

He flushed. "I'm...I'm not ashamed. And I'm sorry if that's the way it sounded. I just meant—"

"I know perfectly well what you meant. Oh, I'm a little slow sometimes, but I've finally got it." Laura stoked her anger, knowing if she didn't, she might fall apart from the searing pain. "You just took advantage of the moment, right?"

His throat worked, and for a moment, she thought he was going to say something. But then he zipped up his jacket, his actions stiff. He didn't meet her eyes.

He was going to leave. He was going to walk away from her. Suddenly she wanted to hurt him the way he'd hurt her. In her coldest voice, she said, "That's what you do best, isn't it? Run away from your problems?"

He flinched, and she knew her arrow had found its mark. "Laura, nothing you can say about me will be worse than what I've been thinking about myself. I don't blame you for hating me. You have every right to."

Then he opened the door and disappeared into the night.

Too miserable to move, Laura stared after him. She heard the slam of the truck door, the rasp of the ignition as Neil started the truck, then the crunch of gravel as he backed out of the driveway.

It wasn't until Phoebe hopped down from the back of the couch and began rubbing against her legs and meowing that Laura moved, like a sleepwalker, toward the kitchen. And as she did, tears streamed down her face, and she collapsed onto one of her kitchen chairs, laid her face against her arms, and wept as if her heart would break.

* * *

Laura finally called Celeste. She didn't know what else to do. For two weeks she suffered, reliving that night over and over again. When she could stand it no longer, she placed the call. She was in luck; Celeste wasn't working the evening shift at the hospital. And Laura found her at the home she shared with three other nuns.

"Laura, why didn't you call me before this?" Celeste said after Laura haltingly told her the entire story.

"I don't know. I guess I was afraid of what you'd think."

"Think? You mean about you?"

"Yes."

"You know me better than that."

Some of the tension left Laura's body at the lack of censure in Celeste's voice. "Do you think what we did was wrong?"

There was no hesitation on the other end of the long distance line. "Not in the sense Neil thinks it was wrong. I don't think what happened is a betrayal of his brother. His brother has no real claim on you."

Laura hadn't even been aware she was holding her breath, but now she let it out in one great gust. She felt grateful Celeste didn't lecture her about sin or morals or sex without marriage. Laura's own Catholic upbringing, as sketchy as it had been with a mother who didn't much care whether her daughter had any religious training or not, had enough guilt built into its foundation to have given her some bad nights since she and Neil had made love. On one level she could tell herself this was the 90s, not the 50s, but on another level, a deeper level, Laura was still striving to be a good girl in everyone's eyes.

"But Laura," Celeste said softly, "I understand how Neil feels. From what you've told me about him, I don't think he has any choice. He's doing what he has to do, regardless of what he feels for you."

Laura seized at Celeste's words. "You think he loves me?"

"Yes, I do. I think he feels exactly the same way you feel. And I think he's hurting as much as you are now."

"Oh, Celeste, I don't know what to do."

"There's really nothing you can do. Unless, of course, you want to tell Norman yourself."

"Oh, no, I can't do that. Neil would hate me. I...I can't hurt Norman that way." Now that she'd said it, she knew it was true. A great tide of weariness spread over her.

"Well, it doesn't sound to me as if this is going to result in a happy ending for you. You've got to face that."

"I don't know if I can."

"Of course, you can. You're a lot tougher than you think."

"I love him, Celeste. I can't stand the thought of a future without him." She could hear her voice tremble. "Oh, God, I sound like such a weak, stupid fool, don't I?"

"I'm not going to waste my breath answering," Celeste said. "If it makes you feel better to call yourself names, go right ahead."

Laura sighed.

"What I can't understand," Celeste said in a thoughtful voice, "is why these interesting things always seem to happen to you. Why is it that no good-looking man ever makes a pass at me? Do you think it's the habit that puts them off?"

Laura, taken off guard, didn't respond for a minute. Then she burst out laughing. Trust Celeste to steer her back when she started toward the deep end.

"Come on, Laura," Celeste said when their laughter faded. "This really isn't the end of the world, you know. You're a strong woman. You'll survive." Then very softly she said, "I'll pray for you."

But the next morning after another restless night where she'd once more dreamed of Neil, Laura wondered if she was going to need more help dealing with her problems than an occasional phone call to a friend. Maybe it was time for her to get some outside help, something she'd been considering lately anyway.

Still thinking about her problems, she began to get ready for work. At seven-forty-five, she walked outside and scraped the ice off the windshield of her car. It had turned cold during the night.

Her car wouldn't start. At first she thought she just needed a jump, and she went next door to ask Jett if he'd help her.

"He's got the flu. He's in bed," Denise said, as she poked her head out, "but I'll do it. Wait'll I throw some clothes on."

A few minutes later, Denise came outside, shivering in the frosty morning air. They hooked up the jumper cables, and Laura tried once more, but the car still wouldn't start. Sighing with frustration, she went inside and called the local mechanic, who promised to send a tow truck to pick up the car sometime that morning.

"Wonderful," Laura said, looking at her watch. "I'm going to be late."

"Well, you couldn't help it. Let me just go tell Jett, then I'll run you down to the office," Denise said.

When Laura finally got to work, she decided she would give the office a good cleaning. She'd been so down in the dumps the past two weeks, she hadn't felt like doing anything. She began her cleanup efforts by first tackling Norman's desk—she always kept her own desk in meticulous order—then, after lunch, she opened the supply cabinet with the intention of straightening it out. She'd only been working on the cabinet about five minutes when the phone rang.

Denise's harried voice greeted her. "Laura, something must be in the air because you're not the only one having car problems today."

"Why? What happened? Something wrong with yours?"

Denise sighed tiredly. "No, but Mama just called and said that the truck Neil's driving broke an axle out near Bayou Sorrel, and he wanted Papa to drive over there and bring the other truck, but Papa went to Lafayette. With Jett home sick I can't leave here. Can you close up the office and go?" Sounds of dishes rattling drifted through the wire as Denise stopped talking.

Laura frowned. "Why doesn't Neil just call the road service?"

"He did. But he has to do something with all the equipment in the pickup. He can't have the truck towed and leave the stuff in it," Denise said.

The last thing Laura wanted right now was to spend what would probably amount to hours in Neil's company. But she couldn't refuse. "All right, I'll go. I'll leave in a few minutes. Is Neil going to call you back or what?"

"No. I told him I'd send someone. He's waiting." Denise chuckled. "But probably not patiently."

Laura wrote down Neil's exact location, turned on the answering machine, grabbed her coat and the keys to the other truck, and within ten minutes she was on her way.

Bayou Sorrel was located about twenty-two miles south of Patinville on Route 75. Laura was grateful the sun was shining, even though the temperature had dropped down into the thirties during the night and hadn't risen much above it all day. If she hadn't been so edgy about seeing Neil, she might have really enjoyed the drive. The sky was such a brilliant blue it almost hurt her eyes to look at it, and only a few wispy clouds floated overhead. The air felt crisp and clean and smelled fresh, with a tangy nip. It was exactly the kind of day Laura usually loved. But the closer she got to Bayou Sorrel, the more tense she felt.

It didn't take very long for her to reach Neil. He was standing on the side of the road, leaning against the disabled truck, hands shoved into the pockets of his jacket. The sunlight had turned his hair into gleaming ebony, and

Laura's stomach flip-flopped as he turned and watched her pull over. When she shut off the ignition, he straightened, feet apart, his face enigmatic as she climbed down out of the cab and walked toward him.

"Hi," she said, heart quickening as their eyes met. "I was sent to the rescue."

"Hi." For one unguarded moment, his eyes were filled with emotion. "The tow truck should be here soon." His voice sounded rough and uneven. "Thanks for coming."

"No problem." She felt tongue-tied, as if they were strangers. Her awkwardness seemed to have permeated her body, as well, because she wasn't sure where she should stand or what she should do with her hands. *Is he glad to see me? Is that what I saw in his eyes?*

"You can sit in the cab if you like."

"No, no, that's okay."

There was a strained silence for a few minutes, then he said, "At least it's not raining anymore."

"Yes, that *is* a blessing," she agreed. *Good grief, we sound as if we hardly know each other, as if our last meeting was as casual as this one, as if we've never even touched, let alone shared the most intimate experience two people can share.*

Was this how men and women acted when they'd once had a relationship and no longer did? Were they always this stilted and remote? Suddenly she desperately wanted to touch him, to talk to him. She wanted to know he cared about her, even if he could never do anything about it. She wanted to tell him how she'd been feeling the past two weeks, how unhappy she'd been, how much she'd missed him. She also wanted to tell him she was feeling better now, that if guilt was causing him to close her out, to treat her so coldly, he didn't have to feel that way, because she really *did* understand. She wished she could tell him about calling Celeste, about everything.

And if he'd given her any opening at all, she might have chanced it, but he hadn't. If Celeste was right, if Laura's own instincts were right, and he cared for her, how could he act this way? Pain constricted her chest. Maybe she was just kidding herself.

Maybe she didn't matter to him at all.

The thought hurt so much it was hard for her to maintain her calm exterior. She thought she'd faced the possibility that Neil really didn't love her.

Well, she'd better face the truth now. Just because she loved him didn't mean he loved her. And if that were true, she'd have to learn to live with it.

Starting right now.

"I'd better get this stuff loaded into the other truck," he said, gesturing toward the ladders, lumber, boxes of tools and nails, and other paraphernalia loaded in the bed of the broken-down truck.

"I can help," Laura offered.

Following him, she stood quietly by, and when he handed her something small and light enough for her to carry, she took it over to her truck. The work took them about ten minutes, with Neil doing most of it. When they were finished, he shoved his hands into the pockets of his jeans and squinted down the road.

He can't even look at me, she thought. Giving him a covert glance, she propped her arm against the truck, half facing him. His forehead was creased, as if he were preoccupied or worried, or both. The hollows and angular planes of his face seemed more pronounced than normal. She thought he looked lonely, but his stance didn't invite intrusion. She wished she had the right to walk over to him, smooth back his hair, touch his cheek. She would have given anything in the world to see a blaze of love fire his eyes, even if that love was doomed. She just wanted to know, even if that knowledge could never be acted on, that she was important to him.

Cars and trucks whizzed by them, the sun shone down with impartial brilliance, across the roadway a squirrel scampered up the trunk of a gnarled oak tree, a monarch butterfly danced through the air, and somewhere in the distance someone was using a chainsaw. Laura was aware of all these extraneous sounds and sights but nothing was as vivid as the curve of Neil's shoulders, the tight resolution of his lips, the glossy shine of his hair.

"Here comes the tow truck," he said, startling her.

As they watched, the wrecker, looking like a giant bird of prey, swooped down on them, its tires grinding to a halt a few feet away. The driver leaned out of the cab, and Neil walked over to talk to him. Within minutes the tow truck had been maneuvered into position and Neil's truck hitched to it.

"I'll drive," Neil said as they walked toward the truck she'd driven over, and she tossed him the keys wordlessly.

They followed the tow truck to a garage just outside Indian Village, which was about six miles closer to Patinville than Bayou Sorrel. They didn't talk. Neil stared at the road, tapping his fingers against the steering wheel in time to the Oak Ridge Boys singing "Elvira," and Laura stared out her window. When they reached the garage, she waited in the truck while Neil went inside to talk to the owner. She tried to empty her mind, but it wasn't possible, not with Neil so close. Not when all she had to do was turn her head and see the top of his dark head through the grimy office window. Not when she knew within minutes he'd be back inside the truck, sitting within inches of her. Not when the memory of their lovemaking was still so vivid in her mind, causing her knees to go weak everytime she remembered how it felt to hold him in her arms as they shared an unforgettable passion.

She watched as he walked out of the office and strode across the parking lot toward the truck and she wished she didn't care so much. She wondered what he was thinking as he started the truck and they were once more streaking toward home. They still didn't speak. The silence between them grew until it was almost palpable, a heavy tension that thrummed in the air.

Say something, she thought, willing him to talk to her. *Whether you like it or not, I'm here. I exist. Even if you'd like to pretend nothing ever happened between us, you can't, because it did.* The urge to say these words was so strong, she almost blurted them out, but something held her back.

She glanced over at Neil. His hands were gripping the steering wheel, and the set of his jaw was fiercely determined. She realized he intended to drop her off at home without ever saying another word. As if he could exorcise her from his life by ignoring her.

Running away.

She'd been right, even though she'd flung the words at him in anger and hurt. He was dealing with his problems by running away, even if it were only mentally. He still hadn't come to grips with his past.

But wasn't she just as bad? Hadn't she always run away from her problems, too? The question reverberated in her mind like the sound that reverberates through the concert hall when the cymbals are clashed together. With a sharp intake of breath, Laura realized that she had dealt with her problems in exactly the way she'd accused Neil of dealing with his. She'd run away from her home and mother by spending most of her time at Celeste's house, pretending Celeste's family was her family. She'd run away from her phobias by pretending they didn't exist and refusing to discuss them with anyone as if not talking about them would make them go away. She'd run away from her real life and into the world of her fantasies by leaving California to move to Louisiana as if moving to Louisiana—Celeste's childhood home—would somehow make her a different person. And she was still running away by refusing to acknowledge the existence of her mother. Every time anyone asked, Laura told them her mother was dead. But the last time she'd seen Ginger, Ginger had been very much alive. And she probably still was.

Suddenly Laura realized that if she were ever going to get herself and her life straightened out, she had to confront her fears and overcome them. She had to put the past behind her so that she could face the future. No more running away.

Once more, she looked at Neil. If only she could tell him all that she was feeling. Maybe she could help him. Maybe they could help each other. Because she knew he also needed to put the past behind him. She knew his feelings of guilt about his partner's death were affecting his actions now.

But she couldn't say anything. The barrier Neil had erected between them was too high, and she knew he'd have to be the one to break it down.

From the minute he'd seen her walking toward him, coat open, hair blowing in the wind, eyes sparkling blue in the sunlight, Neil knew he had to keep a tight clamp on his emotions. Because if he didn't, he was afraid of what might happen. He only had so much strength.

So he'd said as little as possible while they waited for the tow truck, and nothing at all during the drive back to Patinville. And now they were approaching Beauregard Street, where the office was located. Two or three more minutes, and then he could relax.

"Where are we going, Neil? Aren't you going to take me home?"

The question startled him, and he looked at her. A mistake, he thought, as the impact of her astonishing blue eyes hit him in the solar plexus. "Uh, don't you want to pick up your car?"

"Didn't Denise tell you? My car's in the shop. She drove me to work this morning."

Why did she have to look so much like a woman who needed him? Like a woman who would, if he let her, always be there when he needed her? Like a woman who would be sweet and warm and welcoming and who would always love him?

Why couldn't he forget what they'd shared?

Why couldn't he forget her?

"How were you planning to get home?" he asked, a tightness in his chest causing his words to sound odd. He was already passing the office and driving toward her apartment.

"I was going to keep this truck overnight."

"I'm sorry I screwed up your plans."

"It's not a problem. I'm sure Denise will take me in to work tomorrow if my car's not ready." She made a disgusted sound. "Darn. I was supposed to call the garage this afternoon."

"Want me to swing by there?"

"Do you mind?"

"Of course not."

Now it was his turn to wait for her. She wasn't long.

"They're waiting on a part. It'll be ready tomorrow morning," she said, climbing back into the truck.

He nodded, and once more they were on their way. He wondered what she was thinking as he turned the corner onto her street. He wondered when he would see her again. He wondered if they'd ever talk to each other again, or would their meetings become more and more impersonal? He gripped the steering wheel harder as the truth settled like a dead weight into his stomach.

This might be the last time they were ever alone together.

And there wasn't one damn thing he could do about it.

Chapter Twelve

The following Tuesday night, Laura paused outside Norman's door. Telling herself not to be a coward, she knocked softly.

"Come in," Norman called.

Smiling brightly, Laura pushed open the door. "Hi! How are you feel—" She broke off, noticing for the first time that he had another visitor, a small blond woman with wide gray eyes and a friendly smile. "Oh, hello."

"Hi. You must be Laura," said the woman in a soft, breathy voice. "I'm Alice Kendella."

"It's very nice to meet you," Laura said, walking over and extending her hand. As they shook hands, smiling at one another, Laura was struck by the oddest sensation—a sensation almost like déjà vu—a feeling of recognition. When she looked into Alice's clear, gray eyes, she sensed many things all at once, but the most compelling feeling was that Alice was a kindred spirit, a woman she could trust.

Although Laura would have preferred to concentrate her attention on Alice so that she could explore this strange bonding she felt so strongly, she turned to Norman. "You look chipper tonight." He did. His face had more color, and he just plain looked better.

"I feel good today," Norman said. "And having two pretty gals here tonight is certainly nice." He grinned, first at Laura, then at Alice. "How'd I get so lucky?"

"Hey," Alice said, grinning back, "how often do we get a chance to practice our wiles on a captive male audience?"

"So I'm a guinea pig, huh?" Norman said with mock reproach. "And here I thought I was just irresistible."

"That, too," Laura said, laughing. Amazing. She felt more relaxed than she had in weeks, and she'd been dreading coming tonight. Alice's presence had defused the tension Laura normally felt when she was alone with Norman. Alone with Norman and her own guilty feelings.

The thought had hardly formed when there was a short rap on the door. A second later Neil walked in, and Laura's heart somersaulted. Her entire body tensed.

"Neil, hi!" Alice stood on tiptoe and kissed him.

Laura saw how his face immediately brightened up and watched with mixed emotions as he gave Alice a big hug. Jealousy knifed through her. She knew she had no right to be jealous. She knew she had no claim on Neil. He had made that perfectly clear. But she was jealous anyway, and it was a horrible feeling. She wondered how he would greet her. A second later he looked her way.

He smiled, but she saw the almost imperceptible tightening of his facial muscles, the flicker of torment in his dark eyes, and the way he quickly shuttered off the emotion.

For the next hour the conversation swirled around Laura. She tried to take part, but all she could think about was Neil, and she had to concentrate all her energy on smiling casually and acting normal. Norman and Alice carried the brunt of the conversation, but Neil joined in, too. Even if Laura hadn't been so uncomfortable, she still wouldn't have had much to say because they all had so many friends and memories in common. Watching them, she was sharply reminded of her own status as the outsider. *I'll never be a part of this circle,* she thought forlornly. At one time, she could have been. If she'd married Norman. But that chance was gone forever, now that she was hopelessly in love with Norman's brother.

While they talked, Laura watched the interplay of emotions on their faces. Inevitably, she supposed, the talk turned to Jimmy. A sweet sadness settled over Alice's face. "I'll always miss him," she admitted, "but lately..." she turned her pleasant smile toward Neil "...lately, since you've been home, Neil, I'm coming to terms with his death. I thought I had before, but I hadn't, really. But seeing you, talking about it, has helped. I know now I have to stop mourning Jimmy's death and go on with my life."

"Even when you know that's what you have to do, how do you make yourself do it?" Norman asked.

All three of them looked at him, and Laura wondered if the others were as startled by his question as she was.

Norman looked at Alice and grimaced. "I know you're right. In my own case, I know that nothing can change what's happened to me, that I...I have to get used to the fact that I lost a leg. That I can no longer do some of the things I did before. That my life is going to be different from now on. I know all that. But how do I make myself accept it?"

Laura swallowed. She heard the pain behind the question. She saw the anguish Norman couldn't hide. And she knew he wasn't nearly as accepting of his fate as they'd believed him to be. As he'd pretended to be. At that moment she wished she were anywhere but in that room.

Alice sighed. "I don't know. I don't have all the answers. It's taken me more than three years to reach this point. I do know that bitterness over what's been lost doesn't help, though. Bitterness is corrosive. It gradually eats away at you until there's nothing left. I saw that happen with my mother when my sister died. Mother has never accepted Betsy's death, and she's a bitter, miserable woman because of it."

Laura thought about her own situation. She'd had to fight against the bitterness she felt toward her mother all of her life.

"But it's important to put the past behind you," Alice continued. "People have to learn not to dwell on what might have been. Instead, we have to try to take our experiences and make them work for us instead of against us."

Alice is right. I have to do that. Neil has to do that. And Norman has to do that. As Laura thought about what Alice had just said, she watched Neil's face, wondering what was going through his mind. He'd been very quiet throughout this exchange. His expression was thoughtful but noncommittal, and he didn't meet her eyes.

"Well..." Alice stood up. "Enough preaching." She grinned. "I'd better be on my way. I told Tammy, my babysitter, that I'd be home by nine." She glanced at her watch. "And I'm going to be cutting it close. It's already eight-thirty."

Laura stood, too. "It's time for me to leave, too." She gathered up her coat and scarf, leaned over the bed and gave Norman a kiss on the cheek. He smiled at her, squeezing her hand.

"I'm glad you came." Then he released her hand and turned toward Alice. "I'm glad you came, too, Alice. I hope you'll come again. I enjoyed talking to you."

Alice hesitated only a fraction of a second, then she also leaned over the bed and kissed Norman on the cheek. He colored with pleasure.

"Why don't you walk the girls outside, Neil?" Norman suggested, his genial facade back in place.

"Oh, that's not necessary," Alice said.

"No, he doesn't have to bother," Laura said. She knew Norman didn't like her to walk through the parking lot alone at night, but she had never been afraid. The lot was well lighted, and the guard always watched from the door.

The brothers exchanged looks. Neil stood and put on his jacket. "It might not be necessary, but I'll do it anyway."

As the three of them approached the elevators, a tremor passed through Laura. She avoided Neil's eyes. A silent prayer whispered through her mind. *Let the other one come. Please, God, let the other one come.* Looking straight ahead, she concentrated on keeping her breathing even and her emotions under control.

The two elevators inched upwards. Laura's heart lodged itself somewhere in her throat as the one on the right stopped on four. Dear heaven. The doors to the elevator on the left slid open. Like a robot, Laura followed Alice inside, and she knew Neil was right behind her.

The doors closed. Alice pushed the button for the ground floor. The elevator hummed to life.

"I hope Tammy got the kids to bed on time," she said.

Neither Laura nor Neil answered. Laura couldn't have spoken if her life depended on it. She felt battered, hot and cold, assaulted by memories. She stared at the back of his neck where the hair curled over the edge of his white turtleneck sweater. She wondered what in God's name he was thinking. Was he remembering their desperate passion? Their greedy kisses? Their tumultuous union?

Was his stomach knotted with tension? Was his body flushed with heat? Was every sense alive with a shimmering awareness?

The thirty second ride stretched into infinity. The air sizzled around them, and Laura wondered if Alice felt it, too.

Finally the car settled to a stop, and the doors opened, and fresh air rushed in. Neil stood back so that Alice and Laura could exit the elevator first, and as he did, for one crystal moment, her eyes met his, and what she saw there rocked her, for his eyes contained a naked longing so raw and so powerful, it ignited a wild hope inside her. But the moment passed, and the longing disappeared as if he'd taken a cloth and wiped it away in one swoop.

It was a bitterly cold night, and their breaths misted in front of them as they scurried across the windy parking lot.

"Where's your car?" Neil asked, turning toward Laura. She pointed to the far left side of the lot.

"Oh, good. I'm in that direction, too," Alice said.

As luck would have it, Alice was parked closer, so the three of them stopped at her car first. She unlocked the driver's side of the small Ford, then turned back to Neil and Laura. "Neil, I almost forgot! I found that check stub you asked me to look for."

"Oh?" he said.

Alice's frown was clearly delineated in the circle of light cast from a large lamp a few feet away. "The thing is," she continued, "it doesn't say anything."

"It *does* have a check number, doesn't it?" Neil asked.

Laura didn't know what they were talking about, but obviously it was important to both of them, and she was glad to have something else to think about other than her feelings for Neil.

"Yes," Alice said, "and the date, and another number."

"We should be able to find out who purchased it, then," Neil said, his voice thoughtful. "Do you know anyone at the bank well enough to ask them to go back through the records and check this out?"

She shook her head slowly. "Not really. You don't think we could just go through channels to find out?"

"I don't know. If there *is* something funny about that check, or the motives of whoever sent it, we might not want to take that chance. Do we really want to alert them that we're checking into it?"

Laura shivered.

"Look," Neil said, glancing at Laura. "It's too cold to talk about this out here. I'll call you tomorrow, Alice. We'll talk about what to do then."

Alice agreed and Neil held her door open for her. "Laura," she said as she got in, "now that we've met, let's get together again."

"I'd like that," Laura said, knowing Alice wasn't saying it to be polite, knowing, too, that she wanted to be Alice's friend.

After Alice left, Neil took Laura's elbow and they walked silently until they reached her car. Even this impersonal touch caused her pulses to race.

"What kind of check were you and Alice talking about?" she asked.

"It's a cashier's check that Alice received after Jimmy's death. It was sent anonymously, and I asked her to look for the stub. I'm curious about who sent it."

His voice sounded tense, or was that just her imagination? "If it's a cashier's check, the bank would have a record of who sent it."

"That's what I thought," he said.

"I know someone at the First National Bank," Laura said softly. "She's a loan officer, and I've dealt with her on company business. I could check it out for you."

"Would you?"

Laura's heart warmed at the eagerness in his voice. She wasn't sure it was wise, but she wanted to do this for him. "I'll try. Get me the information, and I'll call my friend."

"I'll get it tomorrow," he promised. "But I want to be there when you make the call."

"Okay." Laura was suddenly very glad she'd come to see Norman tonight instead of tomorrow night, as she'd originally planned. Meeting Alice was one of the reasons, but finding a way to do something for Neil—and to see him again she thought in a burst of honesty—was even more important.

"Be careful driving home," he said as he helped her into the car.

"I will." Their eyes met for a moment before Laura looked away to fasten her seat belt. There it was again. Only a flash, but still there—that unspoken longing—a longing he quickly concealed behind a mask of casual concern.

He does care for me. He does. He hasn't forgotten what we shared. He's as aware of it as I am. He's just better at concealing his feelings. And all the way home her heart was singing. Because if he still cared that much, there was still hope. The irony of her thoughts wasn't lost on her. She and Norman and Neil were an impossible triangle, she knew, but like Norman, she couldn't help hoping that somehow things would work out the way she wanted them to.

And in the meantime, she had the memory of that naked emotion that had flickered through Neil's eyes to keep her going.

Because Neil and the main crew had finished a major job the day before, Neil had the day off. He decided to call Alice and see if it would be all right with her if he came over and picked up the check stub. It would also give him an opportunity to talk to her. Last night he'd realized he needed to talk to someone. Foolishly, he'd thought he was dealing with his feelings for Laura. That illusion had been shattered last night. His reaction to seeing her had been immediate and strong, but he'd been able to hide his feelings while they'd all been in Norman's room.

But then he'd walked out with the two women. And when that damned elevator came—the same one, he still couldn't believe it was the same one!—he almost came unglued. He had no choice but to follow Laura inside, and he stood in front of her, and all he could think about was the last time they'd been in that same small space together. He felt as if all the air had suddenly disappeared. He could hardly breathe. And he was acutely aware of Laura behind him. And Alice just off to his side.

Riding down was bad enough, but then the elevator stopped, and he had to face Laura. When her blue eyes met his, he almost lost it. He felt such a rush of torment and love and helpless need. If Alice hadn't been there, he didn't know what he would have done. The way he felt in that moment, he might have grabbed Laura's hand, rushed her out to the parking lot, and run away with her. But somehow he managed to get himself under control, and he thought he was going to be all right until he was actually saying goodbye to Laura and telling her to be careful driving. He made the mistake of looking into her eyes again.

It shook him. It really shook him, the strength of what he felt for her. He couldn't even remember what he said. All he knew was that he had to get away from her.

Afterward, when Laura was gone and he was back in Norman's room, he felt so alone. He talked to Norman, but his mind was on Laura. He kept asking himself why he had to fall for the woman his brother loved?

Yes, he thought now, it's a good idea to talk to Alice. He waited until he knew Alice would be home again after her morning shift. She drove a school bus both mornings and afternoons, she'd told him. The information had bothered him. She hadn't worked when Jimmy was alive.

"Sure," she said when he asked if he could come over. "Come now. I'll give you some coffee as well as the check stub."

Thirty minutes later he was sitting at her kitchen table drinking a cup of strong coffee. He'd already told her about Laura's offer to call the bank, and Alice had agreed that Laura might be able to find out what they wanted to know easier than either of them could. The check stub was safely tucked into the pocket of Neil's jacket.

Now, with his hands wrapped around the warm mug, he wondered how to introduce the subject that had been on his mind all last night and today.

"I've got to start thinking about getting a full-time job," Alice said, breaking into his thoughts. "Lisa's old enough for me to leave her now. Besides, she'll be starting school in the fall."

Neil struggled to push his own concerns aside and focus on Alice's statement. He frowned. "I hate the idea of you having to work full-time."

Alice looked surprised. "Why? I'm dying to go to work full-time. I need to get out and be around adults. My whole world is kids right now—my own and other people's."

"But if Jimmy were still alive, you wouldn't have to go to work. I can't help feeling guilty about that," Neil admitted.

Alice reached over and laid her hand on his arm. "Neil, quit beating up on yourself. If Jimmy were alive I'd probably still want to go to work. But Jimmy's gone. And life goes on. I need to look toward the future."

"It's going to be hard on the kids," Neil said. "Maybe I could help more."

"I don't want more money from you. In fact, I don't even want you to continue sending what you've been sending. I don't need it." She squeezed his arm and smiled at him. "Neil, I appreciate everything you've done. And I understand how you feel. But I want you to understand how I feel, too."

He looked into her solemn gray eyes. Saw the determination and the strength. Jimmy would have been proud of her. She was one special person. The thought crossed his mind that his life would certainly be less complicated if he could have fallen in love with Alice instead of Laura.

"I *have* to start standing on my own two feet," she said. "I don't want anyone to feel responsible for me, least of all, you. Besides, you need to concentrate on getting your own life straightened out."

Neil knew she was right. He'd been thinking about what she'd said to Norman the night before and knew the advice applied to him as well. "Okay. You've made your point." He smiled. "And speaking of straightening out my life, there's something I've been wanting to talk to you about."

"Oh?" She searched his face. "This sounds serious."

"It is serious. In fact, I'm in a helluva fix, and I don't know what to do about it."

Alice's face wore a quizzical, half amused, half confused expression as she waited quietly.

"I'm in love with Laura Sebastian." Once the words were out, Neil felt about a hundred pounds lighter.

Alice stared at him, gray eyes thoughtful. Finally she spoke. "Does she know you're in love with her? And what about Norman? I somehow got the idea that she was *his* girl."

"That's the problem. Norman's in love with her, too."

"And how does Laura feel about all this?"

Neil shrugged. "She's not in love with Norman. She said she loves me, but maybe she's changed her mind." He looked down into his coffee cup. "We haven't talked about it lately."

"Why don't you tell me everything?" Alice said softly.

So he did. From the beginning. From the first time he'd heard her name. He told her how he'd felt when he first saw Laura. What he'd thought. He told her about Laura confessing she wasn't in love with Norman. He told her everything, including the growing awareness of his feelings. He told her something had happened between him and

Laura, but he didn't elaborate. The episode in the elevator was too personal and nobody's business except his and Laura's.

"I've tried to put her out of my mind, but I can't seem to do it. Every time I see her, my feelings for her are stronger."

"How does she feel?"

He looked away. "I'm not sure. I know I've hurt her. I hope she's dealing with this better than I am."

"Gosh, Neil, I don't know what to tell you. I have no magic answers." She gave him a sympathetic smile. "I'm flattered that you told me, but you're right, you're in a helluva fix."

Then they both laughed, because Alice never swore, and because they needed to laugh. They needed something to break the tension and lighten the atmosphere.

But then Alice's face sobered, and she bit her bottom lip. "You know, I can't tell you what to do. It's your life, and you have to live with your decisions, but I *will* tell you something I believe in very strongly."

"What's that?"

She gave him one of her clear, honest gazes. "The truth."

"The truth? You mean you think I should tell Norman how I feel, what I've done?" Neil shook his head. "I can't do that. He couldn't handle it. Hell, *I* couldn't handle it." He could just see the shocked look Norman would give him—the disappointment and the betrayal Norman would feel. "No. It's impossible."

Alice shrugged. "Well. You asked me. But you have to do what you have to do. And if you feel you can't talk to Norman about this, well, then I guess you're right. You'd probably better leave Patinville and go back to Florida just as fast as you possibly can." She hesitated, then added, "Before something else happens and you hurt Laura any more than you've hurt her already."

* * *

At five minutes after nine two days after she'd promised to help him, Laura heard Neil coming down the steps. When he opened the door to the office a few seconds later, she smiled, happiness curling itself around her at the sight of him, even as her insides fluttered with nervousness.

"Ready to call the bank?" he asked, taking off his jacket. He walked over to the coffeemaker and poured himself a cup.

"Sure." Why did this love she felt for him seem to be an impossible mix of euphoria, desire, and misery?

He leaned against Norman's desk while she picked up the phone and called First National Bank and asked for Bobbi Cameron. Laura could feel his eyes studying her. Her hand tightened on the receiver.

"Yes? This is Bobbi Cameron." Bobbi's words were clipped, and she sounded irritated.

"Hi, Bobbi. This is Laura Sebastian. Isn't it too early in the morning for you to be having a bad day?" Laura said lightly, proud of herself for her casual tone. She didn't look at Neil. She needed all her wits about her.

"Oh, hi, Laura. I'm sorry, but I just spilled a cup of coffee on a brand new wool suit, and I could scream. Now I look like a slob, and I've got a meeting in twenty-five minutes so I don't have time to go home and change." Disgust dripped from her voice.

Laura made a sympathetic sound. "I can't imagine you ever looking like a slob, spilled coffee or not."

"Thanks." Then, in a more businesslike tone, she said, "What can I do for you today?"

"I was hoping I could get some information from you."

"I'll try. What kind of information?"

Laura explained about the check. "What I'd like to know is who purchased it. Can you find out?"

"I'm sure I can, but I don't have time to do it this morning. It'll have to wait until after the bank closes at three. Is that all right?"

"Perfect."

"Are you sure the name of the donor isn't on the check stub?"

"Yes, I'm sure."

"That's odd, you know. There must be a reason, unless it was simply an oversight on the bank's part."

Laura heard the thread of uncertainty, and she said quickly, before Bobbi could have second thoughts, "Oh, I'm sure that's what happened. Will you call me when you have the information?"

"Will you be at the office?"

"Yes. All day."

"Okay. I'll see what I can find out and call you back around four."

"I appreciate it, Bobbi." Laura kept her voice casual. The last thing she wanted was for Bobbi to get the idea there was anything wrong with her request.

"By the way, I heard what happened with Norman. How's he doing?" Bobbi asked.

"Much better. He's now in rehab, and next week he's supposed to be fitted for a prosthesis. We're all very hopeful." She was very aware of Neil listening to her end of the conversation.

"I'm glad to hear it. I saw René in the bank last week but I didn't get a chance to talk to him. Give the family my love."

"I will," Laura said.

After saying goodbye, Laura thoughtfully hung up the phone. Then she relayed what Bobbi had said to Neil.

He finished his coffee. "Okay, good. I'll be back about four, then. Thanks, Laura."

His smile made her heart ache with longing. Oh, she was a mess. Why did he make her feel this way? For the remainder of the day Laura tried not to think about Neil. But about three-thirty her skin tingled with a feeling of expectancy. And twenty minutes later, when his truck pulled into the yard, her heart quickened. For the second time that day she felt almost weak with pleasure when he walked in the door.

He'd barely said more than "hi" when the phone rang, and Laura nodded "yes" to his quizzical look.

Bobbi's words were blunt. "Laura, why do you want this information?"

Laura hedged. "I promised Alice Kendella I'd try to find out who gave her the money."

Bobbi was silent for a long time. Just as Laura was about to say something else, she said, her voice oddly distant, as if she were thinking out loud. "There's a notation on this transaction that the name of the donor is to remain anonymous. So you can see that I really can't release the information that Willis Fontenot is the person who purchased the cashier's check. If I were to tell you that, and the fact that I did so were to get out, I could lose my job. So I'm really sorry. But you *do* understand, don't you?"

"I understand perfectly, Bobbi." Willis Fontenot, the mayor of Patinville. She tried to keep the elation out of her voice as she thanked her friend, but she knew her eyes were shining with triumph as they met Neil's. He immediately walked over to her desk.

"Who?" he mouthed.

"I'm really sorry I couldn't help you, Laura," Bobbi was saying.

Laura picked up her pen and wrote WILLIS FONTENOT on the legal pad in front of her. "I know you are. Just put the whole thing out of your mind." She watched Neil's face as he read the name. His body became very still.

"I already have. Now, when are we going to have lunch together? Every time I see you, you say you'll call me, and you never do," Bobbi said briskly.

Although everything in Laura was in tune with Neil right now, she forced herself to respond to Bobbi. It was Laura's own fault that Denise had been her only friend in Patinville, and here was an opportunity to change that. The second opportunity she'd had in days, she realized, as she thought about Alice Kendella's overture. "How does next Wednesday sound?" she said smiling.

"Good old cousin Willis. I don't know why, but I never expected it to be him." Of all the people Neil had imagined might have been responsible for the ten thousand dollars sent to Alice, Willis Fontenot had not been one of them. Not that Willis couldn't have afforded the money—he had inherited a considerable amount from the Fontenot side of his family—but he had always been selfish.

"Neil, please be careful not to let anyone know how you came to have this information. I don't want to get Bobbi in trouble," Laura said, her blue eyes concerned.

"Don't worry," he assured her. "I won't." Willis. He still couldn't believe it.

"What're you going to do now?"

Distracted by the surprising piece of information, Neil looked at her, only half hearing her question. She looked beautiful today, much too beautiful for his own peace of mind. She was wearing a matching skirt and sweater in some kind of peach or pink color, and its glow was matched by a corresponding glow on her cheeks and in her eyes.

Remembering his conversation with Alice the night before, he deliberately thrust his thoughts away from the dangerous turn they'd taken. "Sorry, what did you say? I guess I was thinking about something else."

"What are you going to do now?" she repeated patiently.

"I don't know yet. I've got to think about this for a while before I do anything."

"I guess I knew Willis was related to your family, but I didn't know he was a cousin."

Neil sat on the edge of Norman's desk. "He's my second cousin, or maybe he's my half cousin, twice removed.

Hell, I don't know. I've never understood how it works." At the look of confusion on Laura's face, he tried to explain. "See, my grandfather on my father's side was married twice. He had two sons from his first marriage, André, who is now eighty-two, and Claude, who's eighty. My own father and all the other children came from my grandfather's second marriage."

Laura rose from her desk and began to fix herself a cup of tea. Neil's eyes were drawn to the way the soft sweater hugged her rounded breasts and slender torso. "So how does Willis Fontenot fit into this picture?" she asked.

"He's the oldest son born to my Uncle André's oldest daughter." Neil absently tore a piece of tape from the dispenser on Norman's desk, rolling it between his fingers.

"But why is your cousin involved in this?" Laura was once more settled into her desk chair. She took a sip of her tea, and now Neil watched how her slender hands curved around the cup. Her wrists seemed so delicate and fragile, yet Neil knew she wasn't a delicate or fragile woman, even though he'd once thought so. Over the past couple of days she'd exhibited a strength that surprised him. In fact, she seemed to be dealing with their awkward situation with more aplomb and dignity than he was.

"That's what I'm not sure about," he said thoughtfully. "Willis and I spent a lot of time together as kids. Although his mother grew up in Lafayette, she and her husband eventually settled in Patinville, so the families have always been close." He grinned. "You know how Cajun families are." He lapsed into the Cajun patois. "We're real tight, *chère,* you know?"

She laughed, the tension she always felt around him ebbing at the warmth in his eyes and voice. "Do you know, that's the first time I've heard you talk with an accent?"

Knowing he shouldn't, but unable to stop himself, he said, "I like to hear you laugh."

A faint flush crept over her cheeks. "Do you?"

Her voice had taken on a husky edge, sending a quicksilver reaction through his veins. He nodded slowly, mesmerized by the expression in her eyes. "When you laugh," he said slowly, unable to look away, "the sound reminds me of wind chimes or bells. You have a beautiful laugh." He wanted to walk over to her and take her in his arms. He wanted to kiss her slowly. He wanted to touch her. He wanted a miracle to happen.

Her eyes were dreamy as she said, "It's odd you should mention bells because the sound of bells always reminds me of one of the happiest memories of my life."

He knew he had no right to feel what he was feeling, but he wanted to hold on to the closeness they were sharing, at least for a little longer, so he said, "Tell me about it."

The faraway look still in her eyes, she said, "I went up to the convent to see Celeste take her final vows, and I'll never forget how I felt. The convent itself was like something out of a Brontë novel, a huge walled fortress that sat high on a bluff overlooking the Pacific just south of Anchor Bay. I drove up the coast, it's the first and last time I ever had the opportunity to do it, and the scenery was incredible. The day I arrived, it was overcast, and the convent was shrouded in fog. It was nearly noon, and I was driving up the twisting driveway that led to the convent, and suddenly the sun broke through. At almost the same moment, the convent bells began to ring."

Neil watched the emotions drifting across her face, and a futile possessiveness gripped him.

"It was so beautiful," Laura said, her voice so soft it was almost a whisper. "The sun like golden fingers sliding through the swirling fog, the sound of the bells echoing around me, the convent looming ahead like a great, gray castle...." She shivered, hugging herself. "At that moment I wanted so badly to be a poet or a great writer so that I could capture my feelings on paper." She laughed in embarrassment. "I fell in love that day. So much so that I even considered becoming a nun myself." She sighed deeply. "But I didn't really have a vocation. I was just romanticizing the whole thing. Young girls can be pretty impressionable, you know."

Neil could see how the young Laura's romantic streak and the ugliness of her past would combine to produce the feelings she'd had when she'd visited her friend. The otherworldly picture she'd painted of that day would have been very appealing to the girl she was.

"But I've really gotten us off the subject," she said matter-of-factly. "Finish telling me about Willis."

Neil had to wrench his mind away from his feelings and back to the reason he was there this afternoon. "Well, Willis was always jealous of me, and I was never sure why. He had a lot more money than I did, but that never seemed to satisfy him. He always wanted everything. He especially wanted all the attention, and when he didn't get it, he'd pout. When he grew up he wasn't much better. In fact, anything I did, Willis tried to best. He joined the Baton Rouge Police Department three years before I did. I always thought the only reason he joined the force was because he knew that's what I planned to do and not because he had any great desire to be a cop."

"Why would he send Alice Kendella ten thousand dollars? Was he a good friend of Jimmy's?"

"No. In fact, he made fun of Jimmy behind his back. We had words about that a couple of times. I always thought he didn't like Jimmy because Jimmy and I were so close."

"Did he know Alice?"

"Not that I know of. Oh, he knew who she was. He probably knew her well enough to say hello to her on the street. But they weren't friends. Why?"

"I just thought maybe . . . well, I know this might sound stupid . . . but I thought maybe he was interested in Alice."

Neil didn't even have to think about her suggestion. "No. Willis wasn't interested in Alice. Believe me, I know that."

Laura frowned. "How can you be so sure?"

Neil smiled wryly. "Trust me. I have my reasons." He saw the curiosity on her face, but he didn't want to tell her about his suspicions concerning Willis's feelings for Erica. He'd flirted with danger once today by allowing their conversation to become personal. He'd better not risk it again.

"All right. We've eliminated friendship for Jimmy, and an interest in Alice. What does that leave? Humanitarianism?"

Neil thought about Willis. The kind of kid he'd been. The kind of adult he'd turned into. "I have a hard time believing Willis would give up ten thousand dollars strictly out of the goodness of his heart. I *might* believe it if it had been done with a lot of fanfare, because then Willis would have gained something from it. But anonymously? Nope. Not Willis."

"What then? Guilt?"

"But about what? That's what's bugging me."

"Well, then, that's what we need to find out."

An alarm went off in Neil's mind. He was headed for even more trouble if he spent too much time with Laura. "Look, I appreciate all your help, but you're not involved in this, Laura." As soon as the words were out of his mouth, he was sorry they sounded so abrupt.

She shrugged, and turned away, but not before he'd caught a glimpse of the hurt in her eyes.

There were some things that were just too much to ask of a man. "Do you really want to help?"

She nodded. Then she looked up, and Neil knew he was lost. He was stupid. He was playing with fire. He shouldn't have even let her do what she'd done so far. He should avoid her company at all costs.

He knew all these things. "Okay, you can help me by doing some research," he said, and was rewarded by the most beautiful smile he'd ever seen.

Chapter Thirteen

Laura didn't see much of Neil for the next two weeks, but her unhappiness had eased. She had the memory of the way he'd looked and acted toward her the day she called Bobbi Cameron to keep her hope alive. And he did stop by the office a couple of times. He only stayed a few minutes, but he brought her up to date on his attempts to find out more about Willis Fontenot and why he'd cared enough about Alice Kendella to send her money anonymously.

In the meantime, Laura was making a few positive changes in her life. She bought herself some new clothes, making a special effort to choose things in brighter colors and more fashionable styles than she'd ever chosen before. She also had lunch with Bobbi Cameron twice and enjoyed both outings. But the most satisfying change was her evolving friendship with Alice.

A couple of days after she'd called Bobbi Cameron about the check, Alice phoned her at the office.

"Hi, Laura. It's Alice Kendella."

"Oh, hello, Alice," Laura said, pleased.

"I wondered if you might like to come over tonight and have dinner with us."

"I'd love to."

She fell in love with Alice's kids and Alice's house before she'd been there five minutes. Little Lisa, with her pixie face, was adorable, and Jimmy, Jr., with his shy grin and endearing smile, stole her heart. The kitchen, with its bright colors and cozy clutter, reminded her of the kitchen in Celeste's house. Laura felt instantly at home.

She stayed for hours that night. She even helped Lisa with her bath and little Jimmy with his math homework. Alice protested, saying, "You don't have to do that, Laura."

"I want to," she insisted.

She stayed far too long. She realized it when Alice sat back in her chair and yawned, running her fingers through her short, curly hair. "I'm sorry. It's not the company, believe me. It's just that I got up so early this morning." She sighed. "I have to be at the school bus parking barn by seven each day."

"Who watches the kids?" Laura asked.

"My next door neighbor."

Laura realized that Alice's life, even though fuller, was much more complicated than her own. All she had to worry about was herself. Alice was responsible for the lives of two young children. But still, she'd trade places with Alice any day of the week. Alice was needed. And loved. She was a part of that elusive circle.

Since that night, Laura had visited Alice two more times. And now here she was again. She'd stopped in impulsively on her way home from work and Alice asked her to stay for dinner.

"We're just having spaghetti and there's plenty," Alice urged when Laura, out of politeness, started to say no.

They had just finished their dinner and Laura was helping Alice clear the table with the doorbell rang.

"Wonder who that could be?" Alice said. She disappeared in the direction of the front door. Laura opened the dishwasher and began putting the dirty dishes inside. But when she heard Alice open the front door and say, "Neil!" her heart zoomed into her throat.

She only had a couple of minutes to get her emotions under control before Alice, followed by Neil, entered the kitchen.

"Look who's here," Alice said, watching Laura's face intently.

Laura was too flustered and too busy trying to act nonchalant to take the time to wonder why Alice had looked at her so oddly. "Hi, Neil."

"Well, hi." He smiled, and Laura's heart flopped over. His smile had a way of turning her knees to water. "I'm glad you're here. I came over to tell Alice what progress I've made concerning Willis."

A few minutes later they were all sitting around the table with cups of coffee in front of them.

"So what have you found out?" Alice asked Neil.

"Well, I've called everyone I could think of who might be able to give me some clue about why Willis would have sent you that money. I've had to be careful because I didn't want to tell anyone about the money. It was pretty tricky. Also frustrating because I know no more than I did when I started. No one seemed to know anything, or if they did, they were hiding it."

"There's got to be something," Alice said.

"I don't know. Maybe we're just blowing smoke. Maybe Willis was just being a good guy, and there's nothing to learn."

"Why don't we go over everything that happened that night?" Alice suggested. "Maybe we're missing something."

"Are you sure you want to?" Neil asked. "If it's going to be painful for you, we don't have to."

How nice he is, Laura thought. How stupid I was to be jealous of him and his feelings for Alice.

Alice smiled sadly. "This might seem strange to you, Neil, but I need to talk about it. Everyone has avoided the subject for so long."

"Talking helps," Laura said, giving Neil an encouraging look.

"Over the past three years, the only person who seemed to understand my need to talk about Jimmy has been my father," Alice said, "but Dad wasn't there that night, and I wasn't there, so the only thing we've been able to discuss is our feelings." She sighed deeply. "And now I want to know everything else. I *need* to hear the rest if I'm ever going to put this completely behind me."

So they went over everything. Detail by detail.

"Neil..." Laura said when they were finished. She'd just had an idea. "Why did your wife follow you, do you know?"

"Yes, I wondered about that, too," Alice echoed.

His brows knitted. "I guess because she didn't believe me when I told her I was on a stakeout. I don't know. It's one of the things I've always wondered about."

"Had she ever doubted you before?" Alice asked.

"No. We'd had plenty of arguments about my being gone so much of the time. And about my not paying enough attention to her. You know, the usual stuff..." His voice trailed off, and he looked at Laura.

She knew he was uncomfortable talking about what he viewed as his shortcomings in front of her.

"But had she ever acted as if she didn't believe you when you said you had to work?" Alice persisted. She turned to Laura. "She was jealous of the time Neil spent away from her, but I'd never known her to think he might be cheating on her. Everyone who knew Neil knew he would never do anything like that, anyway."

"No," Neil said slowly, "she was too sure of her hold on me to think I might be interested in another woman."

"Then *why,* that night of all nights, did she follow you?" Alice said.

"I don't know."

Laura hesitated, then said, "Didn't you ever ask her?"

"No." He looked down at his cup. "I'd been unhappy with my marriage for a long time, and what happened that night was the final straw. I was so sickened by everything that I didn't care if I ever saw Erica again. In fact, the only time I *did* see her was when I went home to pack my clothes. The divorce, everything, was handled by our attorneys."

"Well, I think you should ask her," Alice said slowly.

"I just don't see what her reasons have to do with Willis Fontenot and his gift to you," Neil said.

"Weren't you always telling me he was in love with her? Didn't we sit at this very table—you, me, and Jimmy—and talk about that very subject?"

"Yes."

Laura digested this surprising information. She wondered how Neil had felt about that. Had Erica been interested in Willis Fontenot? How could she be, with Neil as her husband?

"Well, then," Alice continued, "there could be a link between her following you and Willis's interest in her."

"That's really stretching things, isn't it?"

"I think Alice is right," Laura said, hoping he wouldn't think she was interfering.

"Besides," Alice added, "you've got to start somewhere."

"So you two think I should call Erica and ask her why she followed me?" He didn't sound irritated, just thoughtful.

"Yes," Alice and Laura said in unison. Then they both laughed.

Neil scowled at them, but Laura could tell he wasn't really angry. "Okay, you win. If it'll make you happy, Alice, I'll do it. I'll call her tomorrow."

"Tomorrow! Call her tonight. Use my phone." Her gray eyes were eager.

Part of Laura wanted him to call Erica tonight, too. The other part of her didn't want to be anywhere near him when he talked to his ex-wife.

"No, I can't," he said quickly, darting a look at Laura.

Comprehension wiped out the eagerness in Alice's eyes. "Oh, sorry. You don't want to talk to her in front of us. That was pretty stupid of me to suggest it, wasn't it?"

"That's not it."

But of course, that was it, and Laura knew it.

For the rest of the evening, the three of them didn't talk about Erica, or the night Jimmy died, or anything to do with the past. Instead, Alice provided some much needed relief from serious subjects with a funny tale about how Baron, the family dachshund, had eaten little Jimmy's homework. "He took one look at that paper with jelly beans pasted all over it, and before I knew what had happened, the homework was inside Baron's stomach, and little Jimmy was outraged."

Laura and Neil both laughed.

Laura wasn't sure if she was glad or sad when the evening was over. She hugged Alice goodbye, then turned awkwardly toward Neil. But he covered the awkward moment by saying, "I'll walk out with you."

For a few minutes, as they emerged into the navy night, Laura pretended they were going home together. She took a deep breath of the balmy night air filled with the scent of spring and wished with all her heart for a miracle.

Neil walked around to the driver's side of her car and opened the door for her. He waited.

She looked up, and their eyes met. His were dark and gleaming in the moonlight.

"Good night, Neil," she said softly. She wondered if he could hear her heart beating.

"Good night, Laura." Then he bent down and kissed her cheek lightly. "Drive safely."

Before Laura had time to react or even think, he helped her into the car and shut her door firmly.

Then he walked away.

Neil had enjoyed watching the two women together. They were nothing alike physically, and until lately, he would have said they were nothing alike, period. But obviously, he had been wrong, for they shared an inner strength and a sense of humor that had helped them survive some tough times.

When it was time to leave and Alice and Laura hugged, he could tell how much they liked each other. He couldn't help but compare their budding friendship and mutual admiration to the relationship between Erica and Alice when he and Erica had been married. Alice had tried to be nice to Erica, but Erica had resented Alice. She'd called her "simpering" and a "goody-goody" and she hadn't made any real attempt to get to know Alice. Now that he thought about it, Erica had not had any women friends. *Fool. That should have told you something.*

The whole evening he wondered if Laura had any idea just how difficult it was for him to maintain emotional distance from her. He wondered if she thought about him the way he thought about her, if she still thought she was in love with him or if maybe over the past weeks she'd had a change of heart. He also knew he couldn't ask her. He had no right to ask her.

As he drove home, and later, as he lay in bed, he continued to think about Laura and the differences between her and Erica. Too bad Erica couldn't have been like Laura. If she had been, his entire life would have been different. But she hadn't been, and no amount of wishing or thinking would change the past. The most he could hope for was that he'd learned a few things and he wouldn't repeat his mistakes.

The next morning he called the drugstore and asked to speak to Margaret Chase, Erica's mother.

"Margaret, this is Neil. I'd like to call Erica. Would you mind giving me her phone number?"

"What for?"

Neil clenched his teeth. "It's personal, Margaret."

"Mebbe she don't want to talk to you."

"Then she can hang up, and I won't bother her again."

She grumbled for a few more minutes, then finally read him the number. Neil wrote it down, repeated it, then thanked her civilly.

Two minutes later he was listening to the ringing at Erica's home in California. After four rings, a soft Spanish-accented voice, said, "Savage residence."

"May I speak to Erica, please?"

"Who is calling, please?"

Neil hesitated. He had hoped he wouldn't have to announce his name first, but he had a feeling the maid wouldn't call Erica unless he did. "Tell her it's Neil."

"Neil? Is it really you?" Her voice sounded just as honeyed, just as seductive as he'd remembered it. The only difference was that it no longer elicited the response it once had. Now all he felt was curiosity.

"Yes, Erica, it's really me."

"I can hardly believe it. It's been a long time."

"Yes, it has. How have you been?"

"I've been wonderful! Didn't my mother tell you? I'm assuming that's how you knew where to find me."

Erica had always been sharp about some things. "I *did* talk to Margaret. You're right—she gave me your number."

"Are you calling from Florida, or wherever it is you went? Or are you home—in Patinville?"

"I'm in Patinville." He gave her a brief report on Norman's accident.

"I'm sorry, Neil. Give Norman my love."

She sounded sincere, which really didn't surprise him. Erica was selfish, but she wasn't completely thoughtless, and she'd always liked Norman. She'd laughingly referred to him as a "big teddy bear" and enjoyed teasing him and making him blush. "Thanks. I will."

"So... to what do I owe the honor of this call? I'm sure you didn't call to check on my health."

"Erica..." How to start? "Listen, there's something I have to know. A question I want you to answer...."

"Ahh, I sense a little mystery here." Now her voice sounded coy.

"No mystery. It's just something I should have asked you three and a half years ago, but didn't."

"Well, come on, don't keep me in suspense."

"That night...the night Jimmy was killed...why did you follow me?"

"What do you mean?"

"Why did you follow me? You never acted like you didn't believe me before that night. Why, all of a sudden, did you doubt my story and follow me? Was there a reason?"

She was silent so long, Neil almost asked if she was still there. Finally she spoke. "It was because of Willis."

Neil stiffened. "Willis?"

He could almost hear her shrug. When she spoke, there was a ring of apology in her voice. "I'm sorry, Neil. I should have told you then, but I was so angry with you and our relationship was so strained by then, I purposely didn't tell you, even though I had a pretty good idea Willis planted the idea knowing full well what I'd do."

"Start from the beginning."

"Willis came over that afternoon. He used to drop in a lot, and I... I encouraged him because I was feeling neglected. Anyway, when I complained about the stakeout, he acted as if there might not really be a stakeout. He hinted that maybe you were seeing another woman."

That snake. Willis knew damn well the stakeout was authentic. Everyone in the department knew about Tony Abruzzi and his girlfriend.

"I was furious to think you'd been lying to me. Up until that moment, I never considered that there might be someone else. I always thought your job was my rival, not another *woman!*"

"I never saw another woman while I was married to you, Erica," he said. "I know I had my faults, but unfaithfulness was not one of them."

"I know that now. But at the time, I was so angry with you... anyway, I guess I... wanted to believe it."

Neil was amazed. This was a new Erica he was talking to. This Erica sounded as if she might have grown up in the last three years. "So you followed me when I left that night."

"Yes."

Willis. Willis had planted the seed of doubt in her mind. What had he hoped to accomplish? Surely he hadn't intended for Jimmy to die. Was that why he'd sent the check? Because he'd started something that ended in tragedy? A tragedy he hadn't intended? Neil had always known there was something unexplained about that night despite what Internal Affairs had said. And now, finally, he might be on the verge of discovering the whole truth.

"Neil... can you forgive me? I... I know how much Jimmy meant to you, and... and I've always felt guilty about his death. If I hadn't come that night... maybe Jimmy would still be alive." Her voice trembled.

"It wasn't your fault," Neil said resignedly. "We can't know what would have happened if you hadn't come. Everything might still have ended the same way. But if anybody's to blame here, I think it's Willis."

"What are you going to do?"

She'd asked the same question Alice had asked the night before. "I'm not sure. One thing I do know, though. I'm going to have a nice, long talk with my cousin Willis. A long overdue talk."

Neil hadn't been in the mayor's office for years. But he did remember that old Henri Tremayne, who'd been mayor of Patinville for more than fifteen years, had had a secretary older than he was. Everyone in town knew Esther Riddley, and the smart-looking brunette sitting behind the secretary's desk today was definitely not Esther. Neil looked at the brunette's legs as she walked toward Willis's office to announce him. No, definitely not Esther.

He wondered what Willis would think when the brunette told him Neil was there.

He didn't have long to wait. A smiling Willis emerged from his office only moments later. "Neil! What a surprise. Come on in."

Neil forced himself to smile in front of the secretary, then followed Willis into his office, shutting the door behind him.

It was a nice office, Neil thought, occupying the corner and most of the back half of the third floor of the city building, which also housed the water and sewer departments as well as the rest of the administrative staff. Although Patinville wasn't a big city, with a population of about 30,000, it had a respectable number of city employees.

"Moved up in the world, haven't you?" Neil said, eyeing the plush green carpeting and shining mahogany furniture.

Willis flushed, and his smile slipped a little. "Well, yes, things have worked out nicely for me." Then, as if he'd just remembered his manners, he said, "Sit down, Neil. Can I get you some coffee? Hell, this is an occasion. How about a drink?"

"No, thanks." Neil took the proffered chair, and Willis walked around and seated himself in the swivel chair behind his desk. Neil leaned back in his own chair and tented his fingers. In a slow, thoughtful voice, he said, "Yes, things have worked out nicely for you, Willis." He allowed himself a small smile. "But then, after all, it's only what you deserve, isn't it?"

"Well, I uh..." Willis's voice trailed off uncertainly.

"Not like me, right? I mean, isn't that what you told Lt. Richardson?"

"Now that's all water under the bridge, Neil. I was wrong. I know that now. It's time to forget about all that."

Neil smiled again, and Willis couldn't meet his eyes, although he tried. But the effort only lasted seconds, and for the second time, his gaze slid away. "It's big of you to say that, Willis. Why, if I didn't know better, I'd think there was a reason you wanted to forget about that night." Neil stood and slowly walked to the window behind Willis's desk. He gazed down at the street below. There was the usual flow of midday traffic on Main Street. "But that's crazy, isn't it?" he continued slowly. "What possible reason could the upright, honest, newly elected mayor have for wanting to bury the events of that infamous night?"

"You know, Neil, I thought you came here to mend fences," Willis blustered, "not to make snide innuendos about me."

"Snide innuendos? Is that what I was doing? Gee, Willis, I'm so sorry. I didn't mean to offend your sensibilities. Can you ever forgive me?"

The flush on Willis's face deepened, and his eyes narrowed. "I'm a busy man, Neil. I don't have time to play games with you."

Neil almost laughed. Bluster hadn't worked, so now Willis was obviously going for the bluff. Very deliberately, he walked toward Willis, stopping only inches away, so that Willis had to look up to see him. "I'm a busy man, too, Willis. In fact, I've been very busy. You wouldn't believe how busy. Why, in the last two weeks I've discovered that a mysterious check for ten thousand dollars that some anonymous donor sent to Alice Kendella after Jimmy's death was actually purchased by you, and I've found out that a telephone call came in to the department the very same afternoon of the day Jimmy died—a telephone call from my snitch—a call that you took because I wasn't there. And I've also discovered the reason my ex-wife decided to show up that fateful night is because you planted the idea in her head that I wasn't really working. You very cleverly led Erica to believe that I was seeing another woman. That's why she followed me, and that's why things happened the way they did, and that's why Jimmy died."

Willis's face had gone white. "You're crazy!"

Neil, who had been fighting to keep his temper in check, grabbed Willis by the collar, and even though his cousin outweighed him by a good forty pounds, he lifted him out of the chair effortlessly. "Listen, you worthless bastard," he ground out, "I'd as soon beat the crap out of you as look at you, so don't lie to me."

"I'm...I'm not lying," Willis sputtered, pulling at Neil's hands.

But Neil was relentless. Three and one-half years of guilt and pain and dealing with the knowledge that his life had changed irrevocably because of that night drove him, would continue to drive him, until he knew the truth. Only then would he be able to forget. Only then would he be able to build a new life. "You might as well tell me the truth, because I know it anyway. The only thing I don't know is what you hoped to accomplish by pushing Erica into following me that night. Did you know Tony Abruzzi was going to show up then?"

"I told you! I don't know what you're talking about!"

Suddenly all of it—the pain, the years of sadness and guilt, everything—combined to enrage Neil. He let Willis go, and Willis staggered backward, falling against his chair.

"I'd like to kill you, do you know that?" Neil said through clenched teeth. He wanted to smash Willis's face in, but he knew there were better ways of taking care of Willis.

"You just try it!" Willis shouted, eyes blazing with hate. "My secretary would have the police here so fast your head would spin. You think you're so smart, don't you? You've always thought you were smarter than me. Well, who's sitting here in the mayor's office and who ran away to Florida, answer me that!"

"I don't have to answer anything. You're the one who'd better come up with some answers, and quick."

Willis's eyes narrowed, and his face had turned a mottled shade of red. "Get out of here, Neil. We're not kids anymore. You don't carry any weight in this town, and I do."

"You haven't gotten any smarter, have you Willis?"

"I'm smarter than you'll ever be!"

"If you're as smart as you think you are, you'll realize that I don't have to prove anything to cause you a lot of trouble. All I have to do is start spreading rumors around. The last thing a politician with ambition needs is rumors."

"You wouldn't dare. I'd haul you into court so fast, you wouldn't know what hit you," Willis said, but not before Neil had caught a glimpse of fear in his eyes.

"Fine. If you want to go to court, have the bank's records subpoenaed, have that whole mess opened up again, that's fine with me. I have nothing to hide. I also have nothing to lose." Neil smiled coldly. "You, on the other hand, have a great deal to lose."

Suddenly, all the bluster left Willis, and he sagged into his chair, his face draining of color. "What do you want from me?" he said.

"For starters, tell me why you did it."

Willis didn't look at Neil. He squirmed in his chair and reached for his collar, loosening his tie as if it was suddenly choking him. "I...I didn't think anything like that would happen. I never thought anyone would get hurt. And you're right, Lester, your snitch, did call that day. He said he'd heard a rumor that Tony Abruzzi was going to contact his girlfriend that night. I...I told him I'd tell you. And I went over to your house *to* tell you, but then...Erica was there, and she was mad and she kept on and on about you and your job, how she just knew things would only get worse when you got that promotion...and suddenly, I started to get mad." Now he looked up, and his blue eyes were filled with bitterness.

"You and your charmed life," he said, "you made me sick. I was older, and I was just as smart, smarter even, and all my life I'd had to take a back seat to you. This was my chance to show everyone you weren't quite so great. So I let Erica believe you weren't really on a stakeout. It was easy. I dropped a hint that you were with another woman those nights when you said you were working. I even planted the idea she should follow you."

"Didn't you stop to think that maybe Erica might get hurt?"

"If everyone had done what they should have done, no one would have gotten hurt."

"Except me," Neil said quietly. When Willis made no response, he said, "What if Erica had told someone you goaded her into following me?"

"I pretended to try to talk her out of it. I figured I could always say she'd misunderstood. She didn't have a great track record anyway. She was always callin' you up, causin' trouble."

"But what did you think would happen when she got to the stakeout?"

"I didn't know! I didn't have any plan. It wasn't like that. I just knew it would cause trouble for you. That's all. I just wanted to cause trouble for you...."

Neil stared at him. *Our illustrious mayor.* A weak, stupid man. Neil was sorely tempted to expose him.

"Wha... what are you gonna do?" Willis said.

"I could still take my chances in court."

"You can't prove any of this!"

"There's the little matter of that check. That should raise a few eyebrows, don't you think?"

"I sent that check out of the goodness of my heart."

"Okay, Willis. You're right. I'm not going to bring all that up again. But don't think you're getting off scot-free. I want something from you."

Willis sneered. "I should've known. How much?"

"I don't want your money, Willis. But I do want my pound of flesh. I want you to set up, anonymously of course, an annuity for Alice Kendella and a college fund for her two kids. If you do that, I'll forget all about what you told me today."

"Now wait a minute, I've got some money, sure, but I'm not a rich man. You're talking about an awful lot of money. I'm not sure I can manage it."

Then Neil leaned down until his face was on a level with Willis's. "You'll manage, jerk. I'm offering you a way out, a way to make Jimmy's death worth something. But I could change my mind very easily."

Chapter Fourteen

Everybody in Patinville agreed that the past winter had been the worst one in years. First, there had been torrential rains in December and January. Then, once the rain finally stopped, the mercury plunged down to set all-time low temperatures throughout the month of February. When March tiptoed in with sunny skies and mild breezes, people were almost afraid to believe spring had finally arrived.

Laura usually loved spring. Her natural optimism would bloom along with the flowers poking their faces up through the ground in joyful release. But this year was different. This year, when she flipped the calendar page each morning, the hope she'd nurtured for weeks would dim just a bit more. This year, the passing of each day inched Neil's departure from Patinville twenty-four hours closer. This year, all she saw ahead was a lifetime spent without the man she loved.

Even her desire to put the past behind her and look toward the future and her newfound friendships with Bobbi Cameron and Alice Kendella couldn't lift her flagging spirits for more than a day or so.

"Laura, what's wrong?" Alice asked. "Everytime I see you, you look more unhappy."

The two women were sitting in Alice's kitchen. Their friendship had cemented solidly over the past weeks. Laura had quickly fallen into the habit of dropping in at Alice's two or three times a week on her way home from work. They both looked forward to Laura's visits—Laura because she had missed the close daily contact she used to share with Celeste, and Alice because she spent too much time with children, and most of her other friends were mothers like her whose conversation was mostly about *their* children.

Laura wanted to tell her. She needed to tell her. But she couldn't. It was one thing to talk to Celeste about Neil. Celeste wasn't here in Patinville. Celeste could be an impartial listener, and Laura didn't have to look into her eyes and know she knew. Alice was a different story. Alice was here, a close friend of Neil's. Laura was afraid. What if she yielded to the temptation to spill everything to Alice and Alice's opinion of her changed? What if Alice no longer liked her or respected her? She couldn't take that chance. Even though she knew Alice was a fair and open-minded person, Laura didn't want to risk losing even one notch of esteem in Alice's eyes.

So she made herself smile. "I'm all right, really. I...I just haven't been feeling well." Then she thought, oh, Lord. Why did I say that? Because it wasn't even remotely true. For the past six weeks, Laura had felt physically better than she'd ever felt. It was only her heart that was sick, not her body.

"Have you been back to the doctor since you were released from the hospital?"

Laura felt like a worm when she saw the concern shining in Alice's eyes. "No."

"Laura! Why not? Maybe something didn't heal properly. Do you hurt anywhere?"

"No, no. It's nothing like that. I just feel tired." She should never have said she didn't feel good.

"Maybe you're anemic, although your color is good. In fact, you even look like you've put on a few pounds." Alice grinned. "You're more well-rounded than when I first met you. I noticed it the other day, when you were wearing a sweater."

"Well, I've been eating like a horse," Laura admitted, realizing that her appetite hadn't suffered from her dawning realization that perhaps there was no hope for a future with Neil. She grinned back. "Part of the reason I've been eating so much is your insistence on feeding me mountains of food."

Alice was a wonderful cook, and she'd laughingly confessed a few weeks earlier that she had a need to feed people. "It makes me feel like I'm doing my job, or something. Oh, it's stupid."

"It's not stupid," Laura had protested. "It's perfectly natural." But Laura knew Alice was on a pretty strict budget, so after the second or third time Alice fed her a delicious meal, Laura began bringing groceries with her when she came to visit.

"I still think you should see a doctor," Alice insisted.

"It's too much of a hassle to drive to Baton Rouge."

"Why would you have to drive to Baton Rouge?"

"The only doctor I know is the one who treated me at the hospital."

"You mean you don't have a doctor in Patinville?" Alice said incredulously.

Laura shook her head, feeling more ashamed of herself by the minute.

"Laura! Honestly, how can a woman as smart as you be so dumb?" Alice said. She jumped up. "How long have you been living here?"

"Three years."

"Three years! You mean you haven't had a checkup, or a PAP smear in three years?"

"No," Laura said meekly, knowing Alice was right. She *had* neglected herself.

"I'll bet you don't have a dentist, either!"

Again Laura shook her head. Even though she knew nothing was wrong with her, that both doctor and dentist would give her a clean bill, she also knew it really was dumb not to have yearly checkups. She should probably even schedule a mammogram. If she remembered correctly, her grandmother had died of breast cancer.

Her heart speeded up as she suddenly realized her breasts had been tender lately. She'd noticed it when she was showering. Maybe she *already* had breast cancer.

"Well, we're going to take care of both these little details right now," Alice said and disappeared into the other room. Minutes later she was back, clutching an address book. She tore a sheet off the notepad mounted by the kitchen phone and sat back down at the table.

"Here," she said, handing the scrap of notepaper to Laura. "Here's the name of my own doctor—she's wonderful—you'll love her. Her name's Margaret Winslow, and her office is right down on Main Street, upstairs, over the furniture store. And the other name—Dr. Marianne Theesyn—that's my dentist. She's wonderful, too. But her office is a little farther away—in Port Allen."

"You have a female doctor *and* a female dentist?"

"Sure. Why not?"

"I don't know. It just seems funny."

Alice smiled. "Trust me. You'll never want to go to a male doctor again."

"Okay. I'll call and make an appointment with both of them."

"When?"

"Tomorrow."

"Do you promise?" Alice said stubbornly.

"I promise."

And the next morning, she did call. Dr. Winslow's office said they could see her on Friday morning. Dr. Theesyn's office said she'd have to wait until the end of March.

"I should have been a dentist," muttered Laura when she hung up the phone.

Later that day Alice called. "Did you make those appointments?" was the first thing she said.

"Yes, Mom," Laura answered.

Alice laughed. "Somebody has to look after you if you won't do it yourself!"

"I know, and I appreciate it. I really do," Laura said, some of her unhappiness fading as she realized what a wonderful friend she'd found in Alice.

"So when are you going to see Dr. Winslow?"

"On Friday morning."

"Good. Listen, checking up on you wasn't the only reason I called this morning. I wanted to invite you to a little party I'm giving Saturday night."

"A party?"

"Yes, I think it's time you met more people in Patinville. I'm not inviting a lot of people. Only about a dozen. And I want you to come."

Suddenly suspicious, Laura said, "You're not trying to fix me up with a guy, are you?"

"No," Alice said quickly, "although there *will* be two single men coming, but one of them's Neil, so he doesn't count. The other one's Paul Fontayne, have you met him?"

Neil. Neil would be there. "No, I don't think so. Who is he?" She responded automatically, her brain and heart still processing the information that she would get to see Neil, who, since the night she'd run into him at Alice's, had been avoiding her like someone with leprosy was avoided in the Dark Ages. In fact, it amazed her that he'd been so successful since he was living right upstairs. But he managed to leave for whatever job he was working on before she arrived in the mornings, and he didn't return until after she'd gone for the night. It had been two weeks since she'd even laid eyes on him. No wonder she'd been so depressed. She needed to at least see him—get her daily fix—she thought wryly.

"Paul's a sweetie. He's my lawyer. He's originally from New Orleans—a Creole—handsome and debonair—and he moved to Patinville about a dozen years ago. Anyway, he's getting over a pretty miserable divorce, and he needs to get out and see people. That's really why I'm having the party. To try to cheer him up."

Laura felt relieved to know Alice wasn't matchmaking, but uneasy because of Neil. No matter how much she wanted to see him, she knew the evening would be tough on her. But she couldn't think of any reason for refusing.

"All right. I'll be there," she promised Alice.

"Great. It'll be fun. You'll see. And Laura...call me when you get back from the doctor's office Friday, okay? I want to know what she had to say."

Laura walked out of Dr. Winslow's office like someone in a trance. The steep stairs leading to the street, the warm March sun when she emerged onto the pavement, the bustle of noontime pedestrians on Main Street, the brilliant crimson petals of the clusters of begonias planted along the esplanade—none of these penetrated her dreamlike state. She walked to her car, she unlocked the door, she slid into the driver's seat, she turned the key in the ignition.

Only one thought pulsed through her mind, wiping everything else from her consciousness.

Pregnant.

She was pregnant.

About eight weeks pregnant, Dr. Winslow had said, her kind blue eyes meeting Laura's as she gave her the news.

The words had reverberated around Laura, filling all the available air space. *Pregnant.*

"Are you all right?"

Blindly, Laura looked up. She blinked. When had the doctor gotten up from behind her desk? She opened her mouth, sucking in air. She tried to speak, but no sound came out.

Pregnant. The bright afternoon sunlight faded; there was a buzzing in her ears. Dr. Winslow grabbed her and pushed her head down, and gradually, the weakness and dizziness passed.

"Did you have no idea?" Dr. Winslow said gently when she was once more seated after giving Laura a glass of cold water.

Laura shook her head. "No. I... I've never had regular periods, so..." *A baby. She was going to have a baby.* She couldn't believe it. Neil's baby. She was pregnant with Neil's baby. Images of all the babies she'd ever seen filled her mind. Chill bumps broke out over her arms; her heart thumped heavily. Tears burned her eyes, and her lips trembled.

Neil's baby. Her baby. Their baby. She felt so ridiculously happy and sad and stunned all at the same time. She could feel the tears sliding out of her eyes and down her cheeks, and she hastily wiped them away with the back of her hand.

The rest of the consultation with Dr. Winslow was only a blur in her mind. She knew she was supposed to come back in three weeks, and she remembered that the nurse had given her vitamins and a book of instructions. Everything else had disappeared, and only the knowledge that she carried Neil's baby remained.

Somehow she reached the roofing company office, but afterwards, she didn't remember driving there. Suddenly she was just there, sitting behind her desk, the same thought cartwheeling through her mind, over and over again.

In seven months I'm going to have a baby. Neil's baby.

Nothing would ever be the same again.

"Laura, you're awfully quiet tonight," Alice said. "Are you bored?"

"Hmm? Oh, no, of course not." Laura shook herself. She'd done it again. For the past twenty-four hours she had lapsed into intermittent daydreams, and the world around her had receded.

"Well, come on over and talk to Paul. I've told him a lot about you."

Laura wondered if her first instinct had been right, that Alice really was trying to maneuver her into a date with Paul Fontayne. She wondered what her friend would think if she knew it was much too late for anything like that. Laura unconsciously laid her hand over her flat stomach, a fierce joy shooting through her as she thought about the tiny baby growing inside.

But she allowed Alice to lead her over to the tall, elegant man standing in front of the fireplace. She stood there and made small talk, and smiled and said the right things, but all the while she had one ear trained on the front door as she waited for Neil to arrive.

The party had started at seven-thirty. It was now nine o'clock, and Neil still hadn't shown up. Alice commented on his absence once in Laura's hearing, so obviously he hadn't called to say he wouldn't be there. Laura wanted to ask Alice about him, but she knew it was better not to.

So she tried to concentrate her attention on Paul Fontayne. Too bad she wasn't interested in him, because he really did seem like a nice man, and he was certainly good-looking, and from what Alice had said, successful. More importantly, he was available.

He didn't seem any more interested in her than she was in him, even though he was very polite. But Laura could see no spark of real interest in his eyes. It was a relief then, when another woman joined them, and Laura could ease away.

She escaped the noisy, crowded living room into the familiar kitchen where Alice was taking a tray of egg rolls out of the oven. "Hand me that platter, will you?" Alice said. She used a spatula to remove the egg rolls from the hot cookie sheet to the platter. She frowned, looking up at the kitchen clock. "Darn that Neil. I wonder why he didn't come?"

"Did I hear my name spoken in vain?"

Alice's head jerked up, but Laura turned slowly. Her heart shot up into her throat. She smiled a greeting, trying to keep her mouth from trembling. Her hands were shaking, and she clasped them together to hide the fact that her emotions were tumbling unchecked. Right now she felt as if she'd been flattened by a steamroller as she was filled with the realization that this man was the father of the child she carried inside her. This man was the man she loved desperately and hopelessly. This man was the man she could probably never have.

"Sorry I'm so late." He smiled at both of them, but his eyes lingered on Laura, sending a shivery trail down her spine as their gazes held. Her knees felt like mush.

Neil, oh Neil. She had to get control of herself. She couldn't fall to pieces in front of him. She couldn't. She tried to look away, but she couldn't do that either. Something stirred deep in his eyes. Just as Laura thought she might really lose it, just fall apart right here in Alice's kitchen, blubber like a big baby, he broke eye contact, and when he did, Laura was able to breathe again, and the moment passed.

"Well, where the blazes have you been?" Alice demanded. "I was counting on you to tend bar."

"I went to the rehab center today, and without any warning, Norman's doctor said he could go home."

"What?" Laura was shocked out of her preoccupation with herself by this stunning piece of news.

"How wonderful!" Alice exclaimed. "Did you bring him home?"

"I took him to the folks because it wouldn't be smart for him to try to navigate the stairs at his apartment. They're very steep. He's going to have to find another place to live, I guess." Neil grinned. "But he's home. And he's very happy to be there."

"I'll bet he is," Alice said.

Laura was still assimilating Neil's bombshell news. Somehow she hadn't been prepared for Norman coming home this soon. She was happy for him, of course, but she wondered what this development would mean in terms of Neil and how long he'd stay in Patinville. She felt hollow inside when the realization dawned that Neil might be leaving for Florida very soon.

As if to confirm her worst fears, Neil said, "He's even talking about going in to the office for half days starting on Monday." He reached for one of the egg rolls. "I'm hungry. I missed my dinner."

"Well, there's plenty to eat on the dining room table," Alice said. "Go help yourself."

When he left the room, Alice leaned toward her and said sotto voce, "Pull yourself together, kiddo."

Startled, Laura met her clear, gray eyes. What she saw unnerved her. "What do you mean?"

"If you keep looking at him like that, it'll be obvious to everyone in the room how you feel about him. Is that what you want?"

Laura licked her lips. "You know?"

"I've known for some time."

"Why didn't you say something?"

"I was waiting for you to say something."

Laura slumped into one of the kitchen chairs. She felt so tired. All her elation over the baby, which had sustained her until five minutes ago, faded. Suddenly, she was facing reality. She was still happy about the baby, but now she knew she had a very rocky road ahead. Because the hard, cold, truth was that Neil would be leaving Patinville very soon. His sense of commitment to his family, his sense of fair play, his sense of honor, would all force him to leave. Whether he loved her or not.

Unless...the thought trembled in her mind...half-formed...so tempting.

Unless she told him about the baby.

Chapter Fifteen

Having Norman back in the office was a strain—a strain Laura wasn't sure her nerves could take. She was glad he was home, of course, and happy he was doing so well. Aside from an occasional grimace or whitening around his lips, she would never have known he wasn't entirely comfortable with his prosthesis.

Each day he seemed to grow stronger, rapidly progressing from working four hours a day to working the whole day. If she hadn't known he had an artificial leg, she probably wouldn't have noticed anything physically different or unusual about him.

Emotional differences were another story.

He'd gone from being a carefree, open, jovial man who never worried about anything to being a moody, guarded man who brooded about everything. And she never knew what he was thinking or feeling.

Sometimes she'd catch him looking at her with a bleak yearning in his dark eyes, a yearning he would quickly mask. Since he spent so much time in the office, Laura always felt on edge.

Added to that edginess was the ever-present worry about her future and the future of her unborn child. What was she going to do? If only things had been different. If she had fallen in love with Norman instead of Neil, she could be married now and openly declare her pregnancy. She could be basking in the attention and love of all the Cantrelles instead of feeling so alone.

She wondered now what would have happened if she'd never met Neil. It was entirely possible that eventually she and Norman would have gotten together. And realistically, they might have had an all-right marriage. Norman would never have been the love of her life as Neil was, but he would have been good to her, and she probably would have been contented.

Sighing, she gave Norman a furtive look. She *had* met Neil. She loved him, and now she carried his baby.

Norman glanced up. A frown furrowed his brow. "What's wrong?"

"Nothing." She returned her attention to the bank statement she was reconciling. Darn. She had to stop daydreaming. Norman seemed to have developed a sixth sense during his travail; he was much more aware of her feelings.

"Something's not right," he insisted. "Something's worrying you."

"No, really," Laura said, forcing sincerity into her tone. "I think I just have spring fever." She met his eyes and then was sorry she had, for she could see the genuine concern shining in their dark depths.

"I wish you'd let me help you if you have a problem," he said softly. "I care about you, Laura."

"Oh, Norman..." There was an awkward silence while Laura groped for something to say.

"I'll always care about you."

Laura bit her lip. For one fleeting moment, she had an almost irresistible urge to spill everything, to tell Norman exactly what *was* wrong, but as quickly as the urge had formed, she dismissed it. She could never do that. If anyone told Norman about her and Neil, it would have to be Neil.

She sighed again. "You're a good friend, Norman, and I appreciate it."

His eyes clouded. She pretended not to notice his disappointment and bent her head to her work.

The clock ticked loudly as Laura's discomfort grew. She could feel Norman watching her. Oh, God, she was going to have to do something. This situation was almost untenable.

So as inexorably as her child grew inside her, her awareness that she must soon make a decision grew, too. She knew she'd been marking time, waiting, still holding on to a sliver of hope that somehow she and Neil could work things out between them.

But finally, on a Friday morning toward the end of March, almost two weeks to the day from the time Norman left the hospital, Laura knew the hiatus was nearly over.

"I think I've found a new apartment," Norman said as he took a break from the bid he'd been working on.

"That's good," she answered.

"Funny," he mused, "I thought I'd live upstairs until I got married and bought a house...." His voice sounded wistful.

Laura cringed inwardly. Why must he constantly remind her of how guilty she still felt? Then, at the uncharitable thought, she felt even more guilty, because she knew Norman wasn't purposely trying to make her feel uncomfortable.

"Will Neil stay on in your old apartment then?" she asked in what she hoped was a casual tone. She pretended to be looking at a column of figures, as if his answer wasn't very important at all, as if she'd only asked the question to veer him away from the subject of marriage.

Norman had been in the act of pouring himself a cup of coffee, and he finished, carefully making his way back to his desk before answering. The first couple of days he'd been back in the office, Laura had fussed over him, wanting to help him do everything, and he had quickly let her know he didn't appreciate her misguided attempts. His pride in his physical ability was one facet of his character that his accident hadn't changed.

Seated again, he said, "No. He told me last night he's planning to go back to Florida next week."

Next week. The words knocked all the breath out of Laura. Unable to meet Norman's eyes, she fought to still the trembling of her hands as she turned and lifted her mug of tea. When she trusted her voice not to give her away, she said, "I thought maybe he'd decided not to go back." She lifted her eyes, finally meeting Norman's gaze.

"He said he's glad he knows the truth about Erica and Willis because now he can live with what happened and not feel guilty. He can finally put the past behind him." Norman frowned. "I thought sure he'd stay here in Patinville, but nothing I said would change his mind." He grinned. "He's as stubborn as I am."

Laura's thoughts whirled. So she had less than a week. Should she tell Neil about the baby? That question had been going around and around in her mind ever since the night of Alice's party.

If she told him, she knew he wouldn't abandon her. The same sense of honor that now demanded he leave Patinville would force him to shift his loyalty to her and his child.

And that knowledge, that Neil would feel obligated to honor his responsibility to her, was the crux of Laura's problem.

Do I want him at that price?

That night, as she lay in bed, she still couldn't answer the question. She loved Neil, passionately and with an intensity of feeling she hadn't known herself capable of feeling. She also loved their child, fiercely and possessively. She would defend both with her very life.

She placed her palms on her stomach, feeling the firmness beneath her hands through the sheer cotton gown she always wore at night. Soon that firmness would change shape, and there would be a betraying roundness.

She drifted into a hazy half sleep, and soft, misty images floated through her semiconsciousness. A fat, laughing baby sitting on Neil's lap with Laura bending over them. Neil tilting his head to kiss her, then kissing the top of the baby's head while Laura slipped her arms around his neck and leaned over the two of them. Shimmering images of the three of them surrounded by a nimbus of dazzling light and a thick, sparkling golden circle that enclosed them and kept them safe.

Neil felt numb. He'd known for weeks that he had to leave. He had no other choice. What difference did it make that he loved Laura? He wasn't free to love her. So what if the thought of leaving her made him feel physically ill? He'd get over it. He had to get over it.

But he couldn't rid himself of the picture of Laura's haunted eyes the night of Alice's party. For minutes there, when they'd met in Alice's kitchen, she'd let down her guard, and Neil saw that instead of the acceptance, even indifference to him that he'd convinced himself she felt, she was just as miserable as he was. He'd almost come unglued that night. He wanted to haul her into his arms and kiss her senseless. He wanted to hold her and never let her go. He wanted to claim her in front of Alice and the entire world.

But he couldn't. Laura wasn't his to claim, and she never would be. At that very moment, he knew he had to get the hell out of Patinville. Soon.

Tomorrow he was leaving. All the arrangements had been made.

Tonight his parents were having a welcome home party for Norman. Neil hoped he could get through the evening. It would be one of the hardest things he'd ever had to do. Because he was leaving in the morning he would have to endure a lot of backslapping and good wishes and tearful goodbyes from his demonstrative family.

And he would have to say goodbye to Laura. Laura, who had brought light into the darkness of his soul.

His stomach felt hollow at the thought. Nothing he'd ever done, even the most dangerous assignment, had ever frightened him like the prospect of facing her tonight, of looking into her beautiful eyes and knowing he would never see the light of love shining in them again.

If only he thought she didn't care. He could handle his own misery. What was tearing him apart was thinking about the possibility she was feeling the same way.

She'd get over him. Once he was gone, she'd eventually forget him. Even though she didn't love Norman, she would meet someone else. Someone who could give her that secure family life she craved. Someone who could build that golden circle around her. All Neil could give her would be a life where they'd both feel guilty—a life apart from his family and all the things that were so important to both of them. A life full of too much darkness, something they'd both endured enough of.

So why did the idea of someone else loving her make him feel so terrible? That was what he wanted for her, wasn't it?

Laura. Neil closed his eyes, swallowing against the tightening in his throat. Right now, right this minute, she was downstairs. All he had to do was open the door, go down the steps, and open the office door, and he would see her. He could picture her sitting at the desk, her silken hair falling forward, partially hiding her face, the way her lower lip jutted out, the delicacy of her slender hands as they turned the pages of the general ledger.

Gritting his teeth, he yanked open the door and barreled down the steps, taking them two at a time. He didn't look into the office when he passed the door. He kept right on going, over to the truck he'd been using. He opened the door, jumped in, cranked the ignition to life, and drove out of the parking lot like a man possessed.

Dear God, please help me get through this night. Laura whispered the prayer over and over as she turned off the ignition, picked up her purse, slid from the seat of her car, and stood outside the Cantrelle home in the balmy evening air.

She took several deep breaths. She had to be calm. She had to be cool. She had to acquit herself with dignity tonight. Looking around, she saw that there were already at least a dozen cars at the Cantrelle home. She could hear the rollicking lilt of zydeco music coming from the open windows of the brightly lighted house. The party seemed to be in full swing.

As she walked down the gravel drive toward the house, the sweet scent of Arlette's climbing roses surrounded her. Laura stopped for a minute, closing her eyes and breathing in their fragrance.

Suddenly she was aware of the acrid smell of cigarette smoke coming from the darkness at the side of the house, and she saw the glowing tip as someone raised the cigarette to his mouth. She squinted into the darkness.

"Hello, Laura." Neil stepped out of the shadows.

Her heart stopped, and she felt hot and cold all at once. "Neil," she said, the word coming out like a croak. "I...I didn't know you smoked." She knew that he must think she was nuts. She hadn't spoken to him in weeks, and now all she could think to say was she didn't know he smoked.

He made a sound that might have been an attempt at a laugh but fell far short. "I don't."

She didn't even try to answer. She stood there just beyond the reach of the circle of light shining from the big picture window and pooling on the sidewalk. Neil walked toward her, and her brain took note of his appearance: his dark dress pants—they must be new, she'd never seen them before—his open-necked white shirt, his glossy dark hair which still looked untamed even though it was obvious he'd made an effort to comb it neatly, his strong features set in serious lines.

Her heart began to beat again, an erratic tap dance she was sure must be causing her chest to bob up and down like a punch-drunk fighter.

"I was just on my way inside," she said. *Stupid. Stupid.*

"Yes." He stopped only inches from her. She could smell his unique scent: a blend of body musk, spicy after-shave, and now the lingering odor of cigarette smoke. He seemed tense, his body poised and alert, as if he were waiting for something. His eyes raked her, settling on her face. They glowed with some inner emotion she couldn't identify.

For a minute she had the wild idea that he was going to say something that would make everything okay again. But the moment passed and all he said was, "I'll walk in with you."

Seconds later she was inside the too-warm room, surrounded by the pounding rhythm of the music. People swarmed around her, their excited voices welcoming.

"*Chère,* we are glad you could come tonight," said René, dark eyes aglow. "It is so nice to have everyone gathered together again, no?"

"Laura! You're finally here!" This lively greeting came from Denise, whose face was flushed as she leaned into

Jett's embrace. He grinned and captured her mouth in an exuberant kiss.

Envy pierced Laura at the sight of their loving exchange. What she wouldn't give to be able to show her feelings so openly, in front of Neil's assembled family and friends. She knew Neil was still behind her. She could feel him, his dark eyes, his brooding presence. Was he as unhappy as she was?

"Oh, Laura, you look so pretty tonight!" Desiree said as she walked up to her and grabbed her hands. "I love that dress. And the color! It's exactly the shade of your eyes. Doesn't she look great, Neil?"

"Yes, beautiful."

She felt his warm breath against her neck, and a delicate tremor, like the touch of a feather, whispered over her skin.

Then Norman joined the group, and coming on his heels, Alice, who looked wonderful tonight, Laura thought, in a bright red dress with a deep V neckline. Her short, bouncy blond curls were tied away from her face with a red ribbon. "Hi, Laura," she said. "I've been trying to persuade Norman to dance with me."

Norman blushed as he met Laura's eyes. "I can't dance."

"You can slow dance," Alice said with a twinkle in her eye. "It doesn't take fancy footwork to slow dance. All you have to do is cuddle up close to your partner."

Laura wished she had Alice's ability to tease and be lighthearted. *But she's not riddled with guilt and misery.*

"You dance with the pretty girl, Neil," said René. When Neil didn't immediately respond, René rolled his eyes and grabbed Alice, swinging her out among the other dancing couples. "Somethin' is wrong with my sons, they don' want to hold a beautiful girl close!" he declared.

Norman took Laura's arm and led her off. She wondered where Neil went, for he didn't follow them, but she wouldn't let herself look. For the next two hours, Laura was acutely aware of Neil, although he always seemed to be as far away from her as it was possible to be. She talked to everyone, forced herself to eat even though food was the last thing on her mind that night, drank a little iced tea, and refused to dance, even when Jett tried to pull her to her feet.

"I don't dance," she insisted. She knew she should make an attempt to join the gaiety, but she couldn't. Not even for Norman could she pretend to be happy. She felt numb, the knowledge that tomorrow Neil would be gone turning the blood in her veins to ice. Even though the room was very hot, Laura felt colder and colder as the night wore on. Once she shivered, and Norman, who had barely left her side all night, said, "You can't be cold!" He fanned himself. "It's hotter than hell in here."

"I'm fine," Laura said automatically, but she shivered again.

Neil was standing talking to a beautiful dark-haired girl, and Laura felt as if someone had put a stone in her chest. As much as she dreaded his going, she knew she could never handle watching him with other women, so it was probably best that she wouldn't have to after tonight.

"I don't think you *are* fine," Norman said. "There's no color in your face."

"Maybe it's something I ate," she improvised. "I just felt dizzy for a few seconds, that's all." For once she wasn't irritated by Norman's solicitous attitude. Maybe now she could leave without him protesting. He'd never expect her to stay if she wasn't feeling well. "In fact, I *am* chilled, and my head hurts. I think maybe I'd better go home and go to bed."

"That's a good idea. Wait here." Before she realized what he was doing, he levered himself up from the couch and walked away. A few minutes later he was back, leading Neil by the arm. "Would you take Laura home, Neil? She's not feeling well."

Laura's mouth dropped open. She didn't know what Neil was feeling because his face was closed, his eyes shuttered. Gathering her wits about her, she said, "That's ridiculous. I'm perfectly fine. I can see myself home."

Norman's jaw settled into a stubborn line. "I'd take you home myself, but it'll be weeks before I can manage driving."

Oh, no. "Please, Norman..." She couldn't be alone with Neil. Not tonight. "This is silly. I've got my own car. I'll be fine."

"At least let Neil follow you. I don't want you driving by yourself. What if you get dizzy again?" Norman argued reasonably.

People were starting to look at them. Laura knew if she continued protesting, she'd call even more attention to herself. She looked at Neil. He shrugged.

Great, she thought. "Fine," she snapped, irritated with both brothers. Irritated with herself. "If he wants to waste his time, it's okay with me. Will you tell everyone why I left, Norman?" She looked around, found her purse, slung it over her arm, and after giving Norman a hasty peck on the cheek, she elbowed her way through the crowd toward the front door.

"Are you leaving?" said Alice, who had just finished an energetic dance with a good-looking redhead that Laura vaguely remembered as being one of the Cantrelle cousins.

She nodded. "I'm not feeling well." She didn't meet Alice's eyes. She didn't want to know what Alice thought.

Somehow she made it out the door. Ignoring Neil behind her, she walked rapidly down the walk and up the drive. Gravel crunched under their feet as Neil followed her. Her heart was thumping against her chest wall. *Please, God. Please, God.* It was a silent litany, an almost incoherent plea, for what, she wasn't sure. She fastened her gaze on her Honda.

It seemed to take forever to reach its safe haven, but finally she was unlocking her door. She still hadn't looked at Neil or spoken to him, but she knew he was only inches away. Her entire body felt frozen. She grasped her door handle, her hands like giant stumps. Taking a deep breath, she turned and lifted her head. Her eyes met Neil's. "This really is stupid. There's nothing wrong with me. I said I wasn't feeling well because I wanted to get out of there. You don't have to accompany me."

"It would look funny if I didn't since I said I would," he said quietly.

There was no use fighting it any longer. So she allowed him to help her into the car, closing her eyes at the touch of his warm hand on her arm. He shut her door firmly and walked toward the company truck, which was parked at the end of the driveway.

As she drove toward her apartment, her brain was on automatic pilot. Over and over she told herself that soon she could escape. In minutes, she'd be home. She would say a quick goodbye, shake his hand, wish him luck. She *would* do it. She wouldn't break down. She wouldn't say anything she shouldn't say. Then she would go inside. Once inside, if she wanted to scream and cry, she could. But not in front of Neil.

"Not in front of Neil," she whispered. "Hold on until he leaves."

She pulled into the driveway of the duplex, her actions mechanical. Shut off the ignition. Shut off the headlights. Open the door. Close the door. Walk around the back of the car. Stop. Wait for Neil.

Neil, who had pulled in behind her, opened the door and climbed down from the truck. He walked toward her. When he reached her, she stuck her right hand out quickly. "Goodbye, Neil. Good luck."

"Let's go up there," he said, tilting his head toward the porch.

Laura dropped her hand. Woodenly, she walked to the porch and climbed the steps. The porch was dark. She had forgotten to leave the porch light on, and obviously, so had Denise. But it didn't matter. Nothing mattered.

Laura stared at her feet. Her entire body was numb. Her mind was numb. Her heart was numb.

"Laura . . ." He touched her chin, lifted her face gently.

"Please go," she whispered, closing her eyes. A breeze set her wind chimes to ringing, and the sound tore at Laura's heart, reminding her of the day Neil compared the sound of her laughter to the sound the wind chimes made.

Tears burned her eyelids, clogged her throat. Her hold on her emotions was so tenuous, she was afraid to speak.

"Laura," he said again, his thumb rubbing her chin. "I wish things could have been different. I never meant to hurt you."

A tremor slid down her spine, and she clamped her teeth together to keep them from rattling. *Go. Go. Go. Go.* She couldn't have spoken aloud if her life had depended on it. She whirled around, fumbled for her keys. *I have to get inside. I have to get inside.*

"Oh, God, Laura." The words sounded as if they were being ripped from his throat, and suddenly he was folding her into his embrace, holding her close against his heart, burying his face in her hair, and Laura's heart was thundering like a herd of wild horses. The keys slipped through her nerveless fingers and clattered to the porch.

She began to cry, great wrenching sobs she couldn't stop. His arms tightened around her, and then he was kissing her, a kiss filled with desperation and hopelessness and pain. Laura clung to him, tasting the salt of her tears on his tongue.

They finally broke apart, and his voice, when he spoke, hardly sounded like him. "Oh, Laura, I'm sorry."

Tears still rolled unchecked down her face. She couldn't speak. Now she wished for the numbness, but it was gone.

Every part of her throbbed with pain—like a great, open wound. She had to get away from him. If she didn't, she might weaken. She might tell him. And she had decided days ago that she wouldn't do that. She didn't want Neil out of a sense of honor. She wanted him to come to her freely, because he loved her, and because he felt it was the right thing to do.

Somewhere she found the strength to stop her tears. "I have to go in. Goodbye."

She didn't look at him again. She bent down, picked up her keys, opened her door. Blindly, she walked in, shutting the door behind her. It was dark inside, and she felt the cats rubbing against her ankles. She stared straight ahead. She heard Neil walk across the porch, heard his footsteps slowly go down the front steps, heard him start the truck.

And then he was gone and she was alone in the darkness.

Chapter Sixteen

"Alice, I've decided to go home to California."

"Oh, Laura!" Alice looked stricken. "Why?"

Laura picked at her paper napkin. "I just think it'll be better for me if I do. Besides, I have some unfinished business to take care of."

"You're running away," Alice said softly.

"No, not really."

"Laura, don't go. Please. Leaving won't solve anything. And you have so many people here who care about you. There's nothing for you in California."

Laura sighed. In the weeks since Neil's departure, she had become resigned to her situation. But without explaining about the baby, she knew it would be hard to make Alice understand. "There's nothing for me here except constant reminders of what I've lost. Besides, staying here will only encourage Norman to think maybe someday we'll work something out. And that's never going to happen. It's not fair to him. He needs to get on with his life. Find someone else." She shrugged. "No, it's best for everyone if I go."

Alice's gray eyes were suspiciously shiny. "Darn that Neil!"

"Don't blame Neil." Laura attempted a smile. "I'm just as much to blame as he is."

"Oh, I know. It's just that I wish things could be different." Her eyes were filled with sympathy. "Laura, things will get better. I know you don't think so now, but they will."

Laura nodded.

"I hate seeing you so unhappy."

"I'll live."

Alice reached across the table and covered Laura's hand with her own. The loving gesture brought a lump to Laura's throat. She would miss Alice so much. She would miss all of them so much. But she *couldn't* stay in Patinville. She would begin showing soon. As a matter of fact, if she hadn't been so miserable the past month or so, and lost some weight, she would probably already be showing. And if Norman or anyone else in his family were to find out...well, it didn't bear thinking about.

"How soon are you going?"

"As soon as I tell Norman and help him find someone to replace me."

"No one can replace you!" Alice said stubbornly.

Laura leaned over, and they hugged. "Thank you," she whispered.

"For what?"

"For being my friend. For not judging me."

Alice drew back from the embrace. She assumed a mock frown. "What do you mean, not judging you? I think you're a rotten, terrible person."

Laura laughed, and some of the tension she'd been feeling melted away. Everything would work out. It had to. She didn't just have herself to think about anymore. She had a precious life inside her, a legacy of the love she felt for Neil. She'd made the right decision.

Sixteen days later, on a warm April afternoon, Laura took a deep breath, tried to still the butterflies in her stomach, and knocked on the door of the small frame house in West Covina. It had only taken her two days to track her mother down. It hadn't been hard at all once she'd located Barbara Wasowski, who had been Ginger's best friend for years.

She looked around. The house was in a middle-class neighborhood, eons removed from the kinds of places she and Ginger used to live in. Typical of Los Angeles area homes, the yard was postage-stamp sized and filled with an assortment of hardy plants. Hydrangea bloomed on either side of the front walk, and Laura wondered if her mother had developed a latent green thumb.

She knocked again. This time the door opened, and Ginger stood there staring at her with shocked, aquamarine eyes. She looked the same, but she looked different. Her hair was still a carefully colored platinum blonde, and she still wore too much makeup, but she'd lost weight, and her skin had a healthier hue.

"Hello, Mother," Laura said. "Aren't you going to invite me in?"

"Laura! Well, I'll be..." Ginger smoothed her fawn-colored gabardine slacks over her hips. "Well, sure, come on in." She stood aside, and Laura walked past her into the sunny house. Ginger gestured toward the living room on the left, which was two steps down from the entry hall. Laura followed her, looking around with interest. The house was clean but too modern for Laura's taste. She sat on one end of the white sectional sofa, and Ginger sat across from her in a black leather and chrome director's chair.

"I thought maybe you was dead," Ginger said. She picked up a pack of cigarettes from the glass coffee table, shook one out of the pack, and lighted it with a big silver lighter. Leaning back in her chair, she crossed her legs and blew a perfect smoke ring into the air. Her eyes held a speculative look.

"No, I'm very much alive." Funny how calm she felt now.

Ginger betrayed her own nervousness by tapping the fingernails of her left hand on the chrome arm of her chair, the long, red nails making a clicking sound.

For a long moment, their eyes locked. There were so many things Laura had planned to say, but now she didn't think any of them were very important.

"Whadda you want?" Ginger said.

Sadness filled Laura. "I only wanted to see you," she said softly. "To find out how you were doing." To put my past to rest.

"I'm doing just great! I'm married now. Did you know that?" Ginger's tone was defiant, but there was a flicker of something in her eyes, something that had already disappeared.

"Yes, Barbara told me. That's how I found you."

"Yeah, I thought so. That Barbara always did have a big mouth."

"Are you happy, Mother?"

There it was, that same flash of some emotion, but it was quickly veiled. She shrugged, leaned forward to stub out her cigarette. "Joe gives me plenty of money. Takes me to Vegas. Likes to show me off. Sure. I'm happy."

"I'm glad," Laura said. "You deserve some good luck."

Ginger's head jerked up. Her eyes narrowed. "Still the same goody-two-shoes, aren't you? Who're you tryin' to kid? There's never been any love lost between us, so don't act like you care about me." She stood up, two angry red spots firing her cheeks. "Why'd you come here? Do you need money?"

Laura shook her head sadly. "No." She sighed, picked up her purse and stood. "No. I don't need anything."

Ginger glared at her.

Why had she come? There was nothing for her here. There never had been. She had known that all along, but somehow she'd had to see her mother one last time.

She looked at her mother. She no longer hated her. She just felt sorry for her. Ginger was missing out on so much. But it was her loss, not Laura's. Laura put her purse protectively in front of her stomach. "Good luck, Mother. I hope things continue to work out well for you."

As she turned to leave, she saw the uncertainty slide across Ginger's face. Laura stopped. Quickly, before she could change her mind, she walked over and put her arms around Ginger. Ginger's body was stiff and unyielding as Laura hugged her, but as Laura broke the hug and moved back, Ginger's right hand fluttered up as if she wanted to touch Laura, then dropped back to her side. Her face twisted.

"Goodbye, Mother," Laura whispered. She didn't look back as she walked away from her past and into the light.

Neil laid aside his volume of poetry. He'd been reading Longfellow, one of his favorites, but it was no good. He might as well give up. He sighed, and at the sound Zoe staggered to her feet, yawned and stretched, then padded quietly over to where he sat on the top step of the porch. She nuzzled against his hand, and he absently scratched behind her ears. Her silky fur was warm from the sun.

It had been a hot day. Neil's olive drab T-shirt was damp with sweat. The whole summer had been relentlessly hot, and it was only the end of July. Hurricane season was just around the corner. Then winter. Then Christmas.

Christmas.

As a kid, Neil had always loved Christmas. Bittersweet memories of past Christmases floated through his mind.

The big family reunion that always took place, with relatives from all corners of Louisiana and Texas converging on his parents' home in Patinville. The toe-tapping frenzy of the Cajun music that played around the clock. The laughter and backslapping of his father and uncles as they played *bourrée,* a favorite card game. The chatter and gossip of his mother and aunts and sisters as they stirred endless pots of steaming gumbo and spicy jambalaya. The redolent smells of the turkey roasting in the oven and the boudin sausage grilling on the outdoor barbecue. The giggles and shouts of his cousins as he and Norman and his sisters joined them in noisy games of tag and hide-and-seek. Those had been happy, carefree days.

And then last Christmas. Last Christmas seemed an eternity away. Last Christmas . . . and Laura.

All day he'd been fighting thoughts of Laura. But that was nothing new. Ever since he'd returned to Cudjoe Key, thoughts of her had never been far away. It didn't matter what he was doing or where he was, everything reminded him of her. Here at the shack, he heard her whisper in the sound of the surf, her laughter in the music of the brass wind chimes he'd hung in a moment of weakness. When he was out with a group fishing for permit or bonefish or tarpon, her ocean-blue eyes and sun-golden freckles were everywhere he looked. Her crystal image danced through his mind like the rays of the sun danced over the sea. He'd thought memories of her would fade. Instead, they seemed to grow stronger with each passing day. He couldn't seem to let her go.

Getting up, he walked inside. He opened the battered footlocker that served as his chest of drawers, and slowly, from under a stack of clean underwear, withdrew a cigar box. He opened it and removed the photograph. It was a picture that had been taken the night of the party—the night before he left Patinville. His mother had snapped the photo. Norman had sent it to him. Neil had handled it so many times, it was frayed around the edges.

He studied it now. Norman had his arms around Laura on one side and Alice on the other. All three were smiling, but Neil looked only at Laura. She'd looked so beautiful that night. So very beautiful in her turquoise dress that echoed the color of her eyes. An old, familiar pain throbbed within as he remembered the feel of her slender body, the scent of her skin and hair, the taste of her mouth.

Laura.

The pain settled into a dull ache as he drank in the details of her face, which was tilted toward Norman. How was she?

Where was she?

That was the question that had been torturing him for days. Ever since he'd received Alice's letter.

He'd had very little news of home after his return to Cudjoe Key. Norman's letter-writing skills were still impossible. He had only written twice, and neither letter contained any reference to Laura. Only the picture with a cryptic note. *Look at me with the two prettiest girls in town.*

Denise, whose letters were more informative, had only written once. She did mention Laura but only to say she was worried about her because she hadn't seemed to be feeling well. *She seems unhappy. Even Jeannine mentioned it the other day.* Those words haunted Neil for weeks.

Finally, in desperation, hungry to know anything at all, Neil wrote to Alice. She was the only person he could openly ask about Laura.

And one week ago today, he'd had his reply. He'd picked up his mail at Gastin's, and when he saw the return address on the pale yellow envelope, he wanted to tear the letter open then and there. But Gastin was standing there expecting Neil to have a cold beer with him—their regular ritual whenever Neil came to the store—and Neil knew the letter would have to wait. For the first time, his visit with Gastin seemed interminable and he could hardly concentrate on the garrulous old man's conversation. But finally, he said he'd better get going. Zoe was waiting at home, and she was probably hungry.

"Shouldn't wait 'til you're outta dog food 'fore you come shoppin'," Gastin said. Then he grinned and threw a big rawhide bone into Neil's grocery sack. "Present from me."

"You spoil her," Neil said, but he gave Gastin an affectionate shoulder squeeze, then waved goodbye.

He almost stopped his bike as soon as he knew he was out of earshot of Gastin's place. But he told himself not to be crazy. He could wait another fifteen minutes or so. Hadn't he already waited months?

Even after he got back to the cottage, he forced himself to wait. He put his groceries away and shook some dry dog food into Zoe's bowl and grabbed a can of cold beer from his refrigerator. Only then did he take the letter, along with his beer, and walked outside. Leaning his back against the porch post, he sat on the top step and opened the flap of the letter. He scanned the beginning quickly, only slowing down when he reached the part that most interested him.

> You asked about Laura. I couldn't believe you didn't know. I thought surely Norman must have written to you. But then I realized Norman probably isn't much of a letter writer. Neil, Laura left Patinville back around the end of April. We all tried to talk her out of going, but she was determined. She explained to me that it wasn't fair of her to stay, that Norman would never get on with his life if she were still around. I knew she was right, but I hated to see her go. And Neil, I have to be honest with you, she wasn't handling your going back to Florida as well as you'd

hoped she would. I was very angry with you, but she told me not to be. She said what had happened between the two of you was as much her fault as yours. I know that you will want to know where she is, so before you write back, I might as well save you the trouble. I don't know. She said she was going back to California, that she had some unfinished business to take care of. And that's all. I haven't heard from her, and I have no idea how to get in touch with her.

The end of April. Laura'd been gone from Patinville for months and he hadn't known. His heart beat in slow, heavy thuds as the import of Alice's words sank into his brain.

Neil hadn't slept well that night. He dreamed of Laura and the way she looked the evening at Alice's. And every day since, everything that had happened between them was replayed in his head. He remembered Alice's words of advice months ago, when she'd told him she believed in the truth and its strength. All week he'd been thinking and thinking.

He put the photograph back in the cigar box. He walked outside, put two fingers into his mouth and whistled. Within seconds, Zoe came bounding through the pines and buttonwoods that surrounded the cottage. She ran up to Neil, and he gave her an absentminded head rub. Her body felt moist from the salt spray and smelled faintly of the sea.

"Come on, Zoe," he said. She followed him as he walked slowly toward the shore.

Had he been wrong to leave Laura? Had his sense of honor become skewed? Was he so hung up on how he'd look in his brother's eyes, he'd failed to recognize what was the right thing to do? Had he been fair to Laura or Norman by hiding the truth?

These questions went round and round in his head. Frustrated and confused, he walked down to the water's edge. He stared at the spectacular vista spread before him.

Brushstrokes of golden rose painted the surface of the sea as the sun slipped over the horizon. Man-o'-war birds swooped through the dusk with effortless grace, casting amethyst shadows in their wake. Feathery coconut palms swayed in the breeze, the sound of their branches a rustling accompaniment to the rhythm of the sea. Neil could see the dark silhouette of American Shoal lighthouse marking the reef in the distance. The twilight hour was alive with the sound of insects and foaming surf.

He kicked at a pebble, watched it arch across the water and disappear. Zoe panted at his feet. He glanced down. The dog's eyes gleamed in the dusk. There was a small piece of driftwood a few feet away, and Neil stooped over to pick it up.

"Go get it, girl," he said softly, throwing the driftwood down the beach. Zoe lunged toward the stick, and when she did something shook itself free inside Neil.

When the dog came bounding back, Neil patted her on the head and beckoned her to follow him. Trustingly, she wagged her tail and trotted behind him. Hours later, when he dropped her at Gastin's, she was still wagging her tail.

Neil rented a car in Baton Rouge. He decided he didn't want to be dependent on anyone this time. As the miles ticked away and he got closer to Patinville, he wondered how his family would react to his sudden reappearance.

He didn't have long to wait. He headed straight for Norman's new apartment, a ground level modern garden apartment on the west side of the city. When he pulled into the parking lot of the apartment complex, his palms were clammy but he felt calm.

He had no trouble finding Unit #20. Lights blazed in the apartment. Good. Norman was home. As Neil approached the door, he could hear the muffled sound of a television show as well as the drone of the air-conditioning unit. He rang the doorbell. The door swung open within seconds.

"Hello, little brother," Neil said, grinning. He wished he had a picture of the look on Norman's face.

"Neil! My God! Neil! I can't believe it." He grabbed Neil's hand, almost dragging him into the apartment. "What are you doing here? Do Mama and Papa know you're home? When did you get here?"

Neil laughed. "One question at a time, okay?" He looked around, inclining his head toward the kitchenette. "You wouldn't happen to have a beer in the refrigerator, would you?"

"Yeah, sure. I'll get you one." He grinned. "Hell, I'll get me one, too."

Neil watched him walk into the kitchenette. If you didn't know he had an artificial leg, his gait would never have revealed it, Neil thought. He was amazed at how fast Norman had adjusted, how naturally he moved. When Norman came back, Neil accepted the cold can of beer and popped the top. Norman pointed to the small round table in the dining area.

"Why don't we sit over there?" he said, dark eyes full of questions.

When they were seated across from each other, Neil cradled the cold can in his palms. He looked at his brother. He hoped he could find the right words to say what needed to be said. "Norman, there's something I have to tell you. That's why I came home. I...should have told you long ago, but I didn't want to hurt you." He shook his head. "No, that's not right. I didn't want you to think less of me. That's the truth."

Norman frowned. "What is it?"

"There's no easy way to say this, so I'm just going to say it. While you were in the hospital, I fell in love with Laura, and she fell in love with me."

Norman's face went completely still.

"I know it shouldn't have happened. I fought against it, and I think she did, too. But it *did* happen. I thought I'd forget about her. I told her we had no future together."

Norman still didn't say anything. Neil couldn't figure out what he was thinking, but he had to tell him everything.

"That last night, when you insisted I follow her home, she cried, and I felt as if my guts were being torn out. But I didn't want you to know. I thought you'd think I was a scumbag. So I walked away from her and went back to Florida."

Norman rubbed his chin. "A lot of things are clear to me now," he said.

What was he thinking? "I'm sorry. I know it seems as if we were doing something behind your back, but it really wasn't like that. I can't explain it. It all just happened. I wasn't looking for it, and she wasn't either."

Norman looked at his hands. "I won't pretend this isn't a shock. I never thought..." He stopped. From outside, Neil could hear some children at play. Their voices sounded innocent and happy.

Norman's eyes finally met Neil's, and their gaze was clear and steady. "I can see exactly how it might have happened." He smiled wryly. "I won't pretend it doesn't hurt, because it does, but it's not like Laura was ever mine." He sighed. "I don't blame you, Neil. I... I understand."

Neil felt an enormous rush of love for this man who had already endured and overcome so much. He searched Norman's face and eyes, but he saw no censure there—only love. Neil swallowed against the lump in his throat even as relief gushed through him. He felt freer and lighter than he had in months, in years. "Thanks, little brother," he said, his voice unsteady.

"So what are you gonna do now?" Norman asked, making a visible attempt to keep his own emotions under control.

Their eyes met again.

"I'm going to find Laura," Neil said quietly. "No matter how long it takes."

Chapter Seventeen

The nun was his only hope.

Over the past two weeks Neil had looked everywhere. He'd tried everything. But he hadn't been able to find Laura. Frustrated, he walked out onto the balcony of his hotel room and stared at Alcatraz in the distance.

He'd been in California for nearly two weeks. He'd started his fruitless search here in San Francisco, and now he was back once more.

End of the line, he thought, unless he could find Laura's friend Celeste. All his other leads had been dead ends. And he'd been so sure he'd find her right away. Before he even left Patinville, he checked with the post office and found that Laura's mail-forwarding instructions were to a post office box in San Francisco. But when he got here, the post office wouldn't tell him anything except that the box was still rented to her. Neil spent the better part of four days standing inside the lobby watching her box. But no one came to pick up her mail.

Giving up on that angle, he called a friend still on the Baton Rouge police force, who contacted someone in San Francisco's P.D. The contact, a burly Irish cop named Kevin Flanigan, checked phone listings for him throughout the bay area. That turned out to be another dead end. There was no listing for Laura Sebastian. There was one L. Sebastian, but when Neil checked out the number he discovered it belonged to a grizzled old man named Louis Sebastian. All the other Sebastian, L. listings were numbers that had been in service more than six months, so they couldn't be Laura.

Next he tried Los Angeles but had no luck finding her mother. He knew she'd once played a part in a teen scream movie, but that was no help. Even if he were to find out the name of the movie, there'd be no record of where Ginger Sebastian might be now.

His next approach was the junior college in San Diego where Laura had gone to school. But the records office, although they acknowledged her attendance there years ago, had no updated address for her.

"And even if we did, sir, I'm afraid I couldn't give it to you," the dark-haired registrar said.

Neil wondered if she thought he was an ax murderer or something, but he knew the procedure. If she'd admitted to having an address, he would have called in more favors and found someone on the San Diego P.D. to help him out.

So he made his way back to San Francisco and checked the post office again, but he could see that the box still contained the same amount of mail it had earlier.

That left the nun. How would he go about finding her?

Lost in thought, he watched a cable car trundle up California Street, bell clanging and riders hanging out on all sides.

Where should he start his search for Celeste? The only thing he ever remembered Laura saying was that Celeste was now a nurse, working in some hospital somewhere. He had no idea where, what the name of the hospital was that she was assigned to, or even what her full name was. He frowned, trying to remember what Laura had told him about her.

The cable car came closer, its bell louder.

Bell.

Bells.

The sound of bells.

Laura's words came back clearly. *The sound of bells always reminds me of one of the happiest memories of my life... the convent was like something out of a Brontë novel... a huge walled fortress that sat on a bluff overlooking the Pacific just south of Anchor Bay....*

Surely they kept records of where their nuns were assigned. Even if there were more than one nun named Celeste, it shouldn't take long to figure out which one she was.

Neil looked at his watch. If he hurried, he could make it up the coast to Anchor Bay before dark.

The narrow road leading to Villa Marie Convent was just as Laura had described it. A light fog had rolled in, a silent mist that shrouded the bluff in mysterious beauty. As Neil rounded the last curve of the road, the convent loomed before him, its gray walls thick and forbidding.

Neil stopped the car in front of the wrought iron gates. For a moment he sat there, staring up at the fortress-like structure. His stomach felt hollow with apprehension at the intimidating prospect of breaching the barrier of the convent walls.

He looked around. He could hear the crashing surf far below and the muffled bray of a foghorn. The air was cool and damp. Rhododendrons were clustered at the base of the wall, their deep pink color a counterpoint to the encroaching silvery mist.

Neil got out of the car and walked to the gate. Just then, the bells in the tower began to ring. The Angelus. It was six o'clock.

Neil pressed the buzzer to the side of the gate. A speaker crackled to life, and a young female voice said, "Yes? Who is it?"

"Uh, my name is Neil Cantrelle. I've come all the way from Louisiana to find someone. I wonder if I could speak to the Mother Superior?"

"Wait one moment, please," the sweet voice said.

A few minutes later, the voice was back. "Please come in." Simultaneously, he heard the lock on the gate release. He grasped the handle and opened it.

Inside was a giant courtyard, cobbled and empty. There were several buildings, all of gray stone, but Neil walked unerringly toward the largest. As he approached, the double walnut doors swung wide and a young nun dressed in a black habit smiled and beckoned him forward.

"This way," she said.

He followed her down a wide hallway with a highly polished floor of terra-cotta tiles. There was a strong smell of furniture polish and candle wax. In the distance he could hear muted voices and the clink of dishes.

The young nun stopped in front of an open doorway. She waited for Neil to enter, then closed the door behind him. The room he'd entered was large and had great floor to ceiling windows. The fog obscured the sunlight, but the room was still bright. Seated behind a big mahogany desk was a nun he judged to be in her sixties. She had shrewd blue eyes behind granny glasses and she gave him a thoughtful look.

"Mr. Cantrelle? Is that right?" she said, her voice brisk with a slight accent he couldn't place.

"Yes."

"I'm Mother Ambrose. Please sit down."

Neil sat in the proffered chair. He felt just like he'd felt as a kid in parochial school when he'd done something wrong and knew he was going to be found out. He cleared his throat nervously. "Mother, I'm looking for someone, and she was once a novice here at the convent. I'm hoping you can help me find her."

"I see. And what is her name?"

"I don't know her last name, but her first name is Celeste. She would have been a novice here about nine or ten years ago. She came from the Los Angeles area."

Mother Ambrose lowered her head and peered over her glasses at him. Something about the way she looked at him caused his heart to bump against his chest. "Tell me something," she said slowly. "Why do you want to find Sister Celeste?"

Her sharp eyes demanded the truth. "I hope she'll give me some information about a mutual friend of ours—a woman named Laura Sebastian."

"I see," Mother Ambrose said again. "And just what is the nature of your business with this Laura Sebastian?"

Neil had known she might not tell him what he wanted to know. After all, she didn't know him. He looked her straight in the eyes when he answered. This was the most important plea he'd ever make, his last chance to find Laura, so he'd better make it good. "I'm in love with Laura. We had some problems, problems I didn't think we could solve, and I left her. Now I realize I never should have. I have to find her. I have to try to make things right between us. I've looked everywhere. I've been all over California looking for her. Sister Celeste is my last hope. She's the only one who might know where Laura is."

Her eyes reminded Neil of cloudless summer skies as she quietly studied his face. The room was very still. From somewhere in the far reaches of the building, the sweet, pure notes of a flute could be faintly heard. Neil held his breath.

Finally Mother Ambrose nodded, apparently satisfied then said briskly. "I believe I can help you, Mr. Cantrelle Will you follow me?" She stood, the keys on her belt rustling as she moved.

Neil's heart turned over, and he scrambled to his feet Without another word, she motioned for him to follow her and like a sleepwalker, he did. She walked swiftly down the long hallway toward the back of the building. She opened a door that led to a second courtyard, and he was right behind. They passed a building that looked like a school house, another that looked like a chapel, and yet another Finally she stopped. She pointed to a greenhouse a few fee away. She smiled faintly. "You'll find her in there."

Then she walked away.

Neil walked slowly toward the greenhouse. He was afraid to hope. Would Celeste be willing to help him? Or would she know the whole story and hate him? He could hardly believe he'd been lucky enough to find her here, at the convent.

He pushed open the greenhouse door and walked in. The air was thick and moist and warm. Plants and flowers and vegetables of every description were growing from pots and beds and tubs. Despite the fog, the greenhouse was full of light. Someone was working at the far end.

Neil's heart stopped. He would have recognized her anywhere. Her back was to him; she wasn't aware of his presence yet. She was wearing pale blue cotton pants of some sort and a long, blousy cotton top with rolled up sleeves and gardening gloves. Her silky hair was longer, and had been pulled back and tied with a red bow. Her slender back looked vulnerable and defenseless as she knelt there working. Pete and Phoebe were nosing around at her feet, and Pete turned, his yellow-green eyes big and unblinking.

"Laura." Her name came out like a croak. Neil swallowed. His heart had started beating again, and it pounded against his chest wall like a demented prisoner trying to escape.

She stiffened. For agonizing seconds, she didn't move. Then, slowly, very slowly, she rose awkwardly to her feet. For one heart-stopping moment, everything went still. Neil was sure she could hear his heart carrying on inside him. He was acutely aware of everything. All his senses strained toward her.

Then she turned, and Neil felt as if someone had slammed into him with a truck.

He stared, unable to believe what he was seeing. Their eyes locked, hers so incredibly blue, so incredibly clear, so incredibly beautiful. She didn't speak, but her eyes answered his question. *Yes,* they seemed to say. *Yes. This is your baby.*

His gaze slid down her body, fastening on her swollen stomach.

Pregnant. The knowledge beat against his brain like a thousand moths' wings. The night he'd left her crying as if her heart would break. Even then. She had known, but she hadn't said a word to try to keep him.

He closed his eyes, stunned by what he now knew. My God. No wonder she'd left Patinville. She must have felt so alone. He felt like crying, and he swallowed against the lump in his throat. He took a step toward her.

Laura couldn't move. She couldn't think. Her mind whirled in senseless frenzy. What was Neil doing here? How had he found her? Why didn't he say something? And then he took a step forward.

Her nerveless fingers dropped the trowel she'd been holding. Her hands were shaking as she clutched them protectively against her stomach. She could feel the baby kicking.

Why *didn't* he say something?

And then he reached for her, pulling her into his arm and he was kissing her with frantic, greedy kisses. Th kisses landed everywhere. On her nose. On her eyes. A over her face. "Oh, Laura, my God, Laura," he mu tered, over and over again. "Thank God I've found you.

"Neil," she cried, her voice thick with tears. "Oh, Neil.

"I looked everywhere for you. Everywhere. I was ju about crazy. I thought if I didn't find you soon, I'd g nuts!"

His mouth captured hers in a deep, urgent kiss that Laura's veins with liquid fire. She clutched at his hair, an his hands were all over her, touching her as if he couldn believe she was real. When he finally dragged his mout from hers and lowered his head to her neck, her mouth fe bruised, but her heart was singing.

"Finally I decided the only chance I had was to com here, try to find Celeste." He groaned, holding her clos against him.

"I can't believe you're here," she cried, and the tear she'd been trying to suppress ever since she'd seen hin standing there slipped down her cheeks.

"Oh, *chère,* don't cry," he whispered, gently wiping he tears from her face and tilting her chin up. "I love you s much. I was such a stupid fool. Can you ever forgive me?"

Laura smiled through her tears and lifted her face like flower lifts itself toward the sun. "All that matters is tha you're here now."

"I'll never leave you again." He touched her stomach his hand gentle as it caressed the sloping curves. He ben down, placing his lips against the rounded swell, and sh felt the heat of his breath through her clothes. She was s happy she wanted to cry again.

"Oh, Neil, I love you so," she said.

"And I love you."

"I couldn't believe it when I heard your voice."

"I know. I know. I couldn't believe it when I saw you standing there. When did you come here? Why did you come here?"

She looked at his dear face. She could see all the worry lines etched around his eyes, the love shining in their dark liquid depths. "After I left Patinville, I went to Los Angeles first. Then, a few days later, I went up to Crescent City, where Celeste is. I . . . I didn't know what else to do."

His arms tightened around her, and his face twisted. She knew he was thinking that he hadn't been there for her when she needed him. Her heart was so full it was hard to continue. "Celeste put me in touch with a friend of hers in San Francisco. I stayed with Jackie for a couple of months and worked temporary jobs. Then, last month, Celeste called Mother Ambrose and arranged for me to come here until the baby was born." She smiled. "The nuns have been so kind. I've been helping Mother Ambrose in the office, with the books, and she lets me putter around out here."

"Oh, Laura, Laura, *chère*. I'm so sorry for putting you through all this. Thank God you've had a good place to stay and people who care about you. But I intend to make all this up to you. I want you with me. We belong together. You, me, and our baby." Then he kissed her again, but now the kiss wasn't so frenzied. This was a gentle kiss, a loving kiss, and warmth spread itself everywhere, filling her with a sweet radiance. "Will you marry me, Laura?" he whispered as the kiss ended.

"You know I will," she whispered, her breath mingling with his.

"I have something for you," he said. He reached into his jacket pocket and withdrew a small velvet box. "I've been carrying this around with me ever since I bought it in Baton Rouge."

In the red-gold rays of the evening light, Laura saw him lift a thin band of gold encrusted with tiny diamonds out of the box. "Oh, Neil," she said as he slipped the ring on the third finger of her left hand.

"Look at it, Laura," he said, his voice gruff. "It's a circle, and it's my promise to you. Every time you look at it, I want you to know that it represents that circle of love you told me about, a circle that's going to enclose you and me and our children, forever."

And as his arms enfolded her once more, Laura was filled with wonder and joy and a deep, rich contentment and peace.

She had finally left the darkness behind. She was home. At last.

* * * * *

COMING NEXT MONTH

#751 HEARTBREAK HANK—Myrna Temte *Cowboy Country*
Principal Emily Franklin was meeting with local bad boy Hank Dawson to discuss his daughter's schoolwork. But when the meetings continued, rumors raged—had the rodeo star lassoed the learned lady?

#752 AMAZING GRACIE—Victoria Pade
Gabe Duran collected antiques; his new neighbor Gracie Canon restored them. Desire for the same collection had them fighting over something old; desire of another kind had them trying something new....

#753 SWISS BLISS—Bevlyn Marshall
Consultant Susan Barnes had jetted to the Alps on business. Brusque Swiss hotel owner Maximillian Kaiser was as corporate as they came... until passion burst in—without an appointment!

#754 THERE AND NOW—Linda Lael Miller *Beyond the Threshold*
When Elisabeth McCartney appeared in 1892, the townspeople called her a witch. Jonathan Fortner called her the love of his life. How could she tell him a lifetime lay between them?

#755 MAN WITHOUT A PAST—Laurie Paige
Sutter Kinnard was determined not to disappoint the woman he'd protected like a sister. But Meredith Lawton's dream of a perfect marriage was a terrifying challenge to a man without a past....

#756 BRIDE ON THE LOOSE—Debbie Macomber
Those Manning Men
Straitlaced secretary Charlotte Weston was mortified! Her teenage daughter had tried to bribe Jason Manning, their laid-back landlord, into asking Charlotte out. He'd honorably refused... and made the dinner date for free...!

AVAILABLE THIS MONTH:

#745 SILENT SAM'S SALVATION
Myrna Temte

#746 DREAMBOAT OF THE WESTERN WORLD
Tracy Sinclair

#747 BEYOND THE NIGHT
Christine Flynn

#748 WHEN SOMEBODY LOVES YOU
Trisha Alexander

#749 OUTCAST WOMAN
Lucy Gordon

#750 ONE PERFECT ROSE
Emilie Richards